The Mason Wright Series

THE
BONES
OF
SAINT PIERRE

Steven Knapp

Can't Put It Down Books

The Bones of Saint Pierre
The Mason Wright Series Book 1
Copyright 2019 By Steven Knapp

ISBN: 978-0-9994623-3-1

Printed in the United States of America

Published by
Can't Put It Down Books
An imprint of
Open Door Publications
2113 Stackhouse Dr.
Yardley, PA 19067
www.CantPutItDownBooks.com

Cover Design by Eric Labacz
www.labaczdesign.com

Author Photo by Lori E. Chapin

To the "Greatest Generation."
Ordinary people who did the
extraordinary.

Chapter 1

January 1940
Metropolitan Museum of Art
New York City

BREAKING INTO A RESTRICTED ROOM in the Metropolitan Museum of Art is serious, especially for someone who works there. Mason Wright felt his pulse quicken as he stared blankly at the open drawer in the cabinet. The room was cold, but beads of sweat formed on his forehead. He rifled through the drawer once more: nothing. He opened the other three drawers and achieved the same result: nothing. Where was it? How could it be gone? He had seen it just yesterday, and now twenty-four hours later, it had disappeared. His perfectly executed plan had just shattered. He decided to put everything back and get out as fast as possible. He had planned for a quick in and out, never thinking the map would be missing. This old map with very little value to anyone had apparently just become quite popular; someone else was looking for the same thing, and Mason had to find out who. He closed his eyes and took a deep breath.

Then he heard the voice.

"Mason? Is that you? What are you doing in here?" The strident voice rang out across the room, startling him. He knew the voice very well; it belonged to Dr. Margaret Heckler, a highly respected art curator who had been recruited by the Metropolitan Museum five years before as the assistant director of antiquities acquisitions for the museum. She had worked here ever since. Mason did not know much about her, other than that she was extremely gifted in her knowledge of art and Museum valuables, cared for an elderly mother at home, and sorely lacked social skills. Mason had known her for a little over a year, and during that time, if it was not work related, she kept to herself. She was very private about her personal life, brilliant at her job, and right now she was growing more impatient with every passing second. Mason didn't work "with her," at the museum, he worked for her: She was his boss, and he now needed to explain why he was in a restricted rare documents room in the bowels of one of the most famous museums in the world.

Mason Wright was twenty-eight years old, an assistant to the director of art curation at the Metropolitan Museum of Art. The title sounded more prestigious than it actually was; he was really just a low-level paid intern, but his experience in archaeology and rare artifacts far exceeded most people his age. He came from a famous and wealthy treasure-hunting family; his father, Aldon Wright, was well known in the art and antiquities world.

Growing up all over the world while his parents searched for rare artifacts, he had met some of the most famous names in the art world before his sixteenth birthday. His parents had slowed down a few years ago when his mother became ill. He returned home from studying at the Sorbonne in France after his mother passed away, to spend more time with his father, who was also now dealing with health problems. Many of the artifacts attributed to his family could be found exhibited in this very museum.

After Mason returned to New York his father reached out to a family friend, a director at the museum, and was able to get him an entry level position in the curation department. Mason and the museum were a natural fit, and he had enjoyed the experience up until now; at this moment, Mason wished he were somewhere—anywhere—else.

Room RD 3 was filled with rare maps; the room was restricted to a short list of Museum employees, and Mason was not one of them. He quickly began concocting reasons for why he was standing over a table containing old maps and charts from 1800s Europe.

"Mason?" Dr. Heckler again called out. Her voice echoed against the walls of the cold cement room. She was becoming more concerned with each passing second, and Mason was trying quickly to formulate an explanation.

Dr. Heckler held an undergraduate degree from Princeton University, a master's degree from Fordham, and a Ph.D. from the International Art School in Berlin. She was forty-six years old, and quite attractive compared to many of the women Mason had met who spent their lives researching ancient artifacts. She was easy to work for, but a stickler for protocol, and the rules of the museum. She kept a very precise schedule, so Mason was shocked that she was even in the building at this time. She always left at 8:30 p.m. sharp.

Mason finally turned around and acknowledged his boss, "Oh, Dr. Heckler, good evening." Dr. Heckler's serious look told Mason she meant business and was waiting impatiently for an explanation.

"I was walking by the room and saw the door slightly ajar. I thought someone might be in here, so I peeked in to have a look. I found these papers on the table and was in the process of putting them back. They seem to have been left out. Someone must have left in a hurry and forgot to put them away."

Dr. Heckler started across the room. "Mason, you know this is a restricted room. You are not even allowed to be in here, let alone handle documents." Her serious gaze never left Mason's eyes as she approached. "What do you mean the door was ajar? It is always locked. Only a few people have access to this room, and as far as I know, except for Director Montgomery, they have all left for the evening."

"Yes, I know, I was surprised as well," Mason said in a very agreeable voice. He tried to sound as surprised as Dr. Heckler, hoping that they could align their concerns, and she might forget about him. "That's why I thought someone was in here. When I found no one, I thought it strange that the room was open with documents out on the table. Someone must have left the maps out and forgotten about them. I was going to phone the director as soon as everything was back in order." Mason tried to shed the aura of a guilty man.

Dr. Heckler did not look as if she was buying his story, and truth be told, neither was he; her serious stare had turned suspicious. He knew who had opened the room; he knew what they were looking for, because it was him. Mason was looking for an old map of the Paris catacombs, which was supposed to be in these drawers, but was not. The map was split into two pieces due to the size and detail. While rare, the map was not considered to be of a high monetary value. Its importance came from its age, and he really needed to locate it; people were counting on him. Someone had been in this room and got to it first; he was not sure who, but unfortunately, if Dr. Heckler found the map missing, it would not matter because he was going to be blamed.

"Mason, I am not sure you understand the severity of your actions. These are extremely rare and fragile documents that if mishandled may be gone forever. The museum's benefactors would be astonished to find an intern handling old maps and documents." Mason's title of assistant to the director of museum curation had just officially been lowered to intern.

"This is very serious; I like you Mason, but I will have to notify Director Montgomery of what I have witnessed here. As a world-renowned museum we have certain rules that need to be followed. That is the reputation we have built, and it is extremely important we take every measure to maintain top standards."

"I understand," Mason said, trying to sound somber and apologetic. "I was just trying to help." But he knew she did not believe him; she was not the least bit concerned that he had told her someone had entered the room and left it open. She was not fazed at all over a possible breach of security.

He shifted uncomfortably while trying to appear calm. The key to the room was tucked away in his sock; he had swiped the key from her office weeks ago while she was away for a few days on a curating trip. He'd made a copy and returned it to her office. Now, as it rubbed against his leg, it felt more and more like a shackle.

Dr. Heckler put away the last of the documents and motioned Mason toward the door. He walked around the table and headed to the exit. She did not believe him, and he knew Director Montgomery would absolutely not believe him; this was starting to become a long night.

Mason exited the room first, followed by Dr. Heckler. She locked the door and started to lead him upstairs to the Director's office. Mason was in trouble. If they found out what was missing, they would pin this whole thing on him. He was starting to feel very uneasy. He needed to get out of this building as soon as possible.

Who had gotten to the room before him? He had successfully located both pieces of the map, but due to the size of it, and the fact that he needed to conceal it, he had been able to only take one piece at a time. He had taken the first half of the map last night and had come back for the second tonight. But when he got back to the room, it was gone.

He had his piece taped to the underside of his desk in his office, but someone had the other half of the map. He needed the other piece as much as that someone needed his. The map was not well known; most people, even the experts who worked at the museum, were not aware it even existed. It couldn't be a coincidence that it was missing.

If the second half of the map was gone, Mason mused as he followed Dr. Heckler up the stairs to the main floor, someone was on to him. They headed down the hallway and cut through a room in the European Arts section of the museum. They entered the large room filled with Greek sculptures, most of which were missing limbs, an irony not lost on Mason as he thought of his possible fate. Luckily, these days a breach of protocol at the museum did not call for a maiming. Dr. Heckler walked a few steps ahead of him, saying nothing. The only sound heard was that of her heels on the famous black and white mosaic-tiled floor.

Mason noted the Andrea Solario painting, "Solome with the Head of John the Baptist," as he passed it and hoped it wasn't a premonition of his fate. It depicted a hand holding the head of John the Baptist over a tray as it was presented to Solome. Mason pictured the hand of Dr. Heckler delivering his head on a silver platter to Director Montgomery. He managed a smile and a chuckle to himself as they continued.

They exited the European Arts wing and entered the Medieval wing. They passed the Medieval armor display where four life-sized soldiers on their horses in full armor, readied themselves for battle. Another cruel irony. Maybe she was purposely leading him past all the signs of his apocalypse. They turned left and walked through the corridor of 18th century stained glass, arrived at the stairs, proceeded up, and came to the office of the director of the antiquities department.

Mason followed Dr. Heckler into the director's outer office where they found his secretary, a lovely woman named Rita, seated at a large oak desk.

"Is Director Montgomery available? It is quite urgent," Dr. Heckler said in a serious tone. Rita looked at Dr. Heckler and then at Mason, who managed a slight smile.

Rita rang the director informing him that Dr. Heckler was there to see him. "Yes. Okay, I will send her in." She nodded, hung up, and told Dr. Heckler to go ahead.

Director Montgomery was a bear of a man, he had a booming voice, and his handshake would fell lesser men. He had studied all over the world and had come back to New York City to run the antiquities department at the museum. He was brilliant when it came to artifacts, had a photographic memory, and could discuss almost any period in history. He had directed countless excavations in Italy and Greece. He had helped discover the Valley of the Kings in Egypt and had helped museums track down their art after World War I. The director also happened to be a close friend of Mason's father, Aldon Wright. They had worked together on digs, remaining close over the years. When Mason's father had taken ill two years ago, he was the one who had offered Mason a position in the department so he could be closer to his father. Montgomery used to joke that only death would take Aldon out of the field, and sadly that was looking more and more likely to be the case.

Dr. Heckler went into the office and closed the large oak-paneled door behind her. Mason remained in the waiting area next to Rita as she typed away. She gave him a sympathetic smile as if she, too, knew his fate was sealed. Mason looked around at the wood-paneled walls and the sculptures that adorned the tables as the tap of the typewriter keys filled the room.

Several minutes later the director opened the door and asked Mason to come in. Dr. Heckler nodded at Mason and left. Mason sat in the firm, brown leather chair in front of the large wooden desk and took a deep breath. He felt as if he was in the principal's office back at school. He sat silently as the director closed the door, came back around his desk, and sat down. He looked at Mason for what seemed like an eternity before he spoke up, "You know Dr. Heckler is right, the room you were in is a restricted room. Only a few people are allowed access, and that does not include you. How did you get in there, Mason?"

Mason shifted uncomfortably in his chair. He had known Montgomery for many years through his father, and the last thing he wanted to do was put him in an awkward position.

"I was walking down the hallway and noticed the door was open so I went in to have a look. There was nobody inside and I started poking around; I noticed a drawer not fully shut so I opened it to see the contents. The drawer had some old maps from Europe. There were a few maps on the table so I put them back in the drawer. I thought someone had left in a hurry and forgot to put them back."

Director Montgomery sat stoically looking at Mason with his eyebrows raised over his glasses. "Mason, I have known you a long time, and I am inclined to overlook this incident, but Dr. Heckler is adamant that your job here be terminated. I know you enjoy your work here, but I think your real calling is out in the field, like your father. I hate to see you behind a desk when you should be leading a dig or tracking down some lost artifact or lost piece of art. I know your father has a long list of things he could not find, and if he was in better health, he would have you out there looking for them."

Mason nodded. Montgomery was right; it was his intention to get back into the field. He just needed some time with his father to figure out what came next. Mason's father was not well, but he would never hold Mason back from going off into the world exploring. Mason had enjoyed his time in the city and had no plans to leave anytime soon until he received the letter from Jacques Moulié, which changed everything.

The letter asked Mason to find the old map of the catacombs. Moulié was not only an old family friend, he was a legend in the art world. Mason agreed to look for the map. Such a random old map, ordinary when compared to the rest of the museum's collection, surely would not be missed for a few weeks, but apparently there was more to this ordinary 1800s Paris underground map. Mason did not know why Moulié had requested it, but someone else clearly wanted it as well.

"Mason, can I ask you something?"

"Anything, sir," Mason replied.

Montgomery stood up and came around to the front of the desk. He leaned back on it, facing Mason, and crossed his arms. "Why are you still interested in working here? You have more experience than people twice your age, you have been on digs, and traveled the world with your father. Isn't it about time you started to burn your own path through history? There are a lot of things still out there waiting to be found. Lord knows your father is still obsessed with finding lost treasures. Something tells me this little incident is more than just an open door. Come on, Mason, what were you really doing in that room?"

Mason stared at Montgomery. He was not sure how to respond so he decided to come clean…well almost.

"Ok, the maps were not out on the table when I entered the room, I took them out. I was looking for a map of France from World War I. I have decided to write a book on the toll the war had taken on the art world, and the people of France, and I thought a map was a good place to start my research. My plan is to travel to several towns to interview people about their experiences during the Great War, before things in France get worse. I think it can be an interesting story someday, a unique perspective on the horrors of war."

Montgomery nodded as he walked over to the seventeenth century cabinet in the corner. He poured two glasses of scotch and walked back to Mason, both glasses in hand. He handed one to Mason and said, "Mason, I am happy that you are pursuing a career as an author. I also am thrilled that you are so interested in the experiences of the people of France during their dark days. I believe their stories should be shared; but the one thing that bothers me is that I do not believe a word you just told me. You inherited many things from your father, and unfortunately for you, one of those things is your father's blinking eyes when you are being less than truthful. He would always blink excessively while bending the truth; believe me, I have often stood right next to him as he did it—one of the qualities only those closest to him know. I don't know what you are up to...I almost don't want to know...but please tell me you have not stolen something valuable from my museum."

Mason stood up and reached out his hand. "Thanks for the scotch. I appreciate the words of encouragement. My father is a great man, and there are many qualities of his that I am proud to bear. I always knew that with all the good he has taught me there were bound to be some flaws. I will keep that blinking thing in mind...and no, I have not stolen anything from your museum. I would not stoop to that level to dishonor your friendship with my father. I have too much respect for you, and this museum. I also have too much respect for history and would prefer to pave a path through it with dignity. I would not dream of taking anything from your museum without your consent, though...," Mason paused, "I do need to borrow something for a short while. The less you know, the better, and I promise to bring it back in one piece."

Montgomery took the glass from Mason and shook his head. "I am going to pretend I did not hear that. You and your father better not get me in hot water. If Dr. Heckler finds out she will string me up as well. I have always thought she secretly wants this job and would find a way to get it. I plan on working out my days in this office. I don't need the Wrights ruining my plans. Give my best to your father, and Mason, be careful out there; the winds of war are blowing in Europe, and the world you are about to enter is filled with legions of the most unsavory characters."

They shook hands and Mason exited the office. He said goodbye to Rita and headed off to his office to collect his things. He would stop by Dr. Heckler's office on the way to apologize again and thank her for this opportunity. He was still wondering what she was doing in the building at this late hour. For two years she had left at 8:30 p.m., and the night he made his final move, she turns up at the door. *I guess it is just as well; it gave me a reason to end this internship.* It was not exactly the exit strategy he had planned, but it would do.

Mason decided to take one more walk through the museum for a last look at some of his favorite pieces. He did not know if he would be returning, or if he would even be allowed entry if he did. He had spent many years in and out of this museum and had seen almost everything, but always seemed to return to the same works that moved him.

He started down the hall toward the stairwell, took the stairs down to the first floor, and entered the Medieval wing. One of his favorite pieces was a recreation of a French Church from the 1500s. This small room off the main corridor was often missed by visitors, who were unaware of its existence. Mason entered the room and took one final look at the beautiful, inlaid wood panels. The detail of the panels on all four walls amazed him every time he sat here. He paused and said a small prayer for his father and a slightly bigger one for himself, and then continued down the hallway back to the stairs. He was not a very religious man, but it seemed to work for everyone else.

Mason took the stairs down to the main floor where the American exhibit resided. He turned left and continued down the hallway through the large wooden doorway where he entered the room to his right. The wall directly in front of him was dominated by the Emanuel Luetze painting, "Washington Crossing the Delaware." This very large painting measured about ten feet high by twenty feet long and was one of the anchors of the American wing. Possibly the largest painting in the museum, Leutze's was one of the most popular. The oil on canvas was a magnificent sight, with General George Washington in the center of the boat commanding the Delaware crossing on Christmas Day 1776. Mason would come and sit in front of this piece at least once a week to reflect. He would sit in silence and try to envision what that day was like, crossing the cold and icy Delaware River on the way to fight the Hessians. He sat for the last time staring at the majestic look on General Washington's face; confident and regal, it was the look of a great man fighting incredible odds. It always made him wonder how great men became great. Were they born with something that made greatness inevitable or did they have to work hard for it?

Mason stood up and left the room, saving his last goodbye for a woman who had mesmerized him since the first day he laid eyes on her. Her name was Madame Pierre Gatreau, and she was known as Madame X, an American expatriate who married a French banker. John Singer Sargent painted her likeness in 1883. She was wearing an elegant black dress as if she was attending an upscale cocktail party. Sargent painted her with the strap of her dress falling down her shoulder, a scandal at the time, and the painting became a source of ridicule. People were outraged at the sight of an elegant French woman with her dress strap falling off. Sargent bowed to public pressure and repainted the strap back up on her shoulder. He eventually sold the painting to the museum and asked that her true identity not be revealed in his lifetime, for he did not want any scandal to descend on her memory. Mason always sympathized with her. She was incredibly beautiful and did not deserve the ridicule the painting had received. Mason sat in Gallery A11, The Hearn Gallery, and gazed at her face and said farewell to the woman he had adored from the time he first saw her here at the museum. This was not goodbye; she would forever wander the corridors of his mind.

Mason took the stairs all the way down to the Main Floor

Minus 3—it was how they referred to the lower floors of the museum. The front entrance was the Main Floor. The five floors below were called Main Minus 1, Main Minus 2, and so forth. Dr. Heckler's office was just down the hall on the left. Mason was always amazed at how secluded some parts of the museum were. For such a prestigious museum, the lower floors were dreary, and dark. The cinder block walls were painted gray, the plain wooden doors had small signs on them, the endless rows of caged lights hung down casting harsh shadows. Sometimes Mason felt as though he were working in an asylum rather than one of the most respected art museums in the world. After museum hours ended you would not know there were any people around for miles. The museum sat on Fifth Avenue in the heart of Manhattan overlooking Central Park, but sometimes he felt as though he was completely alone.

As he approached Dr. Heckler's office, he heard the phone ringing inside. The sound echoed down the hallway like thunder rolling in before a storm. He slowed down to see if she would answer. One ring, two rings…, and finally he heard her pick up the phone and say, "This is Dr. Heckler."

Mason stopped in his tracks: He did not want to interrupt her, though he did want to listen to the conversation as he was sure it was Montgomery calling.

"Oh, I am sorry to hear that," the doctor said. "Yes, I completely understand. He was aware of the rules, and he should not have been in there in the first place. Yes, I agree. He will be missed but I am sure we will see him from time to time. Thank you, Director, good night."

Dr. Heckler hung up the phone. Mason waited a minute and then knocked on the frame of her outer office. She looked up, "Mason, please come in. I just spoke to the director and I understand you will be leaving us."

"Yes, it is time for me to move on," Mason replied.

"We will be sorry to lose you, but I do hope you understand we are charged with preserving history, and if we are not vigilant about security, our benefactors will pull all the funding from our department, and we will cease to exist."

"I completely understand. I never wanted to jeopardize the museum or its people. I just came by to thank you for everything. It has been an honor to work for you, and at this museum. I will always remember my time here fondly. I wish I was departing on better terms, but it is time for me to pursue new challenges."

Dr. Heckler stood up and reached out her hand. "May your travels take you to places beyond your dreams. I know you will be successful in whatever you choose. Do come by to see us from time to time."

Mason shook her hand and thanked her again. Dr. Heckler managed a smile for him, possibly the first he had ever seen from her.

He turned and left her office. He believed she had been sincere in her well wishes, and he appreciated that. He did not like deceiving her, but there was no other way. The fact that she was here late tonight still did not sit well with him. In two years, he had seen her stay late only twice, and both times the museum was preparing for an exhibit. She never gave more than was needed. There was always something about Dr. Heckler that made Mason want to know the rest of her story.

He headed down the hall, made a left, and continued down the dreary hallway to his office. He arrived at his door and stopped suddenly. Before he even entered, he knew something was wrong. He always closed his door when he left. Now it was open, and a light was on. Mason didn't know if someone was in his office right now, but someone had definitely been there. He came around the corner, slowly pushed the door open, and looked in. Everything looked the same as when he left, but someone had come in and turned on the light. He went over to his desk and sat down. When he leaned down to take a look at his drawer, he noticed something missing. Mason's father had long ago taught him to never take anything for granted. Always assume the guy next to you wants what you have. In the shady world of art and antiquities, he was usually right.

Mason always put a small piece of tape between the bottom of the four drawers and the desk. He always checked when he returned to make sure the tape was still intact. Now, the tape was only attached to the bottom of the drawer and not the desk. The other three drawers were the same. Someone had been in his office, sat in his chair, and gone through his desk. Mason opened his top drawer, pushed in the side clips and removed it completely. He reached into the underside of the desk and removed a large envelope that had been taped there. He put the envelope in his bag along with a few other things. The map inside was protected by a clear plastic sleeve, and the manila exterior blended in with other things in his bag. He thought his best decision right now was to leave the museum as quickly as possible. Someone was following his every move, and it was possible that they were still in the building. He assumed whoever had the other half of the map would eventually come looking for the rest of it, and something told him that, now, they definitely knew he had it.

Mason quickly turned out the lights and exited his office. He knew the quickest way out was up one floor, and then out the employee's exit, but that might be the expected way to go. Mason had to turn in his credentials with security before he left for the evening; he did not plan on coming back. He decided to leave through the main entrance on Fifth Avenue. He would stop at the main desk and drop off his ID with Bruce, the night watchman. He went to the right and headed to the elevator bank. As he arrived at the elevator, he heard a door open down the hall. The door closed, and he heard the sound of footsteps coming his way. He did not want to wait for the elevator so he headed for the stairs. The footsteps were getting closer. Mason ran for the door to the stairs and swung it open. He raced up the stairs like a lunatic, his bag flailing behind him. He stopped on the landing and looked over the edge at the door below. It started to open slowly. He could not see who was there, just someone wearing a long black coat and a hat. Whoever it was did not want to be seen. Mason calmed himself and slowly continued up the stairs, keeping out of sight against the wall, until he reached the next floor. Quietly opening the door to the first floor, he entered the primary wing of the museum.

The museum had closed to the public twenty minutes before; no one was around. Usually security started their rounds at 11 p.m. Mason swung his bag over his shoulder and began to walk briskly toward the main entrance. He stopped briefly to see if the man in the black coat and hat was coming through the door. When he saw nothing, he continued to make his way out. He hopped down the famous main staircase on the sixteen-foot-wide granite steps, glancing back a few times. There were forty-four steps in all. Half down, a small, six-foot wide marble landing divided the staircase.

Mason found Bruce sitting at his desk in the Great Hall as he came running up, slightly out of breath. Bruce looked up, smiled, and said, "Mr. Wright, I am sad to hear the news that you are leaving us. I just heard from the director. I will miss our baseball talks and will still take my Dodgers over your Yankees any day."

"Bruce, hopefully one day, for your sake, that will happen. I will be back to visit from time to time; I'll come by and say hello. Here is my ID and my office keys. I told Director Montgomery I would leave them with you. Take care of yourself." Mason reached out and shook Bruce's hand.

"Stay out of trouble. I know for you it is not easy," Bruce said with a laugh.

"I'll do my best," Mason said as he headed for the exit with a stolen map in his bag.

Mason nodded to the guard at the front who unlocked the large middle door of the three front glass doors. He let Mason out into the cold January night. The city was bustling as usual with traffic and people. Street vendors sold peanuts and trinkets on the sidewalk in makeshift stands while people wandered about. Mason felt safer now that he was outside. He turned up the lapels on his coat, put on his hat, and started his walk home. Passing through the massive Corinthian columns that framed the front entrance of the museum, he hopped down the marble steps, past the ten-foot tall bronze torchère lamps, and proceeded up Fifth Avenue. He was sad to leave the museum but knew something important was happening that required his assistance. Since he had received the letter from France, he had known this day would come and he would need to say goodbye. He stopped and turned around for one more look at the museum. He took a deep breath and resumed his walk home.

As Mason passed the first of several street vendors, he was completely unaware of a man who emerged from behind one of the museum columns to the left of the main entrance. The man calmly started down the steps, and with caution began following Mason up Fifth Avenue, pausing behind some trees to remain out of sight. The man fit right into the winter scene in the city, just another New Yorker on his way home in his long black coat and hat.

Chapter 2

MASON WALKED UP FIFTH AVENUE on his way home to his apartment on East 86th Street. He crossed the intersection at 84th Street and passed an entrance to Central Park on his left. Fifth Avenue was on his right, filled with taxis, cars, and buses. Trying not to walk too fast, Mason appeared calm as he headed up the cobblestone sidewalk. He tried to relax and take in the sights of New York City in winter; snow covered the trees in the park, and many buildings were still decorated for the holidays. He passed the Marymount School on the corner of 84th Street, with its wreaths and colored lights. He did truly love the big city; it was like nowhere else in the world.

He stopped at a newspaper stand on the sidewalk between 84th and 85th Streets. Every night after work Mason would stop to pick up a copy of *The New York Times*, and Andy always had it waiting for him. They would chat about anything new in the world; Andy looked forward to Mason's visits. Today was a little different as Mason was later than normal. Andy closed up at ten and Mason just made it in time. Andy said jokingly to him, "You're working too hard, son."

"Not nearly as hard as you, my friend," Mason said as he grabbed his paper, left some money on the counter for his pal, and nonchalantly looked back down Fifth Avenue toward the museum. He saw nothing strange so he said goodbye to Andy. With everything that had happened so far tonight, Mason was pretty sure he would not be seeing Andy again anytime soon.

Mason paused at one of the wooden park benches to tie his shoe; he tried to act normal as he glanced back down Fifth Avenue. He noticed a figure quickly duck behind the newsstand; it looked like the man from the museum. A lump started to form in Mason's throat as he continued to fumble with his shoe, thoughts racing through his mind as he contemplated his next move. He could run into the park, but that was not advisable at this time of night. He could confront the man in the middle of Fifth Avenue, but that didn't seem like a good idea, either. He composed himself, stood up, and began walking briskly; he stumbled on a raised cobblestone and lurched forward, almost falling to the ground. After regaining his balance, he stopped for a moment. As Mason stood in the middle of the sidewalk, he went over his choices and decided on his best course of action. He darted to the right, ran into traffic, and crossed the street. Horns blared as he ran between cars, and one taxi driver yelled out the window at him. He reached the other side and blended into the crowd of people, waiting for the light to change on the corner of 85th Street. An older gentleman looked at him with a confused, disapproving glare. A policeman walked by, and for a second, Mason contemplated saying something about the man following him, but he did not know who the man was, or if he was actually following him. Mason was also in possession of stolen property, so he nixed that idea pretty quickly. The policeman continued down the street as Mason turned his attention back across the street. As he peered between a young man and his wife, he could see the man looking across the street for him in every direction.

Using the crowd as a diversion, Mason turned and started north on Fifth Avenue, across 85th Street, and ducked into the entryway of an apartment building. He ran up the three steps and concealed himself in the shadows of the entrance. The traffic light turned red, and the group of people on the corner started to cross toward the park. The man became concerned when there was no sign of Mason once the crowd dispersed. While the light was red, the man ran across Fifth Avenue and stopped on the corner that Mason had just vacated. Crossing 85th Street, he headed north toward the entrance of the building, where Mason was hiding. Mason crouched lower and prepared to lunge at him if needed. The man approached the opening, jogging right by Mason. He was bundled up with a scarf around his face, as if he were in the North Pole. Either he was not used to the cold or he didn't want to be seen. Mason didn't get a look at his face as the man ran by.

After a few moments, Mason stepped back into the night and slowly followed him. He watched as he continued north up Fifth Avenue toward 86th Street. A woman emerged from an apartment building with her dog, almost knocking Mason over. She apologized, and Mason quickly dismissed her. Turning his attention back toward his target he watched as the man turned right on 86th Street....his street.

This guy must be going to my apartment. Who is he, and how does he know where I live?

Making a quick choice, Mason immediately ran back to the corner, turned left, and disappeared up 85th Street at a full sprint, his bag swinging off his shoulder. He took this shortcut home often; he hoped to beat the man to his apartment building and wait for him.

The blocks are long in New York City if you are going across town. If you are going uptown or downtown, they are much shorter. Mason's shortcut was through the lobby of the Lankford Towers. He ran into the lobby, almost knocking over a woman. She hollered at him, "Hey watch it, sonny." Mason yelled out, "Sorry," and continued through the lobby, down a short flight of stairs, and passed the elevator banks, clearly annoying several folks who were waiting at the elevators.

As he approached the 86th Street entrance, he slowed to a walk. He stopped to catch his breath as a couple came in through the revolving door. The man said, "Good evening," but all Mason could muster in between breaths was "Un-huh."

His attention turned back to the man in the long coat. Mason was now directly across from his own building on 86th Street. He slipped out the door and glanced down the street. He saw no one; maybe the man had turned back. He could not possibly have beaten Mason to his building, Mason had been in a full-on sprint, dodging people and traffic. He was confident that he had arrived first so he waited a few minutes in the shadow of the Towers. A young couple emerged from the building laughing loudly, startling Mason, and he began to think that the man in the long black coat was probably laughing at him as well. He had just sprinted half a mile to get to his building so he could confront a man he did not know and accuse him of following him home. Was he just paranoid?

Another minute went by with no activity up the street so Mason decided to cross and enter his building. He unlocked the front door after glancing one more time down the street...nothing. He felt confident he was no longer being followed. Entering the front stairwell, he stopped to unlock his mail slot. He could hear Mrs. Stanton's radio blaring through the door of apartment 1A. He was happy he lived two floors up and did not have to deal with that every night. He started up the two flights to his apartment. Mason liked to take the stairs; it kept him in better shape than the elevator. He looked through his mail as he walked, and realizing there was nothing important, he discarded it in the garbage slot on the second floor. He made the final turn to head up to the third floor; Mrs. Stanton's radio no longer audible. He reached the third floor and arrived at his apartment door breathing heavily. Mason checked the small piece of tape on the frame at the top of the door; it was still intact. He unlocked his door, entered his front hall, and turned on the hallway light. Though not the biggest apartment, by New York standards it was a nice place. A tall table adorned the left side of the hallway. On top of the table was a large Italian vase, which he had "borrowed" from a dig outside of Rome. He was pretty sure the Italian Museum was still looking for it.

As Mason took off his coat, he realized it had started to rain. He could hear the annoying dripping of water on his fire escape. The sound of a large drip of water hitting the metal railing made more noise than one would think. It was just one of the joys of living in an apartment rather than a house. He removed his coat and hung it in the front hall closet. As he entered the living room, he put his bag on the chair. He leaned over and tried to turn on the lamp, but it did not turn on. *Damn bulb. I just changed it.*

Mason went into the kitchen to see what food possibilities existed. He was starving; he had not eaten since lunch. He opened the refrigerator and took out a casserole dish of half-eaten pasta from the night before. He turned on the oven, removed the lid, and put the dish in the oven.

He then poured himself a glass of Bordeaux wine. His father had taught him about the great wines of France as a boy. It was very confusing with the 1855 classification, and the different levels of French wine. He never totally got the whole breakdown, but he enjoyed the wine. He always grabbed a few bottles when he went to visit his dad upstate. His father was given many cases of the best wines in the world for all his efforts in preserving history in Europe. He would often receive shipments from Europe from people he did not even know, thanking him for donating various things to museums. He was more than happy to accept them even if he did not know why. He always had the finest on hand for special gatherings at the house. Whether it was a Chateau Lafite Rothschild, a Chateau Margaux, or a Chateau Latour, his father always enjoyed his French wine, and was happy to share it, but only with people he deemed worthy. He would always tell him, "Son, the finest wine in the world should only be enjoyed with the finest people in your life."

With glass in hand, Mason retrieved his bag from the living room and settled in the dining room. He reached for the overhead light switch, and it went on, to his surprise. He opened his bag and took out the map he had "borrowed" from the museum. He laid it out on the table and put four large books on it, one in each corner. The sound of the rain dripping on the fire escape had softened; the rain must be lightening up a bit.

The map on the table was one part of a two-part map depicting a maze of underground tunnels, the Catacombs of Paris. There was no way to navigate the entire system without the two parts of the map, considering that the tunnels had been closed and sealed off at various times in history. The underground tomb had been housing French remains for nearly two hundred years and was estimated to hold six million dead.

Mason stared at the map and followed the maze of tunnels as they wove their way under the streets of Paris. Unfortunately, without the other side, the map was almost useless.

It was the sound of the oven expanding, a pinging noise from the metal, that broke Mason's concentration. He went back into the kitchen to retrieve his dinner. He opened the oven door, took out the bowl of pasta, and placed it on top of the stove. Grabbing a fork and a spoon, he headed into the dining room, placed the pasta down on the table, and grabbed some napkins. Before he sat down, though, he felt a crawling sensation up the back of his neck, the feeling you get when someone is watching you. He turned toward the front door and froze.

"Hello, Mason," the figure standing by the front door said. Mason stood there staring as he realized the voice was that of a woman. A woman he knew but had not seen in a few years. His guts churned. Collette Moulié. They had spent several years together as kids growing up; their families were close. Her father was the reason he had taken the map from the museum. His daughter, now standing in his apartment, was always full of surprises. The night had just gotten even more interesting.

"Collette?" Mason said. "What in the world are you doing here? More importantly, how did you get inside my apartment?"

"Mason, I am sorry to surprise you like this, but I really need your help."

"You need my help?" Mason replied slightly annoyed.

"Yes, I need to talk to you about something very important. May I come in?"

"I think you are already in."

"Mason, please, I really need your help. Can I come in and talk to you...seriously?"

"Let me get this straight. I have not heard from you in three years. I heard you were studying in New York, and you never bothered to contact me. You show up out of the blue, break in to my apartment, scare the life out of me, and ask me for my help. Please don't take this the wrong way, but you really need to work on your social skills."

"I did not exactly break in, I had a key," Collette said.

"Ohhh…well I guess that makes everything okay. I do not have the greatest memory in the world, but I do know that I did not give you a key to my apartment. I have only been living here for two years, and I have not seen you in three. So how is it that you have a key to my place?" Mason said with serious sarcasm.

"Your father told me where you keep your spare key. He said you get locked out a lot so you keep one under the potted plant outside the elevator."

"Oh great, he told you that. Gee, thanks, Dad. Did he add anything else, like maybe where I keep all my valuables, or how much I enjoy being surprised as I'm sitting down for dinner?"

"Mason, I am sorry. May I come in, please?"

"Of course." Mason relented. He was always the sarcastic type, but he could see she was serious. He had to be honest, as bizarre as this was, there were worse people who could have shown up at his apartment. Collette was a close friend from the many years their fathers worked together in France. He'd thought that someday they would be more than friends, but it never really happened. It had just been too difficult to have a long-distance relationship between New York and France. She was twenty-six and had been studying at NYU. He had known she was there, but when she did not get in touch with him, he just let it be. He often thought of her over the years and knew one day their paths would cross again. He'd thought it might be under more normal circumstances.

Collette came in and took off her coat. She looked around closely. "Nice place. I recognize some of the pieces from back in the day. I am pretty sure the Italian Museum is still looking for the vase in the front hall," Collette said returning a little of his sarcasm with a slight smile.

Mason smirked.

"I would like to wash up a little. I have been out in the rain. May I use your bathroom?" she asked, tying her hair up in a knot.

"Down the hall on the left," Mason said. "There are towels in the closet across from the bathroom. Can I pour you some wine? I have a Bordeaux open."

"Maybe some tea if it would not be too much trouble?"

Mason nodded and headed to the kitchen, saying to himself sarcastically, "No…no trouble at all, come on in, make yourself at home, would you like to use my bathroom? Sure, I will make you some tea. Perhaps I can make you some dinner, how about a change of clothes? Would you like me to sleep on the couch?"

Collette always liked to be in control; she had always pushed his limits. Mason, too, was strong-willed, but Collette always broke him down. He was powerless against her. She knew it and he knew it. There were very few people who could get Mason to do things he did not want to do. Atop that short list was Collette Moulié.

Obviously, something was up, but what? Whatever was going on, it must be pretty serious for Collette to show up at his door. Her father was one of the most powerful art people in Europe so for her to need his help, it must be something that her daddy was unable to take care of. He wondered if it had something to do with the letter he'd received from her father. Jacques Moulié had told Mason specifically that no one else knew about it. Did that include Collette? Mason would keep his cards close.

He went into the kitchen and put some water on for tea. He quickly scooped up the map from the dining room table and put it in a drawer. His pasta was still sitting there, and something told him he would not be eating dinner tonight. He covered the bowl and put it back in the refrigerator. He quickly downed his glass of wine and poured another. Now that Collette was here, he was pretty sure that his life was about to get far more complicated.

Chapter 3

COLLETTE EMERGED FROM THE BATHROOM with a towel wrapped around her head as Mason put the tea down on the dining room table.

"Thank you," she said as she sat down.

Mason sat down opposite her and took a sip of wine. He asked about her father, and they had some small talk. Mason tried to seem interested in what she was saying, but he was more interested in the reason for her surprise visit. After a few minutes of back and forth, they both knew it was time to discuss the real reason for her visit.

"So, I have waited long enough; what brings you to my apartment on a rainy January night?"

Collette sighed and took a sip of tea. "Mason, you know of the work my father is involved in for the last few years. Since the end of the Great War he has been put in charge of documenting and preserving the art collections of all the museums in France. It has been a tiresome and thankless job, and over time has taken a toll on many relationships. Everyone has been lending advice on what to do, and the best way to go forward. My father has never been good at taking advice from people he does not care for, so he has a growing list of men asking questions. These men were once friends, but for various reasons, their trust in my father has eroded."

Collette stood up and unwrapped the towel from her head and placed it over the back of the chair. She sat back down took another sip of tea, and continued, "He warned everyone from the beginning that this would be a private affair, shared with but a few. Many of the museum benefactors have become critical of my father and tried to have him removed from his role. He had to rely on the approval of the director of the French Ministry of Antiquity to remain in his position and continue. My father is a man of principle and to see him torn apart in the newspapers, and to hear some of the things being said about him—it makes me so angry." She finished her tea and placed the cup back on the saucer, pushing both aside. "I speak with my parents once a week, and my father always assures me not to worry, but my mother says the pressure is weighing on him. Mason, I am very concerned. My father is getting older and does not need this kind of consternation. He was only interested in preserving the art of France; he has dedicated his life to that cause, he has never been interested in personal gain. Many people believe he has taken art for his own personal collection, which is simply not true; these lies are being perpetuated by his enemies."

Mason could see Collette getting visibly upset, a combination of concern and anger.

"He has become aware of three paintings with questionable histories. He immediately had these removed from the list and set aside, until he could figure out their provenances. He needs time to research them, but given the way things have become in Europe, he does not have the time to do proper research right now.

A contact at the Louvre recently sent the three pieces to my father; they all share a similar story of questionable backgrounds. My father has been given the job of keeping these pieces safe so they can be properly researched at a later date. It is only a matter of time; Germany controls most of Europe, and they soon will have France. We know the Führer is very interested in the arts and will strike at the heart of France's collection. The art of France and all of Europe is under siege. We may never see these pieces again if they are taken by the German forces. This leaves my father in a very delicate position. He is in possession of paintings that do not belong to him, and he needs to keep them safe."

Mason sighed. He had an idea where this was going. Somehow this long, tragic story was going to end up right at his feet. He sipped his wine and continued to listen. He had many questions but wanted the full story before he began to dissect it; besides Collette was not the best person to answer his questions. He would save most of them for her father.

Collette reached across the table and took a sip of his wine. Mason watched without a sound as she slid the glass back across to him. "Very nice wine," she said and continued. "The Louvre has already begun evacuation plans for their museum. They are currently crating up the most valuable pieces and sending them to secret locations. The director of the museum along with my father, is personally involved in choosing the locations. Only a few people can know the destination points for the works of art. A master list is locked away in the director's vault at the museum. It will remain there until every piece has been sent away. After that, the list will be destroyed, and only a handful of people will know where the greatest treasures of France have been sent.

"My father has stored the three pieces he has in his cellar under the barn. He had the cellar dug before the last war to hide his valuables—and his family; thankfully we did not need it. I know when it was built, he prayed he would never have to use it, but I think he is glad he has it now. A secret access door must be triggered to gain access to the cellar. Nothing can be seen through the floorboards, no one would ever know there was a space underneath. The cellar is cool and has no light so the art will be fine down there for now, but who knows what will happen long term? War is coming, and France will soon be overrun."

Finally, Mason could not hold out any longer. "Look, I know that war is at France's doorstep for the second time in thirty years, and I am very sorry about that. We already went through the war to end all wars; this was never supposed to happen again. All the restrictions imposed on Germany after the war in the Treaty of Versailles were supposed to prevent this from ever happening again. Germany has continued to press the issue and be ignored. They slowly condensed all the power into one man, and he began building a war machine right under your noses. Nobody stepped up to stop him, and now it is too late."

"Prime Minister Chamberlain came back from Germany having signed the Munich Agreement, and declared, 'There would be peace in our time,' and received a hero's welcome in Britain. Meanwhile, Hitler is ripping up their non-aggression treaty and laughing at all of Europe. I am sorry, Collette, but Europe allowed this to happen. One of my favorite quotes from history is, 'The only thing necessary for the triumph of evil is that good men do nothing.' I am afraid the good men have done too little this time."

She looked at him with a tear in her eye. "It is easy to judge men from an ocean away. You have no idea who has done what. Hitler is mad. I don't think there are enough good men to ever stop him."

Mason looked up. "I am sorry. You're right. I should not have said that, and I agree Hitler's Third Reich is a very dangerous machine at this moment, and I, for one, am glad I am not living in Europe. But I still don't get what this has to do with me."

Collette looked down at her tea, "I am getting to that. You received my father's letter?"

Mason was taken aback by this question. He was unaware that anyone else knew about the letter. Moulié had asked him to not share any details contained within the letter, but apparently something had happened between then and now and changed the situation.

Collette continued. "I know it was vague, but it is now more important than ever, because we have run out of time. My father does not trust many people anymore; he wants to take matters into his own hands. He asked me to track you down to ask you a favor. I had not spoken to you in a long time."

Mason nodded in agreement.

"So, he gave me your father's information. I contacted him and said I needed to speak to you. He told me where you were living and how to get in if you were not at home. So here I am. He also told me you would be very happy to see me."

"Look, I am happy to see you, but I know you are only here because you need something. I would be happier if you had come by to ask me to dinner or a drink. I understand the predicament your father is in so what favor does he want from me?" Mason asked thinking, *I know exactly what favor your father wants.*

"Mason, he wants you to move the art in his possession and get it out of the country."

Mason laughed and shook his head. "You're not serious. Everyone is trying to get out of Europe, and you want me to go there. It is the absolute definition of a death trip. No way."

"Mason, don't be so dramatic, my father needs your help. He does not know where else to turn. He knows you can handle precious art; you have been around it your whole life. He knows you can go into France and get out without any questions. He knows you received military training, albeit brief. You can handle yourself in bad situations; time is running out. Besides, you are working at one of the most respected museums in the world. You have the perfect place to store some paintings until they are safe to return."

If only she knew. Timing is everything in life. The day he is asked to leave his internship at the museum, a long-lost friend shows up asking him to smuggle some art out of France and store it quietly in his former employer's museum. *Ahh…Collette, if only you had broken into my apartment a week ago, things would be a little easier.*

"I will come with you," she said. "We can fly out in a few days, spend some time at my father's farm, and then you can fly back. It will only take two weeks, in and out, very easy. It will be fun."

Very easy? Fun? he thought sarcastically. Nothing was easy when it involved Collette, and this would be the furthest thing from fun. *If she thought this was so easy, why did she feel the need to break in to my apartment to get my help? Why didn't she just call me on the phone?* He knew there was more to the story, but he would play along until he figured out what the real deal was. Smuggling out some questionable art pieces from France did not seem as if it should be a high priority at this time. What was so important about these three paintings that they needed to leave the country? He was not sure if Collette knew the answer, but if she did, she was not going to share it with him now. If these paintings needed to leave France, they must be pretty important, and during wartime, important things often attracted interest from bad people.

Mason stared at his wine and took a deep breath; he exhaled as he looked up at Collette. "Okay, I will help you and your father. I have too much respect for your father to say no. I am sure he has thought this through and must really be in a bind. There is one condition. If at any time I don't feel comfortable, I am walking away. I do not want to spend the rest of my days in a French prison for stealing the country's treasures, or worse as a prisoner of war in a Nazi jail."

Collette nodded her approval and smiled. "Thank you."

Mason had always loved her smile. He had not seen her in three years, and she was already making him do things he should not be doing. He had always known he would help Moulié, but he would string Collette along for a bit because it was fun. Who knew, maybe the job would be fun, too. After all, he did not have a job to go back to, and he loved a good adventure.

Collette walked around the table and gave Mason a big hug as he sat there finishing his wine. She went into the kitchen to put her cup and saucer in the sink. Meanwhile Mason thought back to his long walk with Dr. Heckler on the way to the director's office as he passed the Andrea Solario painting. His head was still on the silver platter, but this time Collette Moulié was holding it. He shook his head and finished his wine. These next two weeks were going to be interesting.

Collette gathered her things as she got ready to leave. Mason started to walk her to the door. It was really good to see her. He just wished that he was the reason for the visit, not some questionable paintings.

He grabbed his coat from the front hall closet, and they headed out the door. They left his apartment and headed down the hall to the elevator, closing the cast iron gate behind them. The Otis elevator was circa 1900, and had its share of quirks, but was generally a smooth ride. When they got to the main floor, Mason pulled the metal gate back and followed Collette out of the elevator.

As he turned to close the gate, he noticed the figure against the wall behind him. He recognized the man right away. Long black coat, dark hat, and scarf around his face. The man started to approach them, but before he could take two steps, Mason grabbed him by the lapels of his jacket and threw him against the wall. The man fell backwards awkwardly but maintained his balance. Mason grabbed him again and threw him to the ground. The man fell and tried to say something. Mason punched the man across the jaw. The sound echoed through the foyer. Luckily, Mrs. Stanton's radio was still on so no one noticed. The man lay stunned. Mason grabbed him and picked him up. He pushed the man against the wall and said, "Who the hell are you? Why have you been following me? Start talking, or I will snap your neck."

The man gathered himself and stared at Mason, his scarf now off his face. Mason could see straight into his eyes; they stared calmly back at him as a drop of blood clung to his upper lip.

"What do you want with me?" Mason shoved the man back against the wall. Collette looked on terrified.

The man straightened himself, and without leaving Mason's stare, "I am sorry, sir, I do not want any trouble. I have a message I must deliver, and I apologize, I am not looking for you." He nodded over Mason's shoulder and said, "I am looking for her."

Chapter 4

MASON LOOKED OVER AT COLLETTE, "Do you know this man?" She stared back with a blank look and shook her head. Mason turned back to the man still pinned against the wall, blood dripping from his lip, "What do you want with her?"

The man raised his hands and said, "Please? I mean no harm. I will explain."

Mason thought about it and, honestly, did not feel threatened at all. He had thrown the man around like a rag doll without any resistance.

Mason eased up on his grip and let the man stand on his own. He straightened his jacket and wiped the blood from his lip, while continually staring at Mason.

"I have come from France to find Mademoiselle Collette; I have an urgent message from your father." He glanced over Mason's shoulder at Collette. "I was told you would be visiting this address so I was merely waiting for you. That is why I have been following you, Mr. Wright. I am sorry for the confusion." The man's French accent was evident, but Mason was not easily convinced.

He narrowed his gaze, "How do you know my name, and who gave you my address?"

The man once again raised his hands in a defensive surrender, "I only have this information from her father."

"Okay," Mason said, as he relaxed a bit. He loosened his grip on the Frenchman. "What is this important message?"

"I am sorry. I can only deliver it to Mademoiselle Collette."

"Of course, but I am not letting you go near her so you

might as well start speaking," Mason said, dripping with sarcasm.

"Anything you need to say to me, you can say in front of him," Collette chimed in from across the room.

The man turned his head and looked at Collette, then returned his stare to Mason, who nodded with an arrogant smirk on his face. "So…what's the message?"

"I am sorry. My orders are to only relay this message to Mademoiselle Collette."

Mason turned and looked at Collette, she nodded her approval. Mason looked back at the man and took two steps back. He raised his right arm in an inviting gesture for the man to approach Collette. Mason did not like this, first a surprise visit from Collette, now a surprise guest in his building. He had not even made it out of New York, and things were getting complicated. He called it the "Collette Moulié effect," never simple.

The man approached Collette and extended his hand. She backed away and crossed her arms close to her chest in a defensive posture.

"That's close enough," Mason said.

The man obliged and said, "Very well."

Mason wanted to hear the message so he moved in a little closer to them.

The man introduced himself as Paul Ganoux, using English, then noticed Mason inching closer so he changed to French. He gave Mason a disapproving look, then continued, apparently knowing Mason's French was not good enough to allow him to follow along.

Mason rolled his eyes and started to shake his head. He tried to make out what they were saying, with no success. He was already agitated, and this was not helping. He glanced over at Collette again; she was noticeably concerned. She began to raise her voice.

After a couple minutes of back and forth, the man extended his arm to shake Collette's hand. This time, with approval, she shook back, still visibly shaken. He approached Mason and said, "I am sorry for any trouble my visit has caused. I will see you in the morning."

Mason looked back at him with surprise, "Why would I be seeing you in the morning?"

The man smiled and turned to exit the building.

Mason watched the man exit as Collette came over to him. She gave him a little nudge and said, "Look at you, so protective of me."

Mason, still watching the exit, replied, "You? I was protecting myself."

Collette shoved him again and laughed.

"So, what was the big message from Paul Ganoux?"

"He was contacted by my father and sent here to get a message to me. My father told him I would be coming to see you so he has been hanging around you, hoping that would lead to me. Do you remember the list of art I spoke of, the list that was locked in the vault?"

Mason nodded.

"It is gone. The list with the whereabouts of all of France's art collection is now out there." Collette made a gesture with her hand, clearly shaken by this thought. "Only a few people even knew of its existence, but someone has taken it. Therefore, the original plans need to be altered; we need to leave immediately. My father will meet us in Paris and take us to the art. He cannot risk the fact that someone else finds out about the barn. The list only tells of documented pieces. The pieces my father has are undocumented; no one will be looking for them."

"How many people had access to the vault?"

"I don't know, but someone got into it. It could have been someone who does not like my father, or someone who has darker motives, I don't know. With war approaching anything is possible. M. Ganoux has tickets for us and will meet us at the airport in the morning. Let's grab your things and go to my place, we can head to the airport from there."

"So that's why he said he would see me in the morning," Mason said to himself.

"What?" Collette asked as she looked up at Mason

"Can I ask you something? Have you ever met or heard of Paul Ganoux? Why should we trust this man?"

"I don't think we have much choice. I don't know him, but I do believe him. He has known my father for a long time. He explained their relationship as he introduced himself, and besides, if he wanted to hurt us, he very easily could have as we came out of the elevator. Anyway, you will have a chance to get to know him better tomorrow."

"Oh yeah. Why's that?"

"Because he is flying with us to France," she said with a smile.

"You have got to be kidding me. Now we have a babysitter?"

"Relax, Mason, it will all be fine, let's go get your things."

Mason grabbed Collette's arm, and stopped her. "Collette, listen to me. I do not trust people this quickly. I will be watching him closely, and if I get a bad feeling about any of this, I will do something about it."

Collette looked up at Mason and raised her eyebrows with concern. "Mason, please do not embarrass me or my family."

Mason looked back at her with a reassuring smile. "I will try not to embarrass you while I worry about keeping us alive. This Ganoux is a complete stranger to both of us. If he is in fact who he claims to be, then you have no worries. If I find out he is not, I will throw him out of the plane and into the Atlantic Ocean."

Back in his apartment, Mason gathered a small suitcase and packed the essentials: clothes, toiletries, and his Colt semi-automatic M1911 pistol, along with some extra ammunition. He also tucked away his map from the museum into a side zippered pocket, closed the suitcase, and turned off the light. Emerging from the bedroom, he noticed Collette staring at him as he walked down the hallway. She looked at his tiny suitcase, "That is all you need?"

"Yes, this is all I need. Quick trip, in and out, remember? I travel light." He knew this would get a rise out of her. He suddenly had this vision of them arriving at the airport, he with his one small bag, and Collette with ten suitcases. He smiled at Collette and said, "Let's go." She stared at him with a blank look as he walked by her smiling.

The rain had stopped outside, but the ground was still soaked. They would have to dodge puddles if they wanted to walk. Collette's apartment was on the west side of town; it was about a thirty-five-minute walk. Mason wanted some fresh air so they agreed to walk down Fifth Avenue for a few blocks; it would be easier to hail a cab once they were past the museum.

Mason carried his bag in his left hand as he ushered Collette along with his right. They walked up 86th Street, crossing over Lexington Avenue. The streets were mostly empty, but the traffic on Fifth Avenue was still bustling.

As they walked up 86th Street, a black car pulled out into traffic and started to proceed slowly up the street, also. Nobody noticed the slow-moving vehicle. The car pulled over again just before reaching Lexington Avenue.

When Mason and Collette reached Madison Avenue, Mason suggested they cross the street so they could turn left onto Fifth Avenue, just ahead. As they crossed over 86th Street, Mason noticed the black car pull over a block behind them. The car remained running, and no one got out of it; it just sat there, idling.

They reached Fifth Avenue, and Mason looked back again for the black car. It had moved closer but was still parked on the side with the engine running. He wondered if Paul Ganoux was following them.

He suggested to Collette that they cut through Central Park; she did not like the idea at this time of night. Mayor La Guardia had given an initiative to unify the parks system; he hired Robert Moses to clean up Central Park. The park was making progress, but still had some ways to go. Most people avoided it after dark because it was dangerous. Collette tried to avoid the park altogether, and she made this known to him.

The "Hoover Shantytown" was gone, but some of the inhabitants remained. An unsightly group of people wandered the park at this hour: working girls, gangs, drug addicts, and pickpockets.

Collette clung to his arm, even though Mason assured her they would be safe. He wanted to see if they were indeed being followed and, if they were, by whom. The cover of darkness, as well as the park, would give them some protection if needed.

They entered the park at 86th Street right next to the Metropolitan Museum. It seemed like days ago that Mason had left there, but it had only been a few hours. A lot had happened in those few hours, and as they passed it, he hoped to be back in two weeks to return the map to Director Montgomery. He was growing less confident in that possibility with every passing second.

Once in the park and covered by darkness, Mason stopped and turned to watch the black car still parked and idling on the side of the road; two men now stood talking outside it. One of the men pointed toward the park, and the other looked and nodded as he adjusted the midsection of his coat. Mason knew right away he was securing a pistol. The man began to jog toward the entrance of the park.

Collette asked Mason what he was doing. He grabbed her hand and said, "Let's go."

The pathway was lined with wrought iron benches and gas lamps. A few years ago, all these benches had been vandalized, and half the lights did not work. Mason knew his way around the park after spending countless days there after work. He was not afraid; he knew how to handle himself. If someone was following them, the park would give him the advantage.

The winding path was damp from the rain, and empty because of the time. Most of the hoodlums would be farther inside the park; they were still on the outskirts. Mason held Collette's hand as they walked quickly past the benches and further into the park.

They made a left onto a main path which ran behind the museum. Mason told Collette his thoughts about the man who was following them. Collette wondered aloud why they would be followed. She thought Mason was just being paranoid.

"Maybe he is a friend of your father's and has an important

message for you." Mason laughed at his attempt at humor; Collette did not.

Mason stopped and turned to Collette. "I follow my instincts. They tell me this man, whoever he is, is not just strolling through the park on a winter night alone for fun. I am telling you, there is someone looking for us. This is the perfect place to confront someone, because if people hear screaming, or a fight, or see a body, they don't think twice. It happens all the time. I know this park very well. We are in here because I can hide us, and then get us out. I guarantee whoever this man is, he has not been in this park as much as I have so trust me, okay?" Collette nodded, and they continued into the park.

Suddenly the bushes next to them rustled as a squirrel ran across the path. It was very quiet in the park, and the clouds were starting to disperse. The moon was starting to show through the break in the night sky. The sounds in the bushes were becoming more frequent as the creatures of the night began to awaken.

Collette spoke up. "Mason, I don't like this."

Mason held his finger to his mouth, signaling quiet. They crouched down on the path. They could make out the faint sound of footsteps near them. The footsteps were getting closer. Mason grabbed Collette, and they ducked behind a bench surrounded by thick brush. Collette was completely out of sight as a figure appeared in the moonlight and stumbled forward toward them. Mason stood up as it approached.

"Can you spare some change?" the figure mumbled, staggering forward.

"Get out of here," Mason said sternly, pushing the drunken man along.

Collette got up and came from behind the bench. "That was not very nice."

"Being nice is really not my concern right now."

They followed the main path as it snaked its way around the back of the museum, approaching the lights illuminating Cleopatra's needle, a 3,400-year-old obelisk, brought over from Alexandria in 1881, thanks to William Vanderbilt. It was erected in a rather obscure part of the park since it was feared that it was unstable and might topple over. Those fears had since been forgotten, and it stood proudly sixty-nine feet high, illuminated in the New York night directly behind the museum.

As they approached the lit courtyard where the obelisk stood, they could see people huddled on a bench trying to keep warm. Runaways were also a problem in the park. They would gather under the lights of the needle because it was safer. Mason and Collette passed the obelisk on their left and headed farther into the park.

"Who do you think could be following us?" she asked as they approached the stone Greywacke Arch.

"I don't know," Mason answered in between cold breaths. "The last person that was following me turned out to be looking for you so I could ask you the same question."

"Why would anyone be following me?"

"Gee...I don't know. You have just asked me to smuggle stolen art out of your homeland and hide it in a New York museum. I can't imagine why anyone would be interested in stopping that."

"The art is not stolen," Collette replied with disdain.

"I'm sorry. You're right. The art will not be considered stolen until I take it, then it will be stolen. Look, let's just get to your place and we will worry about everything else later. I have a thousand questions you can't answer so I would rather just make it through tonight. We are going to be fine. Let's just get to the fountain, and we can make our way back to Fifth Avenue from there."

Collette stopped and turned to Mason as they approached the opening of Greywacke Arch, an old sandstone archway built in 1862, which runs under the East Drive above. "Thank you." She leaned in and kissed him. They shared a moment in the dark. The memories came flooding back to Mason's mind. The thoughts he always had of them scouring the globe together in search of rare artifacts, carrying on their father's legacies. Those thoughts had ended abruptly when they parted ways. He had always hoped this day would come again. Mason figured if they ever met up again, it would happen under very strange circumstances and, of course, he was right.

"Don't thank me until we are in the air tomorrow. We're going to be fine…I promise." Mason gave her a reassuring look. "Now, we have to get moving." Mason grabbed her hand and started to walk under the arch.

On the path above a man watched their every move, crouched in the shadows behind a bush to the right side of the arch, as they passed under him. Once they had moved farther down the path, he stood and watched as the happy couple continued into the darkness. He knew the pair would soon be in The Ramble, a very secluded section of the park. They were leading him into the perfect spot, far into the park where very few people dare go, and that is where they would all meet. The man smiled as he watched them disappear behind some trees.

Chapter 5

THE RAMBLE IS A 38-ACRE PATCH of Central Park littered with winding paths, rough terrain, and isolation; it is virtually deserted at night. During the day it could be a grueling walk, and at night it was downright treacherous. The rock and gravel paths of The Ramble eventually lead down to The Lake. A former swamp, The Lake was excavated by hand, and opened to the public in 1858.

Mason and Collette entered The Ramble from the East and ventured toward Belvedere Castle. Built in 1869, the Castle had housed the weather station for New York City since 1919; it provided daily weather reports at 5 a.m. and 5 p.m. At this time of night, the station would be closed. The castle turret was visible in the distance as the moonlight peeked through the clouds. They turned left onto a rugged dirt path, which steeply turned downward; Collette slipped on the dirt, and Mason caught her before she fell. The commotion caused a stir in the bushes as a couple of squirrels ran away, chasing each other over the path and up the trunk of a tree.

Most peopled avoided The Ramble after dark; it was an area of the park that attracted unsavory characters. Mason was aware of this, so he stopped briefly and checked his Colt, which was tucked in his waistband; he had no intention of using it, just showing it. Power perceived is power achieved as the saying goes. They continued on through the night with the Bow Bridge as their destination. The bridge would carry them across the narrowest part of The Lake, and deposit them on Bethesda Terrace by the fountain. From there they could find their way out of the park onto Fifth Avenue and find a cab.

The man from the arch followed cautiously. He entered The

Ramble after them and took a parallel route, hoping to confront them before the bridge. His jacket was now open, exposing his gun in case things got ugly. Unlike Mason, he had every intention of using his if necessary.

Mason glanced back now and again, looking for anything suspicious. The coast was clear from his perspective. He felt confident that if someone followed them into The Ramble, the confusion of the landscape would be their best protection. Mason was usually here during the day, so the lack of light made it more difficult to get his bearings; he knew they were headed toward The Lake, so he kept them on the paths leading in that general direction.

As they walked onto a new trail, a group of street kids were gathered ahead around some large rocks. Mason stopped Collette and stepped in front of her as they slowly approached the group. One of the kids came forward and wished the couple a pleasant evening. Mason nodded as they passed by, making sure his Colt was plainly visible in the moonlight. The kid saw the weapon and immediately backed off. Mason glanced back over his shoulder to make sure the group had stayed by the rocks; they had not moved so he grabbed Collette's arm and picked up the pace a little bit.

The man following them witnessed the interaction from a trail that ran above the valley of rocks. He noticed the kids backing away as Mason and Collette approached. He knew this meant that Mason had a weapon clearly visible. These kids would surround anyone and take what they wanted. The only thing stopping them had to be the odds against them. They relied on a gang mentality, maybe a knife. They would not confront a gunman. The man continued up his path, which would wind its way across The Ramble to the mouth of the Bow Bridge.

Collette began to tire as the terrain became more rugged. "Can we rest a minute?" she said, stopping to lean on a tree.

"I would rather not, not here at least," Mason replied. "We are almost at the bridge; we can rest once we cross it and reach the fountain."

The man had arrived at the opening end of his trail. He could see the Bow Bridge through the trees. No one was ahead of him, giving him confidence that he had reached the bridge first. He climbed into the bushes and crouched down. He would hear Mason and Collette coming before they reached him; he waited silently and listened to the sounds of the night. The ground was muddy, and all the leaves were wet; a damp smell filled the air. He sat silently, his breath visible in the cold park air. If he didn't know any better, he would think he was in a forest somewhere upstate, not in the middle of Manhattan. The street sounds of the city were not here; this was seclusion, and he waited patiently for the couple to arrive.

Collette gathered her breath and stood back up. "I can't believe I let you convince me to take this route," she said with a hint of frustration.

"We're almost there. I don't think we are being followed anymore. I think we may have lost him. If you don't know your way around in here, you could be lost for hours. He is probably going around in circles, or maybe he ran into the kids."

They started back down their path heading toward the bridge. They were only about forty feet from the bridge entrance when Mason stopped. He grabbed Collette by the arm and pulled her to the side.

"What's the matter?" she asked.

"Call it a bad feeling. The whole walk we have been hearing the sounds of the park—squirrels, birds."

"I don't hear anything," Collette said as she stared at Mason.

"That's exactly my point," Mason whispered back. "The quiet means all the animals have scattered or been disturbed. When someone approaches all the animals run in a different direction. We have just walked fifty feet on a path, and not one animal has run away. Something tells me they already ran from something, or someone. I just don't like how quiet it is."

Mason grabbed Collette's hand and slowly started to walk toward the bridge, scanning the landscape as he went. A thick bush cradled them on the left side of the path, while the right side was a hill leading down to The Lake. The moonlight reflected off the water, rippling toward shore.

Distant voices broke the silence as a group of drunks yelled at each other. The voices seemed to surround them as Collette moved closer to Mason. After a few moments, the group moved farther away, and the voices became quieter and quieter until barely audible. Mason and Collette stood silently for a moment looking around for signs of life...nothing.

They turned to continue toward the bridge...and stopped short. Standing in front of them was a man with a medium build; he had used the distraction of the drunks to approach them. He pointed a gun in their direction as he approached saying nothing, just staring at them. Finally, after what seemed like an eternity, he spoke.

"You know, the park can be a dangerous place after dark. Two people could disappear without a trace very easily here." The man had an accent, definitely not from New York.

"What do you want?" Mason said angrily. He was upset about being distracted and allowing this to happen.

"I only want to talk."

"How about you put the gun away, then we'll talk."

The man looked at his gun briefly and shook his head, "I don't think so."

Mason kept his hands slightly raised as the man came closer. "So, talk. What do you want?"

The man laughed, "What do I want? Well, I want lots of things, but I don't think you are the person who can bring me any of them so what I want is not important. However, who I work for is very interested in something you have access to; my boss is very interested in a list."

"A list? I don't know anything about a list."

"Oh, I believe you do," the man said as he stopped in front of Mason. Collette stood silently looking back and forth between the two men as they continued.

"You'll have to be more specific, is it a laundry list, perhaps a grocery list, or maybe a class list?"

"Mr. Wright, I don't find you amusing. Both you and I

know the list I speak of. My boss is interested in the contents of that list, certain museum information; he is prepared to pay handsomely for the information. He knows you can get it and would like to offer you a chance at becoming a wealthy man."

"How wealthy are we talking?" Mason replied as Collette pierced her eyebrows in a disapproving stare.

"Oh...quite wealthy, Mr. Wright. Unfortunately, we both know that you do not currently have the list so your interest in the money is inconsequential at this point. I would simply like for you to entertain my offer. Here is a phone number. Should you like to discuss this matter further, simply call that number when you land in Paris, someone will answer; they'll be expecting your call, just ask for Alexander. Try not to take long coming to a decision; my boss can be a little impatient. I would suggest you call immediately after you land."

"What if we're not interested?"

"Mr. Wright, would you like some advice?"

"No, I'm not good at taking advice," Mason said, interrupting the man. He hoped by engaging the man, an opportunity would arise to make a move.

The man continued, his annoyance clear. "I would be interested if I were you, my boss does not make offers of this kind very often. When he does, he likes very much for them to be accepted; if they are not, he feels insulted, and trust me, you do not want to insult my boss, he does not take it well."

Mason stared at the man, who held a piece of paper in his extended left hand. His gun was still pointed at them in his right. Suddenly, a squirrel ran through the bushes next to them, the noise startled Collette, and the man looked into the bushes for a split second. Giving Mason the opportunity he was looking for, he swung his suitcase as hard as he could into the man's arm, sending his gun flying into the brush. The man stumbled and fell to the side. Before he regained his balance, Mason was on top of him. He grabbed the man around the throat and began to choke him. The man fired an elbow into Mason's gut, backing him up, then charged at him, and swung a right punch toward Mason's head. Mason leaned back as the man's fist passed by his face. He grabbed the man's arm, spun him around, and bent the man's arm behind his back. With his right hand, Mason grabbed the Colt from his waistband and pressed it into the man's temple. The man stopped struggling instantly, feeling the cold steel against his head; his puffs of breath showing in the night air.

"Easy now," Mason whispered as he steadied the man. He pressed his Colt harder against the man's head. Collette stood back watching the man's face grimace in pain; she was afraid Mason was going to break the man's arm.

"Mason, don't," she said, trying to calm the situation.

Mason shot her a glance and then leaned into the man's ear.

"Now you listen to me. I don't care who your boss is; there is no list. Either you can tell him, or I will. Understand?"

The man nodded and moaned as the pain in his shoulder grew; he felt his shoulder muscles begin to tear.

"Tell me, what were your instructions tonight? Are you supposed to call your boss after meeting us?"

"My orders are to call tomorrow," the man stammered. "Please, my arm."

"Good, then we don't need to make any hasty decisions. We have time to take a walk. Collette, check him for a wallet."

Collette walked over and retrieved a wallet from the inside pocket of the man's jacket and handed it to Mason; he tucked it in his coat pocket and shoved the man to the ground.

Lying on the gravel path, the man grabbed his arm and gritted his teeth; he moaned as he stared down the barrel of the Colt. "You almost dislocated my shoulder," he said, clearly in pain.

"You're lucky; I would have killed you if she wasn't here," Mason said with a tone that left no doubt he was telling the truth.

Collette retrieved the man's gun that lay in the bushes. She, too, pointed it at him. Mason pulled out the man's wallet and opened it; he slid out his ID, Franz Kolter. His address was in the Bronx; it was clearly fake.

"All right Franz, or whatever your name is. Get up and start walking. I have some friends I would like you to meet."

Franz gathered himself and stood up stumbling, almost falling down. Mason ordered him to put his hands on his head and start back up the trail into The Ramble. Collette handed Mason the gun, he recognized it right away, a German Luger, black steel with a wooden handle.

They continued up the path until they were back in the valley of the rocks. The gang of street kids was still hanging around when the three of them approached from the south. The same kid came forward to offer his greetings. He saw a man with his hands on his head approaching them followed by the couple, who had passed through a bit earlier.

"This is Mr. Kolter. He does not like New Yorkers. He tried to hold us up at gunpoint; as you can see, he was unsuccessful. He has a substantial amount of cash in his wallet; I was hoping you could entertain Mr. Kolter for a while and explain to him what wonderful people New Yorkers are. I suspect he does not need to be anywhere until morning so feel free to entertain him all night. Can you do this favor for me?" Mason said, holding out Franz Kolter's wallet.

"With pleasure," the leader nodded, as the other kids began to approach. Mason tossed the wallet to the kid as Mr. Kolter began to speak, "No, please, I will do anything, do not leave me here."

"Don't worry, you're in good hands, and oh...one more thing. You were right," Mason said as he pushed Mr. Kolter across the path and into the center of the gang. The kids encircled the man and began to grab for his coat.

"Right? Right about what?" Mr. Kolter yelled in a trembling voice.

Mason looked at him, "The park is a dangerous place after dark." He smiled as Mr. Kolter was dragged away.

Mason turned, grabbed Collette's arm, and led her back down the trail. The last sound they heard was the scream of a man who was going to have a very bad night. Mason knew they would not kill him, just strip him of anything valuable and render him a severe beating. A man found in the morning half naked, with no ID, would be picked up by the police for solicitation. He would then spend many days trying to convince the NYPD who he was. Mason felt comfortable that Franz Kolter would no longer be a problem.

Mason and Collette approached the Bow Bridge and hurried across. The Lake was a beautiful site with the moonlight reflecting in the middle. The Bethesda Fountain and terrace were straight ahead.

The Bethesda Fountain, Angel of The Waters, was designed by Emma Stebbins in 1868, and opened in 1873. It was the main attraction as you entered Bethesda Terrace from the north. At this time of night it was pretty empty, save for the occasional hobo sleeping on a bench. Mason and Collette arrived at the fountain and decided to rest for a minute. Collette was noticeably tired. Mason pulled Franz Kolter's gun from his waistband and put it into his suitcase. He kept the Colt in his belt, just in case.

"Who do you think sent Mr. Kolter after us?" Collette said in between breaths.

"I don't know," said Mason. "The person who sent him thinks we have the list or can get access to it. The Luger was an interesting move. German ID, German name, a German gun. It seems to point to Kolter being a German spy. I don't buy it, though; it seems too scripted, and his accent was definitely not German. Why would a German spy try to buy the list from us? An operative would wait until he can locate the list, steal it, and then eliminate anyone with knowledge of it. Nice and clean, no trail, and no contact. This chance meeting in Central Park is a little too exposed, too much is left to chance, not professional at all. If you are going to confront someone, you want to do it on your terms, in an environment controlled by you. Too many things can go wrong in a public setting, it doesn't add up.

"This has all the markings of black-market dealers. They work by intimidation, our fathers talked about it for years. I think someone knows war is coming quickly, and they are trying to locate where France's great art treasures will be stored. When the bombs begin dropping these people will go right for the cache of art, and my guess is they will sell them to the highest bidder or use them to buy their freedom. If you know where these priceless pieces of art are being kept, you become an instant friend to those who want them. Think about it, what more perfect cover for an art heist than an entire continent at war. We have to find out what happened to that list when we arrive in Paris. It may be the only thing we can use to keep ourselves alive."

"M. Ganoux said the list is gone," Collette said as she sat on the edge of the fountain. "Why would someone come after us asking for a list that has already disappeared? My father would have had nothing to do with the disappearance of the list so why are people attaching our names to it. It makes no sense, why would they think we have it?"

"I am not so sure about that. Look, your father is a very smart man, and if he had anything to do with the formation and storage of this list, he would not trust it to just anyone. He would not leave it in a scenario where it could disappear. It just seems too convenient that a list in a vault disappears two days after being locked up. I would suspect that the list which was stolen was supposed to be stolen. Your father clearly does not trust the people in charge of things in Paris; maybe he wanted them to have the list because it is not accurate." Mason paced back and forth in front of Collette as he tried to put the pieces together.

"Besides, if the list is missing, I would also not put it beyond your father to have stolen it himself. Your father knows the difference between friends and enemies. I believe that is why he contacted me. I think he has exhausted his short list of trusted countrymen, and now has decided to export his smuggling job to me, and that is why we are standing here in Central Park in the middle of the night."

"Someone must have the same idea, because they sent Mr. Kolter to find us, and they also knew we were headed overseas. Someone has connected us to the list, possibly your friend Ganoux." Mason paused for a second and brought his hands together in front of his mouth. He stared out across the fountain plaza at the trees as he collected his thoughts. He turned back to Collette, "Our only bargaining chip is the list. As long as people think we have it, or can get it, they will keep us alive. The second the list is out there, we become expendable. I believe your father put the stolen list out there to buy some time. People will be scrambling around for a while trying to figure out how this happened. I think he has the original authentic list, and is keeping it safe, possibly stored under the floorboards of a certain barn out in the country. At least I hope that is the case, or else we need to find that list before I leave France with your father's paintings."

"Collette, this is a very dangerous game we are about to play. Let's hope we are better at it than Kolter. This list is incredibly valuable. There is no telling how many people would like to get their hands on it. France's art collection could literally be open to the highest bidder. We can't let that happen." Mason looked around for a moment as Collette reflected on the gravity of their situation. She was clearly shaken by this whole experience; gone were the smiles and the jokes. She was scared, Mason saw, as she looked up at him.

Mason finally spoke up calmly, "We should get going. You ready?"

As they gathered their things, Mason looked at his watch, two minutes to midnight. Collette's legs felt like rubber. She was tired, scared, and emotionally drained. The only thing that helped her feel any better was being with Mason; he would take care of her. He always had, even when they were young. She had thought about him often over those years in which they did not speak. She had been confused, and after a while figured he had moved on with his life. If they made it out of this alive, she would never let him go again.

Collette was not dressed for a hike, and her boots were meant for the sidewalk, not rugged terrain, Mason still felt energized. The rush of the meeting with Mr. Kolter had injected new life into him. There was something about confrontation that Mason enjoyed. It did not happen often, but he relished it. He had a feeling he would be getting that rush again once they arrived in France. He would be ready.

They headed toward the stairs of Bethesda Terrace and under the lower passage; the moon, now clearly visible, reflected off the panels of the passage. The ceiling and walls were decorated with beautiful tile designs, resembling a European palace. The stone walkway led to the steps taking them up to The Mall, where the path widened, and they walked by rows of benches lining it. They passed through the music pavilion, the site of outdoor concerts in the summer, then up over a hill on their way out of the park.

Once through The Mall they went down to a lower path, which would take them back out to Fifth Avenue. The park was virtually empty. Mason and Collette could hear the sounds of the city approaching as they made their way to the end of the path. They reached Fifth Avenue at 65th Street and waited for a cab. At this time of night there were plenty available. They slid into its back seat and exhaled, relaxing for the first time in over an hour. They gave Collette's address and she quickly fell asleep on Mason's shoulder. He could smell her sweet perfume as she lay against him.

He turned his thoughts to the flight tomorrow; it would be a very long day. On the plane he would have plenty of time to get to know Ganoux. He would take all the time he needed.

Chapter 6

THE NEW YORK CITY CAB pulled up to the curb at Newark Metropolitan Airport on a beautiful New Jersey morning; it was approximately 7 a.m. The two passengers in the back seat had been together for less than twelve hours, though it felt much longer with everything they had been through. Since Collette had showed up at Mason's apartment last night, they had had a confrontation in the lobby with Paul Ganoux, an attempted hold-up by Kolter in Central Park, and now were facing a twenty-three-hour flight to Europe; if Mason's two weeks with Collette were going to be anything like the last twelve hours, he wasn't sure he would survive. Collette was exhausted, and her feet were sore from the night before. Mason hadn't gotten much sleep but felt surprisingly good.

They thanked the cabbie for the ride and got Collette's bags out of the trunk. She did not have ten bags as Mason envisioned but had brought two large suitcases and a handbag. As they closed the trunk, Paul Ganoux was standing on the sidewalk and waved hello. Collette shook his hand and exchanged pleasantries. Mason just nodded a hello and retrieved the bags. A young kid offered to carry them for fifty cents; Mason agreed to the kid's price and he grabbed both bags. The bags were almost twice the kid's size so Mason grabbed one back from him; it would have taken the kid an hour to get the bags to the plane.

"A lovely day for a trip," Ganoux announced, seemingly not speaking to anyone in particular. "I have our tickets. Everything is in order. We can proceed right to the gate. I was only able to get two seats together so I will be sitting by myself for the flight. I trust that is all right with you."

"Fine with me," Collette chimed in. "I plan on sleeping most of the flight anyway."

Mason glanced at Collette. "Perhaps Ganoux and I can start out the flight together so we can get to know each other a little better?"

Ganoux did not seem thrilled with the idea, but before he could speak up, Mason added, "Then it's settled. Paul and I will begin the flight together, and then we can move around once we are in the air."

"Please behave yourself, Mason," came a stern whisper from Collette.

Mason glanced over his shoulder at her and gave a reassuring nod. They were approaching the gate, and their young baggage carrier looked as though his arms were about to fall off so Mason said, "We can take it from here." Mason gave the kid a buck for his attempt at baggage handling; the boy was so tired he could barely get out a thank-you. Mason gave his suitcase to Collette and the heavier of Collette's two suitcases to Ganoux, who took it begrudgingly.

They arrived at Gate 7, where on the board was written, "Newark to Paris Flight A11." The estimated flight time was 23:30, with stops in Bermuda and the Azores for refueling. Collette shook her head at the sign. She had taken this flight before; it was an uncomfortable way to spend twenty-four hours. Mason seemed excited at the idea of flying across the Atlantic. He had usually made the trip by boat. He and his father had crossed the Atlantic countless times, usually returning with a crate full of antiquities. Traveling by boat was much more luxurious, but the trip was almost a week long. The thought of touching down in Paris tomorrow was pretty amazing in Mason's mind.

The call came to board the flight. Their three seats were row 15, seats A and B, and row 21, seat C. The boarding cards were collected, and onto the plane they went. Collette went right to row 21, stowed her handbag, grabbed a blanket, and was asleep before the plane left the gate.

Mason and Ganoux put their bags away and settled into

their seats. Mason sat by the window, and Paul had the aisle. They closed the cabin door, and the plane started away from the gate, approached runway one, and was cleared for takeoff. It started down the runway, sounding like a garbage can rolling down the street. It shook from side to side as if it would break apart at any moment. Mason glanced over at Ganoux; his eyes were closed, and he held the armrests so tightly Mason thought they might break before they got off the ground. The plane lifted off and the shaking stopped. The roar of the engines taking them airborne was deafening. Mason hoped once they were at a cruising altitude the noise would lessen. He needed to talk to Ganoux but did not want to shout at him.

The plane finally leveled out, the noise did lessen, and Mason figured it was time to engage Ganoux in some friendly conversation.

"Is this your first time flying?" Mason said, as Ganoux opened his eyes.

"Regrettably no," he replied. "I usually travel by boat, but unfortunately, we don't have time to sail across the ocean; I really do not enjoy this experience. I have flown a few times before and find myself thanking the Lord when the tires touch down at the end of the flight. How about you? Have you flown before?"

"Only in the U.S.; I don't mind it. I think it is pretty incredible how it all works. It is the future of travel, so you better get used to it. I believe soon that crossing the Atlantic is going to be a routine event." Mason glanced out the window for a moment and then back at Ganoux. "So…tell me about your relationship with Collette's father," he said, quickly getting down to business.

"I was stationed in Paris, and I was assigned to the museum detail. That is how I met M. Moulié. He required my services several times after the Great War. He needed a security detail to transport art pieces within France after the war. I was the head of his security."

"Security? What kind of work do you do? You said you were stationed in Paris. Does that mean military?"

"I fulfilled my military service during the Great War. I was discharged in 1929 and took a job with the Metropolitan Police; I am a freelance inspector. My assignment was M. Moulié; after the war he was in charge of reuniting the art that had been hidden during the war with the correct museum. I would ride with him around the country to make sure there were no issues."

"When I grabbed you in the hallway of my building you did not resist. Why? You have military training, but you let me throw you around. Why did you not fight back?"

"My orders were to deliver a message. If I had resisted it would have escalated into something worse. I handled it that way because the message needed to be delivered. The less I resisted, the quicker the message would be delivered. Besides, I did not want to hurt you," he said with a smirk.

"Oh…well I appreciate that, but I do know how to take care of myself. What has M. Moulié said about our little trip over to France?"

"I was just told to deliver the message, and then deliver the two of you to Paris. Aside from those details, I do not know anything else. Mr. Wright, as much as I am enjoying your interrogation, I am quite tired and would like to get some sleep; I would suggest you do the same so if there are no further questions, I will try to rest."

"Just one more question, and I will let you rest. Do you know a man named Franz Kolter?"

"No, I am sorry. I do not know anyone by this name. Why do you ask?"

"It's nothing, just a name I came across. I will let you get your rest now."

Ganoux grabbed a blanket from his seat front, covered himself, and turned his head to the side. Within minutes he was snoring, and Mason was left to wonder where this all was headed. He had slightly changed his opinion of Ganoux. He felt he was telling him the truth about his relationship with Collette's father so Mason decided he would not throw him out of the plane. Mason still had plenty of questions that needed answers, but he was not getting any more until they were on the ground in Paris; he adjusted his seat and decided to try to get some rest himself. He knew he would have to rest now, because he was not sure when he would have a chance again. Mason closed his eyes and quickly he was in a new world, 1880s Paris with a beautiful woman named Madame X.

~~~

"Do you have it?" the voice came from a man sitting behind the desk in the dimly lit office.

"Yes, and no," replied Lane as he shifted uncomfortably in his seat. "I was only able to get the southern portion of the map. The northern portion was not there. I was interrupted and had to leave the room quickly; someone was coming. I know who has the other half and, coincidentally, he is coming to you. He slid his portion of the map across the desk."

"What do you mean someone was coming? We got you access to the room after hours. It should have been a simple task. Go in, retrieve both parts of the map, and slip out unnoticed. We went through a lot for you to gain access to that room; we paid a hefty sum so that there would be no issues. No one was to be there."

"His name is Mason Wright. I heard someone coming down the hallway, so I slipped out the side door. I left so quickly documents were still on the table. I did not even get a chance to put them away. I heard two voices in the room, a man and a woman. The woman was questioning Wright's authority to be in the room. She left with him and when I returned, the room was locked. I used the key again, but when I entered, the room had been cleaned up, the documents were put away. I opened the drawer where the map would be, and it was not there. I had to leave the museum and catch my flight. I know Wright has it. I am sure of it. It is too much of a coincidence. The map is missing, and then two days later he is arriving in Paris."

"Mr. Lane, we need the full map, understand? One half is useless to us. Don't come back here until you have it. You do understand how very important this is to my country? You are doing a great service, and the church is very grateful. Oh...and one more thing. Do it quietly. We do not want people asking questions, understand?"

"Yes, of course, Father. I will have it by tomorrow night. I can assure you. Mr. Wright will be arriving soon, and I will get it immediately."

"Thank you. Oh...and once again, quietly. We don't want any incidents. I will not be able to protect you should this become public. I shall have your payment upon receipt of both sides of the map."

"I understand, Father."

The priest, in his long robe stood and followed Lane out of the office and to the side entrance.

"Tomorrow night. I will be awaiting your call."

Lane nodded and disappeared out into the French night.

The priest locked the door and stared at the lock for a moment with a concerned look. He knew that an explanation was going to be required. He just hoped it was not tonight. The people he would have to answer to were not forgiving. The priest walked across the room and through the door into the chapel. He slowly walked up the aisle, his footsteps echoing through the stone church. He arrived at the altar and made the sign of the cross. He began to pray. He would ask for forgiveness, even though there would be none to be had.

Chapter 7

AFTER REFUELING STOPS in Bermuda and The Azores, flight A11 landed at Le Bourget airport in Paris, world famous for receiving the cross Atlantic flight of Charles Lindberg in 1927. As the plane touched down with the subtlety of an anvil hitting the ground, Mason reached over and grabbed Collette's hand. She looked exasperated; after twenty-three-plus hours of flight no one was happier than she to be on the ground—well possibly only Paul Ganoux. Collette and Ganoux had switched seats while the plane was refueling in The Azores. It was 8:15 a.m. local time, and there looked to be a light rain falling outside. The plane came to a stop near the entrance to the airport gate. Mason's legs felt as if they were no longer attached to his body. He would need some stretching and walking before he would be back to normal. He looked over at Collette, who was fixing her hair in a small compact mirror. She looked beautiful, even after the long flight. He was pretty sure she would not agree with him, so he kept his thoughts to himself.

The row in front of them began to disembark so Mason stood up and retrieved his suitcase. Collette's bags would need to be collected from under the plane. There were men removing suitcases and placing them on the wet tarmac, to be retrieved as the passengers exited. After gathering her two suitcases, Mason and Collette waited under the overhang near the door to the airport gate for Ganoux to emerge from the airplane. After a few minutes he appeared, looking as though he had aged ten years in a day. Also traveling light, he did not need to retrieve a bag from underneath. He navigated down the airplane stairs and began to walk toward them.

"Well, that was pure misery," Ganoux said as he arrived

under the overhang.

Mason smiled, "I did not think it was so bad."

Collette chimed in, "Sorry, Mason, I am going to side with Paul on this one; that was pretty miserable."

"All right, where do we go?" Mason asked, turning to Ganoux.

"This way." Ganoux picked up one of Collette's suitcases, leaving the heavier one for Mason.

He led them into the airport gate and up the stairs to the main floor. The airport was fairly clean but showed its age. Several cracks were visible in the cement walls, and the stone floor was dirty and faded. After all, the airport was twenty years old. The more modern Orly airport was only a few years old and was starting to receive more traffic. The three of them proceeded down the main hallway past several gates. They could tell who was ready to board a plane and who had just arrived. The looks on the faces of the passengers eager to get on their planes were different than the weariness on the faces of the newly arrived. Mason laughed to himself as he looked around at the fragility of the human spirit.

A large group of people were roped off on the left side of the airport, waiting to go through a small door. French police were patrolling the area.

"Who are they?" Mason asked Ganoux, as they slowed down next to the large line of people. They ranged in age from very young to very old, all carrying large suitcases some pushing large trunks, small children hugging their dolls. For such a large group, there was a somber feel. There was little conversation, and blank stares adorned many of the faces. They looked tired and weak, many almost asleep on their feet.

"They are German Jews. They have fled their homeland and are seeking asylum in France. Hitler has started to oppress the Jewish people, and many are fleeing before it gets worse. I have heard stories of parents sending their children away and promising to join them soon. Some of these people have relatives to take them in, but most will be turned away. France cannot accept everyone. Many are trying to get to America by boat. I understand they need to be accepted by an American citizen to gain entry into the United States. If not, they will be sent elsewhere. You are looking at German citizens who no longer have a country to call home, because their home does not want them anymore. I believe this is the start of Germany's threat to Europe. Hitler believes in a master race, and I think he envisions that master race for all of Europe."

"That is terrible," Collette said as she wiped a tear from her cheek. She noticed a girl at the front of the line carrying a large leather suitcase. She could not have been more than ten or eleven years old and seemed to be traveling alone. The girl was wearing a heavy wool coat and a hat. She stared blankly at the back of the person in front of her. No one acknowledged her presence as the line moved ahead. She struggled to keep up with the weight of the suitcase. She must have sensed Collette looking at her. She raised her head, and turning it slightly returned Collette's stare, then immediately put her head down. She was terrified; Collette could see that. She noticed her dark wool jacket had a yellow star attached to it, almost like a badge. "Why do some of them have yellow stars on their jackets?"

"Hitler has made the Jewish people wear the Star of David on their clothes so they will be labeled as Jews. He also encouraged the German people to boycott Jewish businesses, in hopes that they will close up shop and leave on their own. A Pogrom against Jewish businesses in November of 1938 left most of them looted and destroyed, people have disappeared, it is a terrible situation. He is using propaganda to turn the whole country against the Jews. It is a dangerous place to be at this time if you are not of pure Germanic descent." He paused for a moment and then spoke again in a softer voice. "I am sorry, we must get going."

They proceeded down the main corridor until Ganoux stopped the three of them in front of the restroom. He suggested they split up before entering the main reception area. He did not want them to be seen together. He would go ahead and meet them out front with the car. As French citizens he and Collette would be able to clear customs first. Collette said she needed the restroom so she and Mason stayed back as Ganoux went ahead.

After their bathroom break, Mason led Collette through the double doors into the meeting area. The space was designated for uniting passengers with their awaiting parties. The overall environment was much happier on this side of the doors. Tears of joy and hugs were plainly visible. Many people waved their hands wildly as people emerged through the doors. The passengers needed to proceed to the left and deal with customs before being reunited with their loved ones.

Mason and Collette made their way through the crowds to the customs line. Collette went to the citizens' line, while Mason went to the much longer visitors' line. As they both waited on their respective lines, a face in the crowd watched their every move. Lane had positioned himself with a perfect view of the couple arriving from New York. He had taken a transport two nights ago and arrived last night. He noticed that the woman had two large suitcases, while Wright had a small carry-on bag. It seemed the woman was going to be staying a while, and Mason was going to be in and out. He stared at Mason's bag, figuring the map was there.

A British couple at the front of Mason's line was making a fuss over the treatment they were receiving from the French customs officials. Mason just shook his head and shifted his weight to his other foot. Collette breezed right through with little scrutiny and waited on the other side for Mason.

Finally, he reached the front of his line. He opened his suitcase and handed over his papers. The agent looked at Mason silently, and then at his papers.

"What is the nature of your visit to France?" the agent said in a monotone voice.

"I am vacationing," Mason replied.

"It is a rather odd time to come to France for a vacation, Monsieur, don't you think?" the customs agent asked with a puzzled look.

"My mother said the same thing before I left." Mason smiled at the agent.

The agent was confused by the American, but then again, he had been confused by many Americans since he took this job. They all had a strange sense of humor.

"Have you anything valuable to declare upon entrance to the country?"

Mason thought to himself, *Besides the borrowed map from the Metropolitan Museum of Art and the two guns in my waist, no.* The map was tucked away in a special compartment under the main part of the suitcase, only accessible through the bottom of bag.

"No, sir, just my clothes and toiletries."

The agent riffled through his clothes quickly and closed the suitcase. He stamped the visa papers for Mason and wished him a nice vacation with a still-confused look. He signaled with his right hand to move along. Mason gathered his papers and his bag and continued toward the glass customs doors where Collette was waiting for him. She looked at him and he nodded. "No problems."

He grabbed Collette's heavier suitcase and they started for the main entrance to the airport. Lane was not far behind, walking with a newspaper tucked under his right arm. He figured the map had to be in Mason's suitcase because he would not want it out of his sight.

Collette wanted a little pick-me-up so they stopped at an espresso stand. Mason stayed with the bags while Collette ordered. This gave him a chance to scan his surroundings. Nothing seemed odd. People were coming and going carrying all sizes and colors of luggage, speaking many different languages. Several people were seated on the benches in the airport reading the newspaper. Two policemen slowly walked through the terminal, scanning the crowd for anything suspicious.

Collette returned with a small paper cup of steaming coffee. They sat for a minute as she drank it down. When she was done, they gathered their things and made their way toward the main entrance, Lane still trailing a good distance behind.

They reached the main door and walked out into the gray

drizzle of Paris's outskirts. A row of taxi cabs idled directly in front of the door. Several pushy drivers approached them offering cheap rides to wherever they were going. Mason just pushed them aside and they continued on down the sidewalk to the left. They walked by a few more people and approached a row of benches. Collette stopped suddenly, grabbing Mason's arm.

"Is everything ok? What's wrong?" he asked as they stopped. Collette nodded over toward one of the benches, noticeably upset. Mason turned to see the girl with the heavy leather suitcase sitting alone, wiping tears from her eyes. He turned back to Collette and put his arm around her. She started to cry into his shoulder and in between sobs said, "How can people in this world be so terrible? This poor girl is all by herself, in a foreign land, because someone decided they did not like her. How does this happen?"

"I don't know," Mason replied.

Collette looked up at Mason and handed him her bag. She wiped her face and walked away toward the bench. As she approached the girl, Collette bent down on one knee. The girl looked up and pulled her suitcase closer.

"My name is Collette. I was wondering if you need help."

The girl stared at the ground.

"Are you waiting for someone? I can call someone for you if you would like?"

The girl continued looking at the ground and shook her head.

"Do you mind if I sit down?"

The girl moved over a little and Collette sat down next to her.

"What is your name?"

"Anna," the girl said sheepishly.

"That's a beautiful name. Are you here alone?"

She looked up at Collette, her eyes still wet with tears, and nodded yes.

Mason was watching from a distance. He was anxious to get going, Ganoux was still waiting for them with the car, but he knew Collette needed to finish this without him urging her to go. He felt terrible about this little girl's situation, but there was very little they could do.

Mason watched as Collette and Anna talked for a minute. She saw the girl nod her head in approval, and then Collette stood up, and reached out her hand. Anna grabbed her hand and stood up. With her other hand, Collette picked up Anna's suitcase and they walked over to Mason together. Mason looked at Collette as she approached. His face now showed some apprehension.

"Mason, this is Anna. She is coming with us."

"Umm…I'm…I'm sorry…What?" Mason replied as he looked at Collette with questioning eyes.

"Mason, she has no one here to care for her. She had the papers to enter the country, but she is completely on her own. If she stays here, she will end up in an orphanage, or worse, be picked up by hoodlums and forced to work the streets. I will not let that happen to her. I will bring her to my father's farm, and she will stay with me for now, until I can figure out a solution. I will not leave her here at the airport. I am not asking you for your approval. I am telling you I will not leave here without her."

She gave Mason a stern look, and he knew there would be no changing her mind. He bent down to Anna's height, and said, "Hi, Anna, my name is Mason." The girl looked at him and moved closer to Collette's side as Collette put her arm around her. Mason stood up, exhaled, and nodding said, "Ok…well, let's go then."

Lane watched the scene from across the street. He could not figure out what was happening. As far as he knew there was no child involved in this scenario. He'd agreed to do a job but was told nothing about a child being with the couple.

Mason saw Ganoux approaching as he flashed his car lights. Mason flagged down the car as if he was hailing a ride. Ganoux pulled over to the curb, got out of the car, and opened the trunk, acting as if he was a taxi driver, in case anyone was watching. He looked at Mason for some kind of an explanation.

Somehow in the last half hour they had managed to acquire a young girl. Anna and Collette got in the back seat, and Mason got in the front. Ganoux climbed in the driver's side, and once comfortable, quietly turned to Mason. "Who is the girl?"

"Don't worry about it, just go."

"You know, Mason, kidnapping is a very serious charge in France."

"We are not kidnapping her. She has no family. She is one of the German Jews from the airport. She was sitting out front crying, and she has nowhere to go. Her family sent her here in hopes of saving her life. Collette has decided to help her out. Perhaps you can help Collette find a place for her? She will be safer with us than here at the airport. Now can we go?"

Ganoux put the car in gear and pulled away from the curb. He said under his breath, "I get them all the way to France with no problem, I leave them in the airport for thirty minutes, and they emerge with a child. It was all going so well."

They headed for the exit of the airport, and the quickest way to the warehouse district of Paris.

Lane followed far behind to avoid suspicion. He was still wondering who the little girl was. He just wanted to get the map and be done with this. Once paid he would disappear as he always did until someone came calling again. His work involved getting things done and not asking questions. He did not know who this girl was, but he focused solely on the map, and if a child needed to be harmed in the process, it was all part of the job.

Chapter 8

THEY REACHED THE EXIT of the airport and turned onto the Avenue du Woodrow Wilson, named in honor of the U.S. president after the Great War. Traffic was light at this time of day, and everyone settled in for the ten-mile ride into the Paris warehouse district. Ganoux drove in silence as Collette and Anna spoke quietly in the back seat. Mason watched the scenery go by as he wondered how much time was left before the German war machine arrived in France. They were riding on a street named in honor of a man who helped end the Great War. Before history had a chance to settle, a new war to end all wars was on the horizon. When would it end? *Probably only when there was no one left,* he thought. Man's greatest threat on this earth was his fellow man. He glanced in the mirror at Collette and Anna. This poor girl should be running around with her friends playing games. Here she was in a foreign place riding down the road in a car full of total strangers. Her childhood was over. Her life would never be the same. She would most likely never see her parents again. He could not imagine the thoughts running through her head.

Ganoux broke the silence, "I will drop you at the warehouse, and then go get some groceries. We will need to eat. I will pick up some essentials, and then we will figure out our next move. Your father will meet us later. He is coming in from the country and should be here by dusk. He is very anxious to see both of you."

They had turned on to Boulevard McDonald, which connected with other roads to form a loop around the city. Mason could see the Eiffel Tower through the haze in the distance. One of the most recognized landmarks in the world, he had climbed it when it had first opened to the public. The view of the city had been amazing.

Following the signs for downtown, they continued onto Boulevard Davout. They would take this road to the Rue de Paris, which would take them out of town to the warehouse district. The church of Saint Germain was visible ahead on the right, and Ganoux got in the left lane to turn onto Rue de Paris.

Several car lengths behind, Lane followed in a black Renault. He planned to follow them to their destination, and then wait for an appropriate time to sneak in and get his map.

Anna had fallen asleep against Collette's side, and Collette put her jacket over her to keep her warm. Collette was getting hungry; she was happy that Ganoux would be getting groceries. She would make a nice big dinner for everyone.

They turned onto an old cobblestone road name Rue de Soneaux. The road was lined with warehouses, each with large wooden doors in front. Trucks and cars were pulling in and out of various addresses. The warehouse district became quieter at night as businesses closed, providing an ideal place to make a plan for going forward. Mason started to recognize the area. He had been here years ago with his father when they did some work with Collette's family. He could not believe he was back here, and with Collette.

They arrived at Number 19, and Mason offered to get out and unlock the doors. Ganoux gave him the keys to the large metal padlock, which held the chains together through the large wooden door handles. Mason jumped out into the soft rain and approached the doors. He tried the first key in the lock, and it did not work. He tried the other key, and the old metal padlock snapped open. He removed the padlock and pulled the chains through the handles. He tossed them aside as he grabbed one of the large handles. He opened the righthand door and pushed it until it was all the way open. Then he opened the other side far enough so the car could enter. Once inside he retrieved the lock and chains and closed the heavy doors from the inside, pushing the two big deadbolts through the metal clasps, locking the doors.

Lane pulled past the building, gazing quickly at the number and doing a quick survey of the property. There was not much to go on from the front: two large wooden doors and a smaller entrance door to the left. A dirty window was to the left of the smaller door. He would have to venture around back to see if there was access behind. If not, his job was more complicated. He would have to wait until he saw an opportunity.

Inside, Mason and his ever-growing band of smugglers were getting settled in. After the long flight everyone was happy just to be on the ground. The warehouse had a two-car bay to pull into and a small set of stone steps leading from the ground to the loading area. Inside the office doors was a large room with tables and couches. Off the main office were a kitchen, a storage room, and a room with two beds. Everyone gathered around the large table as it was already approaching 1 p.m. Collette put some coffee on. Ganoux and Mason decided to go to the local market for some groceries.

Anna was still very quiet and would not leave Collette's side. Mason caught her looking at him and smiled; she turned away. She seemed to be doing better. Considering everything she had been through, it was amazing that she was even able to function. Collette had a very nurturing way about her, and it was evident in the way she handled Anna. If you did not know better, you would think Anna was her little sister.

Ganoux returned from the restroom and asked Mason if he was ready to go. Mason nodded; they gathered their coats and headed for the car. Collette gave him a list of things to get at the market. She had underlined some things as necessities: candy, drawing paper, coloring pencils, and juice. Mason understood and promised he would not return without them. He removed his Colt from his waistband and handed it to her. Collette reluctantly took the gun. "Do not open the door for anyone, understand?"

"Yes," she replied. "Be careful."

Mason opened the large wooden doors, as Ganoux backed the car out. Mason closed the doors and gave them a bang with his hand. Collette heard the bang and locked them from the inside. Mason got into the passenger seat, and they drove away, unaware of Lane. Watching the two men drive away, he smiled at the opportunity that had just presented itself.

Collette put the gun on the table. She gathered more wood for the wood burning stove, and immediately the warehouse became a little warmer. Anna was asleep on the couch. Collette laid a blanket over her and gave her a tender kiss on her forehead.

Collette retired to the kitchen and began to set up to cook. She tried to limit the banging of pots; she did not want to disturb Anna. She filled the sink with hot water and began washing some of the pots; a few of them looked as though they had never been washed. *Men,* she thought to herself, *they will eat off anything.* She began to sing to herself a song in French, which her mother would sing to her when she was a little girl. When she turned around to grab the dish towel, Anna was standing in the doorway, a small smile on her face. Collette looked at her and began to sing a little louder. Anna laughed and came and sat down next to the sink. She was still wearing her jacket. Collette found a pair of scissors and crouched down in front of Anna. She began to cut away the thread that attached the Star of David to Anna's jacket. Anna looked down at her jacket as the yellow star began to fall away. Collette cut the last thread, and the star fell into Anna's lap. Collette picked it up and put in Anna's pocket. She looked at Anna and said, "You don't have to wear that here. Here you are not anything but a little girl, and I will make sure it is always that way."

Anna stood up and gave Collette a hug. She had not said anything since they arrived, but now she whispered, "thank you." Collette returned the hug and began to sing the song again.

The special moment was interrupted by a knock at the side door. Collette stopped singing and rushed Anna into the bedroom. She sat her on the bed, and put her finger to her lips, whispering "shhh."

Collette closed the door to the bedroom as there was a second knock at the door. She ran into the main area and grabbed the Colt off the table. She put it in her waistband and went to the window to see who was there. She could barely see out the window, it was so filthy. She noticed a black car in front of the warehouse, with its front hood up, looking as if someone had broken down. She couldn't make out who was at the door. A third knock came, this time louder, then a voice yelled from outside, "Excuse me, I have broken down with my car, might I be able to use your phone?"

Collette stayed silent, hoping the man would go away. The voice came again, "I am sorry to bother you, but I really need help. I am due to pick up my children and need to call my wife so she knows I cannot. I see the light on, can you please help me? I promise to only be a minute."

Collette shook her head. The man sounded truthful and was clearly concerned. She heard Mason's voice in her head telling her not to open the door for anyone. She struggled with it for a minute, then the voice returned. "Please, I need help. I can pay you for the call. I really need to phone my wife."

"Just one minute," Collette relented as she placed the Colt in her waistband under her sweater.

"Oh, bless you, thank you so much," the voice from the other side of the door said with much relief.

Collette walked toward the door and unlocked the bolt. She opened it a little and peered out at the man standing there. He was in his mid to late forties with a heavily receding hairline, almost six feet tall wearing a dark wool suit.

He smiled and said, "Thank you, mademoiselle, I am afraid that my children will be left at the school with no one to pick them up. If I could just use your phone to call my wife, she can pick them up."

Collette nodded to the man. "Of course," she said as she opened the door. The man entered and rubbed his hands together, "Getting cold outside." It was approaching two in the afternoon, and the rain had become a steady stream. The man looked at the warehouse, and asked, "What kind of work do you do here?"

"Imports and exports," Collette said, showing the man to

the telephone. He nodded his approval, "Oh...thank you." He picked up the receiver and dialed a phone number. The clicking of the rotary dial returning to zero after each number echoed through the warehouse. Collette watched impatiently as the man smiled at her. He was moving his head back and forth as if he was waiting for the other party to pick up the phone.

"Oh...hello, Caroline, Yes, it's me. Well everything is not so good. I have broken down near the warehouses. I will need you to pick up the kids. Is that okay? Yes...Oh I don't know. I will have to call him for service. Yes, of course I will be careful. I will call you when I get there. *Je t'aime. À tout à l'heure.*" He hung up the phone and turned to Collette, "Thank you so much. Can I ask you another favor? Could I use your restroom? All this rain is making me need to...well you know."

"Sure," replied Collette. She showed him the restroom in the hallway. He went in and closed the door. She waited for him at the entrance to the hallway. After a minute or so she heard the toilet flush, and the sink water turn on. The man opened the door and came out of the restroom, wiping his hands. "Thank you," he said as he passed Collette and walked back into the main area.

"I will be going now," he added as he started toward the door. "Thank you again, mademoiselle." Collette followed behind him. Suddenly the man turned back. "There is one more thing I need."

Collette rolled her eyes as the man turned around. She was about to speak, when she noticed him pointing a gun at her. She stopped and put her hands up. "Please, I don't want any trouble," she said.

"Good, because if you do as I ask, there will be none." His tone was noticeably colder.

"What do you want?"

"All I want is the other half of the map."

"What map?"

"Mademoiselle, please don't play games with me, I will not hesitate to hurt you. You are a very beautiful woman and I would not want that to change."

"I am not playing games. I don't know what you're talking about," Collette said with a hint of anger.

The man laughed as he looked around the room. "Do not make this anymore unpleasant than it has to be." He looked back at Collette, "What do you think, about one meter thick?"

Collette shook her head. "What?"

"These walls," he answered as he scanned the room. "I figure they are about one meter thick, and with all the noise going on in the surrounding warehouses, there is no sound you can make to get help, no one will hear you. So, get me the map, or perhaps, we will get to know each other a little better." He reached out and tried to touch her arm. Collette backed up and slapped his arm away.

"Do not touch me!"

"Get me the map and I won't have to." He smiled.

"I don't know anything about a map. I have no idea what you are talking about."

The man started toward her, his gun drawn. "I am sorry, you leave me no choice."

Collette backed up to the wall and reached for the Colt. "Uh, Uh, Uh," the man said, shaking his head no. He cocked his gun and Collette froze. He walked over to her and removed the Colt from her waistband. He tapped her on the cheek with the barrel, ran it down her cheek, across her neck, and down the middle of her sweater. He rubbed the outside of her breasts, as he pushed himself closer. Collette closed her eyes and tried to push him away. The man threw the Colt into the corner and held his own gun up to her face. "I am going to ask you one last time. Where is the other half of the map?"

"I...I don't know anything about a map," Collette stuttered as she started to cry.

"Well that's too bad," the man whispered in her ear. He began to kiss her cheek. He ran his tongue down her neck. Collette wept. "Please, no," she said barely audibly. The man rubbed against her when the clicking sound of a gun snapped him to attention.

He turned his head. The young girl from the airport stood

two meters away pointing the Colt at him. He began to laugh at the sight of this girl with the gun, when a searing pain engulfed his midsection. Collette, with all the strength she could muster, had rammed her knee into his groin. The blinding pain made his eyes tear up. He backed up and bent over. Collette kicked him in the face, and he flew backward, the gun falling on to the floor and sliding away. Anna ran over and gave the Colt to Collette, who grabbed it and pointed it at the man. He lay on the floor, moaning. She walked over to him, and said, "Don't you ever touch me again." She kicked him on the side of his head. The man's head hit the ground with a thud, as he lost consciousness.

Collette turned to look at Anna. She was still standing looking on in disbelief, shaking. "Are you okay?" Anna asked.

"I'm fine, sweetheart," Collette replied. She walked over to Anna, knelt down, and said "Thank you."

Collette stood up and walked over to the heap of man in the middle of the floor. She stepped over him and went to the cabinet in the corner of the main room, opened the cabinet, and retrieved some rope. She brought the rope over to the lifeless body on the floor. She thought back to the boat trips she and her father took when she was young. Her mother would always be nervous when they went out on the boat. Collette was taught how to tie knots at a very young age; she always thought it would come in handy one day. Of course, she envisioned tying up a boat instead of a body. She uncurled the rope and tied the man's hands and ankles together in a perfect nautical knot. Whenever he woke up, he would not be able to move his arms or his legs.

Collette walked back across the room and picked up the man's gun from the floor. She popped the clip out and emptied the chamber. She threw the clip and the gun on the table, pulled a chair out, and sat down with the Colt in front of her. Anna came and sat next to her.

"He will not be going anywhere," she said to Anna with a slight smile.

Anna nodded as the man lay there in front of them.

Collette put her arm around her and pulled her close. They

remained like that for a minute as Collette wondered who this man was, and what map he was talking about. Something told her that Mason would know. She and Anna would sit here and wait for the men to return, and then she would have some questions for the both of them, especially Mason.

She knew he would answer them, he always did.

Chapter 9

THE MAN ON THE GROUND moaned as he started to regain consciousness. Collette stood up and grabbed a handkerchief, walked over to him, bent down, and shoved it in his mouth. His eyes opened wide, and he moaned again and shuddered back and forth. He was trying to speak, but only mumbled sounds came out. Collette patted him on the knee, and said, "Shhh. Save your strength. You are going to need it."

She returned to the table where Anna was sitting.

"Why did he want to hurt you?" Anna asked.

"I don't know," she replied. "I don't know who he is."

"What will you do with him?"

"When they return, we will ask him some questions. You don't have to worry. We will not hurt him anymore. We just want information."

The sound of a horn outside the large wooden doors interrupted their conversation. Collette got up and ran to the window. She looked out, turned, and said, "They're back."

She went down the small set of stairs and unlocked the two large deadbolts for the doors. She pushed them outward just far enough to allow Ganoux to fit the car in. Once they were inside, she pulled them closed again and locked the deadbolts.

Mason got out of the passenger side and went to the back of the car to unload. Ganoux also got out and Mason handed him a box full of groceries, then returned to the back to get the rest. Collette grabbed a bag as she went up the stairs and entered the main area.

"Collette, whose car is out front? It looks like someone is broken down."

"Yes, he is definitely broken down," she said as she went

up the stairs and through the door toward the kitchen.

Mason watched her walk away wondering what that meant.

Ganoux followed with his box and put it down on the table. He stared at the man on the floor and turned to Collette. Mason entered, put down his things, and looked up.

"Who the hell is that?"

Collette slapped his arm. "Watch your language."

"Oh...sorry. Excuse me, Collette, but why is there a man tied up on the floor?"

"I don't know. He said his car broke down, and he needed to make a phone call. He was very persistent. I let him in, he made his call, and was in the process of leaving when he turned and attacked me. He kept saying something about a piece of a map."

"What? Collette, I told you not to open the door for anyone. Are you okay?" Mason said with genuine concern.

"Yes, I am fine, thanks to Anna. She came in and startled the man, and I was able to free myself, and then we tied him up. He was making too much noise, so I stuck the handkerchief in his mouth. I was hoping he would choke on it."

"You two are unbelievable," Ganoux chimed in. "First, we pick up a child at the airport, and now we have a grown man tied up in the middle of the room. You have only been in the country for seven hours. Is this how the two of you always operate?"

"Just relax. Let's find out who he is and what he is doing here. Collette, why don't you and Anna start putting things away while Ganoux and I have a little chat with our friend?"

Collette agreed, and she and Anna grabbed some groceries and brought them into the kitchen.

Mason looked at Ganoux. "I think I will let you take the lead on this."

"Have you never interrogated someone before?"

"I have, and I am actually quite good at getting information, but usually it is someone who has done something to me. Since this man attacked Collette, I am just afraid I may kill him before we get any information."

Ganoux nodded. "Ahh...yes, that could turn out to be a problem, one moment."

Ganoux walked into the kitchen and returned with a small glass of water.

"I find that people are more willing to give when they receive," he said as he walked over to the man on the floor. His eyes widened as he noticed them approaching.

Mason sat down at the table as Ganoux approached the tied-up man. He leaned down and removed the handkerchief. The man gasped and coughed. He positioned the glass in front of the man's mouth and Lane took a drink. "Thank you," he said.

"Can I ask you your name?"

"I am not saying anything to you until you untie me. My arms are almost out of their sockets."

"Please answer some questions, and I will see what I can do."

"My name is John Lane."

"Okay, Lane, that was not so hard. What were you doing here? Please tell me you did not come here to attack a woman, because if that is the case, I can pretty much guarantee you will not be leaving here in one piece. My friend over there will never allow it."

The man looked at Mason, who glared back, then looked back at Ganoux. "I broke down in front of the warehouse, and I asked to come in to use the phone and that woman attacked me. I was only defending myself. She is a maniac. She tried to steal from me."

"I see. Unfortunately, that story does not match hers," Ganoux said, remaining stoic.

"She is lying. Please, I am a father of two. I just want to get home to my wife and kids," Lane said incredulously.

"Okay, M. Lane. Let me speak with her and we will see if we can't get this worked out. In the meantime, I will loosen your hands a bit. I cannot untie you, but I will try to make you a bit more comfortable."

"Thank you," Lane replied.

Ganoux walked over to Mason and nodded for him to follow. They retired to the corner of the room.

"For a man in big trouble he is remarkably calm. I don't believe a word he is saying, but he is playing it well. He looks genuinely terrified. Mason, do you know anything about this map, and why this man would be looking for it?"

"I do, but I can't tell you anything until M. Moulié arrives. I promised him I would keep it quiet. He asked me to especially keep it from Collette. I am not sure why, but I think he will explain when he gets here."

"Very well. I will try to find out why he wants the map, or who sent him to get it."

Ganoux walked back to the man on the floor and pulled up a chair. "What is this map you are looking for?'

"What map? I don't know anything about a map."

"Yes, you do. It is why you are here. You know, Lane, the more you tell me, the closer you will get to your wife and family."

"I swear. I do not know what map you speak of."

"That's too bad." Ganoux tightened the knot back up on Lane until he screamed in pain. He grabbed the handkerchief and went to put it back in Lane's mouth.

"Okay, okay. Please...my arms. I will tell you everything. Just loosen the knot. I can't feel my arms anymore."

Ganoux looked at the man for a minute and smiled. "I will loosen the rope, but if I do not like what you have to say, then I will turn you over to him, and trust me, you will not like that very much."

The man nodded rapidly. Ganoux loosened the rope again, and he exhaled. Mason sat at the table, amazed at how calmly Ganoux was breaking this man down. His ability to control his emotions was far beyond Mason's. He was actually enjoying the show. Now he just hoped the man had some information that they could use.

Ganoux gave the man the rest of the glass of water and returned the glass to the table. He leaned into Mason, "What do you think?"

Mason shrugged and said, "Keep going. Let's see what he has to say."

Ganoux pursed his lips and nodded. He walked back over to the heap on the floor, and pulling over a chair, sat down staring at Lane, who was moaning and breathing heavily.

"So, Lane, the map?"

Lane stared at him for a second, and then took a deep breath. "I was hired by someone to retrieve a map, and then deliver it to a church outside of downtown. I don't know what the significance of the map is, but I know the people who want it are very serious."

"What is it a map of?"

"I don't really know. It looks like an older map of the Paris catacombs. It is in two pieces, I have one and need the other."

"How did you get your piece?"

"I was given access to a restricted room at a museum in New York. I took the map and was looking for the other piece when someone approached. I left in a hurry. When I returned later to get the other piece, the room was cleaned up, and the piece was gone."

Mason leaned back in his chair. This was the guy in the restricted room. He couldn't believe his luck. The other half of the map might have just walked into this warehouse.

"What is the name of the church that you are supposed to deliver it to?"

"The Church of Saint-Pierre in Montmartre," the man replied in a broken tone.

"Do you have a contact there?"

"There is a priest that I answer to. I don't know his name. We have only met twice, and he is very brief. I delivered one half of the map last night, and I told him I would have the other piece by tonight."

"Thank you, Lane. You have been quite helpful. I will see what I can do about getting you unbound."

Ganoux stood up and walked back over to Mason. "What do you think?"

"I believe him, and I think we will be using him to lead us

to the church, and his half of the map. If he really has a wife and children at home, he will have to do some work for us before I let him go home to them. Do you know this church?"

"I don't. I only know the Sacré-Coeur, but Montmartre is not that big. It can't be that hard to find."

Ganoux looked over at Lane lying on the ground in pain, and decided it was time to help clean him up. If he was going back to the church tonight, he needed to be in better shape.

Together they untied him and picked him up off the floor. His legs fell to the floor like dead weight. They held him up as he regained his balance. Lane mumbled a thank you as they led him across the room to a chair. Mason sat him down while Ganoux retrieved the rope. They tied his hands behind the chair so he could not move. Lane was far more comfortable, but still unable to move. A honk was heard outside. Mason went to the window and announced that Collette's father had arrived. He went to the large doors to open them. He was anxious to speak to Jacques Moulié, in hopes that some of the many questions might be answered. Mason—or Collette—would need to explain Anna and the situation with Lane. Fortunately for Mason, the second half of the map was now within reach. A little good fortune was a welcome change.

Chapter 10

JACQUES MOULIÉ WAS A STOUT MAN in his sixties. His hair was gray, but still thick, he was fluent in four languages, and sharp as they come. He was a highly respected man in antiquities, in both his native country and throughout the world. He had been in charge of relocating France's treasures during the Great War and was currently involved to the same degree again.

As Moulié pulled in Mason closed the large wooden doors behind the delivery truck. He bolted them and went around to the driver's side door to greet his old friend just as Moulié got out of the front seat.

"Mason, how are you? You look wonderful," Jacques said as he gave him a big embrace. "I can't thank you for enough for helping out."

"My pleasure sir; it is great to see you as well."

"I trust your trip over was uneventful?"

"Nothing is ever uneventful," Mason replied.

"Yes. Unfortunately, I know that all too well. How is your father?"

"He is doing better, thanks for asking."

"Daddy," Collette's voice echoed through the room as she came running to greet her father. She hopped down the stairs and into his arms.

"Collette, my dear, how are you? You look wonderful as always."

"I am well. A little tired but getting there. I am about to start cooking. We have a big meal planned. How's Mama?"

"She is fine. She wishes I was around a little more to help out, and never passes up a time to remind me. I will fill you in over dinner. Mason, can you help me unload a few things?"

"Yes, of course," replied Mason as they both ventured to the back of the truck. Moulié opened the double doors to the truck where a few boxes were sitting. He grabbed one, and Mason grabbed the other two, set them on the ground, and closed the doors to the truck. He followed Moulié through the door into the main area. Moulié nodded to Ganoux, who was keeping Lane company, as he entered.

"Good evening, Paul," Moulié said as he set down his box on the chair.

"Good evening, sir. How are you?" Ganoux replied.

Moulié glanced over at Lane and nodded his head briefly. "I am fine. I see I have missed some excitement already. Who is this man?"

"His name is Lane and he has some information that he is going to share with us, which should hopefully help our current situation."

"Yes, he looks as though he is in a giving mood," Moulié replied with a smirk.

Ganoux smiled, "He needed a little convincing, but I am fairly certain he has come around."

"Good, good. Well, nice to meet you, M. Lane."

Lane stared blankly at the floor, not saying a word.

Mason put the two boxes down on a chair. The top one began to fall, but he caught it just in time.

"Be careful with that one. It is most important. It contains the wine for dinner. We do not want to lose that," Moulié laughed as he walked into the kitchen. As he entered the kitchen, he noticed Anna skinning potatoes. He walked over to her and gave her a smile. "I don't believe we have met; my name is Jacques Moulié. I am Collette's father."

Anna looked up as Collette chimed in, "This is Anna. She will be staying with us for a while."

"Well, Anna, it is very nice to meet you. It smells good already so I will leave the both of you to it. Believe me Anna, the last thing my daughter wants in the kitchen while she is cooking is me."

Anna smiled and looked at Collette, who replied, "Yes, you are right, Father. It is great to see you, but time to go, and please do not touch anything on your way out."

Jacques was about to grab a piece of lettuce from the salad bowl, but he stopped in his tracks, as Collette slapped his hand. "Out," she said as she pointed the way.

Jacques laughed on his way out the door and returned to the main room where Mason and Ganoux were sitting. He pulled over a chair and sat down next to Mason, leaned in and quietly said, "Though I am getting older, I believe I would remember if I had a granddaughter. I don't remember having one, so I must ask you, who is Anna?"

Mason looked over at Lane who was staring straight ahead in a daze and motioned for Jacques to follow him as he headed toward the corner of the room.

"Anna is the daughter of German Jews," he explained quietly when he was sure Lane could not hear. "She was put on a plane by her parents, in hopes of a better life in France. Collette spotted Anna at the airport sitting alone on a bench crying. She was scared, with no family and nowhere to go. Collette talked with her for a few minutes, then brought her back and announced that Anna was coming with us. I was not going to argue with her; she had that look in her eyes," he said with a knowing glance at Moulié. They had both seen "that look" many times. "Any argument from me would have been a losing one. I think Collette would like you to sponsor the girl so she can live here."

"I know that look you speak of. My daughter can be quite stubborn when she feels the need. The German refugees have been pouring into any country that will take them. Most countries are closing their borders, so these people have nowhere to go; they need a sponsor family, or they are turned away. I suppose we can be Anna's, though France is not exactly a safe-haven. War is knocking on the door; I feel we may all be in need of a new country soon. Mason, these are dangerous times. It is no longer a question of if there will be war, it is now a question of when."

Collette chimed in from the kitchen, "Can the men set the table, please?"

Moulié smiled at Mason, "Of course," he yelled as he headed toward the kitchen.

Mason and Ganoux picked up Lane in his chair, moved him to the other side of the room, and put the handkerchief back in his mouth. Mason leaned down and whispered in his ear, "Sorry." Lane looked at Mason wondering what he meant, when he felt the blow to the side of his head; he cringed for a split second, and then blacked out.

Jacques and Ganoux set the table as the food began to arrive. There was a large salad, bread and cheese, a bowl of potatoes, some green beans, and roast leg of lamb. Jacques opened the wine, and everyone sat down, Anna next to Collette. She watched as Collette began preparing a large plate of food for her. The men served themselves as Collette served herself last. Once everyone was settled, Moulié raised his glass. The others followed suit, Anna a little hesitantly, as he made a brief toast. "To family and friends. In times of need may they never be too far away." He looked at Anna, and said in a soft, caring voice added, "Anna, we welcome you to our family with open arms." He raised his glass high, and everyone nodded in approval. They sipped their wine and then silence fell over the table as the feast began.

The meal lasted for over an hour, and there was barely a morsel left at the end. Collette began to clear the table as the men finished the last of the wine, a 1927 Montrachet.

It was time to discuss why they were there, and what needed to be done. Lane was starting to make noise again over in the corner. The table had been cleared and Moulié, Mason, and Ganoux were seated together at one end. The women were in the kitchen cleaning the dishes. Collette wanted to give the men some time to talk; besides she was enjoying having Anna as a helper.

Moulié began by saying, "Time to be serious. Who is this man, and what is he doing in my warehouse? I do hope he has not ruined our plan before it has begun. We have a lot of work to do tonight, and time is becoming increasingly short. When I summoned you from New York, I did not expect you to show up with a child and a prisoner. This makes things a little more complicated; so, gentleman, please explain to me our current situation, and do tell me we have the map."

Mason shifted in his chair; he looked at Ganoux, who returned the glance. Mason had a million thoughts running through his mind as he shuffled through the files in his head one by one, trying to reach the beginning: the museum in New York, the restricted room, Dr. Heckler. The story seemed like a long complex trip, even though it had only been a few days since this escapade started. Though time was ticking, Mason hoped to slow things down a bit so they could gather their thoughts and not make any rash decisions. The journey they were about to undertake would be many things, but it was not to be taken lightly. A simple task, in theory, was never simple.

Jacques was still awaiting an answer. The evening rush had begun outside the doors, and the sounds of rumbling trucks going by became a recurring theme. Mason inhaled deeply and began to recap the events that had led everyone to this dreary part of a Parisian suburb.

He described his search for the map in the basement of the museum, his discovery and dismissal, his meeting Collette, and their encounter with the man who called himself Franz Kolter. "No doubt a fake name," he added. "He was looking for the list from the Louvre; he obviously thought we had it or could get it. He knew we were somehow connected to it. Have you ever heard of a Franz Kolter?"

Jacques shook his head no.

"He was about thirty-five years old and was carrying a Luger, not something you see every day in Central Park. He was not a professional, though he tried to give that impression. He said the man he works for does not like to be told no. He gave me this card and told me to call this number when I arrived in Paris, and to ask for Alexander."

Mason removed the card from his pocket and placed it on the table.

Ganoux picked it up and looked at it. "I will make a call and run it through the Metropolitan Police records to see if we can find a match."

"After the park," Mason continued, "we managed to get to the airport and arrived just after lunchtime here at the warehouse. That's when Lane enters the picture."

"What happened to Mr. Kolter, or do I not want to know?" Jacques interrupted.

"We left him with some friends in the park. I am fairly certain that Mr. Kolter is no longer an issue."

Jacques nodded with a concerned look. "I'm sorry, Mason. I did not want to get you involved, but you two are some of only a handful of people I trust at the moment. Thank you for taking care of Collette and getting her here in one piece; I hope she has not been too much of a burden."

"It has been nice to reconnect with her, though I am constantly reminded she is a woman of strong will," Mason answered with a wry smile. "She is not going to be happy when she finds out what I knew all along. You may need to help me out with that one."

"I will take care of it," Jacques replied. "So, now onto M. Lane, what's his story?"

"Ganoux and I went to the market to get some groceries; I explained to Collette that she should not open the door for anyone or anything while we were gone. When we returned, Lane here," he paused and nodded toward the man in the corner, "was tied up in the middle of the floor, and Anna and Collette were sitting at the table waiting for us. Apparently, Lane came looking for the map, Collette had a run-in with him, managed to get free and tie him up. I don't know exactly how she pulled that off, but like she always told me, she can take care of herself. Lane is scared of us but terrified of Collette; you can see it in his eyes anytime she goes near him. I don't know what she did to him, but he wants no part of her. He says he is working for a priest out of Saint-Pierre in Montmartre and is supposed to meet him tonight with the other half of the map. I think we should use this to our advantage and let Lane take us to this priest. If Lane knows where the other piece of the map is, he can be useful. It's coveted by several people. Can you explain to me why it's so important? An ancient map of the catacombs is the kind of thing my father would look for. I'm not sure what it has to do with art."

Jacques looked at Ganoux and then back at Mason. He nodded. "You're right, Mason, you deserve to know what is going on now that you are directly involved. The story I am about to tell you does not leave this room, understood? Paul and I are the only two remaining people who have knowledge of this. So many people have been misled over the last ten years that if this was ever to get out, none of us would see the light of day for a long time. The only view we would have is from behind bars.

"Many years ago, after World War I, art was being returned to various museums around the country. Henri, my good friend from the Louvre, and I were in charge of making sure the pieces were returned to their rightful owners. We sat over dinner one night and hatched a plan that would change our lives forever. We had become extremely distrustful of the people who were running the museums, so we decided to reroute some of the most famous pieces of art in France to a secret chamber in the catacombs under Paris. We researched the tombs and found a perfect storage area in the ancient part of the catacombs. It was dry, cool, and large enough to house many paintings. Henri and I would go underground through a large iron gate which separated the catacombs from the burial chamber beneath a small mausoleum in Paris. The opening under the mausoleum was used in the seventeenth century to escape—for people and treasure—in the case of a siege upon the city. It was long forgotten. It has since been sealed off but there is an entrance through the mausoleum office. Only a handful of people even knew it existed, one being Henri. His brother was a priest in this religious order, and he would take Henri down after hours to show him this incredible piece of history. So, over dinner when we decided to hide some of these paintings, Henri suggested this as the perfect place. The ancient tombs were believed to be cursed and riddled with disease so in 1900 the French government had them sealed from the newer part of the catacombs."

"They sealed off every entrance with concrete, except one, the one nobody knew about except for Henri's brother and another priest in the order. They thought of the catacombs to be sacred burial chambers and believed the French authorities would desecrate these places of rest if they found out another entrance existed. One night, Henri, Paul, and I went down to find a suitable chamber to house these paintings. We came across a chamber that had been reserved for aristocracy. It was large enough to house everything we wanted to hide. One by one we brought the paintings down. Now, there are only three paintings there—most have been removed and taken to other locations. Last time we ventured underground we were stopped by a blockage in the main hallway. There had been a collapse, and the hallway was filled with debris. You can easily get lost under there, so we need the maps to find a way around the blockage to access the chamber. It is a complicated maze underground, with no light. There are several markings on the walls which we used as landmarks to find our way in and out. I am afraid when war starts, bombs will cause the rest of the chambers to collapse, and then these works of art will forever be lost. We need to get them out of the chamber, and then out of the country."

Mason stared down at the table and then looked at Jacques, "Didn't anyone ask about these particular works when they did not return to their museums?"

"All the museums received their paintings back shortly after the end of the war. Every work of art was spoken for, so no one had any reason to question them," Jacques replied.

"I don't understand," Mason said. "If these paintings in the catacombs are the originals, what paintings are hanging in the museums?"

"We hired a master forger to copy the originals, and then we delivered the fakes back to the museums."

Mason raised his head, exhaled and sat back in his chair.

"You delivered forgeries back to the museums and kept priceless pieces of art hidden in an ancient burial chamber for the last ten years, and nobody knows about this?"

"We have been lucky that no one has suspected anything until recently. There have been inquiries about the ancient parts of the catacombs. One man applied for a permit to excavate an area above the ancient part; he was denied, but that raised my suspicion that someone is trying to get down there or has discovered the secret entrance. Both Henri and his brother have passed away, leaving Paul and me as the only two who know what happened."

"I am guessing this mausoleum is under the church in Montmartre that Lane is talking about?"

"No, though the entrance is not far from the church, and they are connected through the same religious order. The entrance to the catacombs lies beneath the mausoleum of Saint-Pierre, located in the graveyard of the church."

"You said there were a few paintings left down there. I thought Collette told me there are three."

"Yes, there are only three left; these are the ones that I need you to take back to New York. We need to talk to Lane and find out who is paying him. We must negotiate his freedom in exchange for information. Do you think he will help us?"

"I am not sure," replied Ganoux. "A man in his position will say and do anything to get away. If we are to trust him, we must keep him on a very short leash. We must assume he is lying to us about everything—that way he will have to work extra hard to gain our trust. We must have something he wants in order to control him. We need to find out if he indeed has a family as he told Collette. I think we should start by feeding him and cleaning him up. We cannot send him to meet his priest looking this way, it is a dead giveaway that something bad happened."

"I will go talk to Collette and get her thoughts about Lane. Mason, you and Paul help him back to health and get some food in him. Once he is feeling better, Mason, go out to his car and search it for any evidence of a family or something we can use against him."

As Ganoux and Mason approached Lane's chair, he cowered away. Mason removed the cloth from the man's mouth and stared down at him; he looked a little battered as he looked up at Mason.

"What?"

Mason simply replied, "Mr. Lane, we need to talk."

Chapter 11

JACQUES FOUND HIS DAUGHTER in the back bedroom off the hallway, tucking Anna into the bed. Collette looked up as he entered the room and silently motioned for him to be quiet. She leaned over and gave Anna a small kiss on the forehead, then stood up, turned the light off, and led her father out of the room and into the kitchen.

"How is it going out there?" she asked as she put a kettle of water on the stove for tea.

"As well as it could, I guess. How is Anna? Is she still frightened?"

"Yes, she has been through a terrible ordeal and is confused. I am the only person who has tried to help her since she left Germany, so she feels a slight measure of trust with me."

The tea kettle began to sing its tune, and Collette removed it from the heat of the stove. She put out two cups and filled them with the steaming water. She steeped the two cups and handed one to her father. As she did, she asked, "Father, what is going on?"

"Collette, I need to ask about Lane. When he mentioned a map, what exactly did he say?"

"He asked me for *the* map, not *a* map. He was convinced that we had the map he was looking for. I did not know what he was talking about. Do you?"

"Yes, I do. Collette, I asked Mason to bring me a map from his museum in New York. The map is in two sections; Mason was only able to get a hold of one part. I believe that Lane is working for the person who has the other piece. I am sorry I did not tell you."

"Mason knew of this map the whole time we were traveling?" Collette said with an air of annoyance.

"Yes, I asked him not to tell anyone. It was to keep you away from trouble. The less people who know what is going on, the safer we all are."

"I am your daughter; I would think I could qualify as a confidential source."

"Collette, I am sorry. If you had known about it, your run-in with Lane may have ended differently. It is hard to conceal a truth under scrutiny."

"I do understand, but I am going to let Mason know I don't appreciate being lied to, and he'd better think twice about doing it again. He made me beg to get him to come here; all the while he knew he was coming anyway? I don't like that at all," she added angrily.

"Please don't. I told him I would smooth things out with you."

"Oh, you did, did you? I will go easy on him, I promise. I am actually a little surprised he was able to keep it from me; he has a way of telling me things he does not want to. It is kind of a mind trick I have on him. Besides, he does that blinking thing when he is lying; he must be getting better at it, because I did not suspect anything."

"We are going to try to get Lane to help us find the other half of the map. What can you tell me about him? I want to know exactly what he said to you. He may be our only chance at getting this piece of the map."

Collette recounted the story of Lane making the phone call and then attacking her with the gun and his hands. Jacques sat silently as his insides churned at the thought of this man touching his daughter. He had raised a strong daughter, but it was because of him that she had to deal with this. He wanted to go back out in the main area and choke Lane with his bare hands. He knew this would not help anything, so he just walked over to Collette and hugged her.

"I am so sorry," he said as he held her. Tears danced down his cheeks as they both stood there silently.

After a few moments he let her go and she wiped the tears from his face.

"It's okay, Papa. I can take care of myself."

"You shouldn't have to. I am sorry that you are in the middle of this."

"I need to be in the middle because you need me, and so does Mason. He may be strong and stubborn, but he needs to be reeled in every once in a while, and I know how to do that. Even though I can take care of myself, I know Mason will not let anything happen to me. He told me to not open the door for anyone because he knew how dangerous this was. I let my emotions for a man with a broken-down car get the best of me. I should have never opened the door."

"Well, hopefully, this will all be over in a few days, and we can return to some sense of normalcy, though in the current state of the world that seems highly unattainable," Jacques said as he turned and exited the room.

Collette watched him leave and bowed her head. She thought of everything that had happened since she had been in Mason's apartment; she thought of Anna and wondered how in the world any sense of normalcy could ever return. She wiped a tear from her eye and gathered herself. This adventure was just beginning, and she needed to be strong for herself, her father, Anna, and Mason. She took a long, deep breath and finished her tea.

Chapter 12

GANOUX UNTIED LANE AND LED HIM over to a chair at the table. It was obvious from the bewildered expression on his face that he was wondering what would happen next.

Mason left the room to retrieve some food. He walked down the hallway and into the kitchen, passing Jacques just as he was leaving. Jacques turned and watched Mason walk over to the cabinet and take out a plate. "I am going to give Lane something to eat, and we will sit and talk to him."

Collette walked over to the basket on the counter, removed some bread and cheese and placed a few slices on the plate along with some salad. Mason watched as she added a fork. "Thank you," he said to Collette.

She looked at him with a smile, "You're welcome," and then slapped him on the side of the head.

"What was that for?" Mason said as he backed up.

"That was for keeping secrets from me," Collette said with a stern look on her face.

He looked at Jacques who shrugged and silently mouthed "I tried." Mason quickly grabbed the plates and headed out the door as Collette slapped him again with the dish towel. Mason moved faster toward the door, saying as he looked over his shoulder and grinned unrepentantly at her, "I am going back out there where it's safer!"

Mason returned to the main room with the salad bowl and the bread plate. He walked over to the table and placed them in front of Lane.

"What do you want?" Lane said, without making eye

contact with either one of his captives.

Mason leaned toward him. "Why don't you relax and eat something, and then we can discuss what you are going to do for us."

"You are assuming that I am going to do anything for you." Lane took a bite of bread. "I don't know anything about the map."

"We are not interested in the map; we are interested in the people who sent you here to get it."

Lane took some more bites and began to talk with his mouth full. "I don't know them," he said as bread crumbs fell out of his mouth.

"I don't believe you. I think you know exactly who they are, or you would not have taken the job, because someone in your line of work knows what he is getting into before he even gets involved; if you didn't, you would not be long for this world."

"Mr. Wright, I am merely someone who finds things for people, and I believe anonymity is a valuable asset. Can you get me some more water?" Lane said, handing Mason his cup.

"I understand. More water, huh? Sure, I'll bring you some more water. But before I do, I suggest you enjoy your food, Lane. I am a man who can compromise so I am offering you a choice. Either you help us, or I will shoot you in your kneecaps and dump your body in the Seine. It is your decision. Very simply, you can enjoy your final supper, or live to eat again. I will be right back with some more water."

Mason left the room and returned a few minutes later. Lane was almost done with his food. Mason put the water in front of him and sat down, then leaned in and whispered, "The Seine is about 32 degrees right now. I know I wouldn't want to spend my last moments of life gasping for air as my body slowly freezes. That's just me though."

Mason stood up and nodded to Ganoux, then walked over to the door and grabbed his coat. He was going to look through

Lane's car to see what he could find.

Ganoux sat across from Lane with a pistol on his lap to make sure his last few bites went without incident. He did not know Lane, and though he did not look intimidating, people in his line of work were always dangerous.

As Mason closed the front door behind him, he could see that Lane's car was still sitting in front with the hood up. He approached the car as several trucks rumbled by on their way to make overnight runs. The day was winding down, and traffic was starting to minimize as night approached. Mason walked around to the driver's side door; to his surprise it was unlocked. He opened it and sat in the front seat. The first thing he noticed was how dirty the car was; Lane was a slob. The back seat was littered with paper and debris. A box filled with papers sat on the passenger seat; he grabbed a stack of papers off the top. They were advertisements for electronics, particularly a radio. It looked like Mr. Lane sold electronics in the real world. His specialty was the Bedford 200 model with all the newest features, shiny knobs, wood grain exterior, and a built-in clock. A pretty nice radio, Mason thought, wondering about the price.

He threw the advertisements, and the box they came in, on the back seat, grabbed an envelope which had been under the box, opened it, and began to read.

Dear Mr. Dever,

Thank you so much for the wonderful radio, we love it. It arrived on December 13, and we have been using it every day. Please keep us updated on any future electronics, as we wish to do business again.

Sincerely,
Mr. and Mrs. Daniel Koch

Mason looked up and out the window at the raindrops running down the car's hood. He wondered if Mr. and Mrs. Koch had any idea how dangerous their electronics salesman was. He put the letter back in the envelope and tucked it in his jacket pocket. He opened the glove compartment; it was as messy as the rest of the car. Finding nothing of value, he stuffed everything back in and closed it. He grabbed the keys from the ignition and went around to the front of the car and closed the hood. Hopping the curb, he went to the back of the car and tried the key for the trunk, fumbling them as he dropped them on the wet pavement. He bent down, picked them up, and found the right key. With a click the trunk lid opened about an inch. Mason reached down and pulled it open. He immediately covered his nose and mouth with his left hand, and with his right slammed the trunk down. There were no radios in the trunk, only the mangled, bloody body of a middle-aged man whose throat had been slashed. Mason guessed it was the body of Johnathan Dever, the radio salesman.

Mason gathered himself and stared at the trunk for a moment. He returned to the warehouse. Getting Lane to cooperate might prove a little more difficult than he previously thought. He opened the door and entered the warehouse, jogged up the stairs and back to the main area where he found Lane still sitting quietly at the table across from Ganoux. Jacques and Collette sat at the other end of the table. They both looked up as Mason came into the room. He walked over and sat down next to Ganoux.

"Did you find anything useful?" Jacques asked.

Mason shook his head, "No, no useful information, but there is a body rotting in the trunk."

Jacques shook his head exasperated, "Great," he said sarcastically to himself.

Lane looked at Mason with no expression.

Mason stood up and sat down next to Lane. "Lane, we need you to set up a meeting with your man at the church; tell him you have the map and want to meet."

"And why would I do that?"

"Well…I already told you about the freezing water of the Seine, but now I am thinking that is too good for you. The man sitting across from you is a former Metropolitan police detective. He can make one call and you won't see another sun rise in Paris for the rest of your life. They take murder pretty seriously in this country, especially when the victim is a respected businessman."

"It's laughable listening to you tell me about morality when your hands are just as dirty as mine. I have my business and you have yours."

"You don't know anything about me," Mason said as he gritted his teeth.

"I know your name is Mason Wright, your father is quite famous in the art world, you worked at the Metropolitan Museum of Art, you were recently asked to resign, you live in New York on 86th Street, and in your apartment, you possess several artifacts from around the world that are not rightfully yours. Would you like me to go on? I do my research before every job. I know you are looking for another piece of the map. I know where it is. If you can set aside your disdain for me for a moment, maybe we can find a solution, so we all get what we want."

Mason quickly envisioned the Solario painting, with himself holding Lane's head over the silver platter.

"What is it that you want?"

"I know it sounds rather shallow, but I just want to get paid. I will lead you to the person who has the map, but you must allow me to give him your half so that I can get paid. Once I am paid you can move in and take both pieces, and you will never see me again."

"Do you always betray your clients at the first sign of trouble?"

"I am a businessman Mr. Wright; business can suffer if you are deemed unreliable. This way, I can complete my job, and you can do whatever it is that you are doing, and we will never meet again."

"Okay, but I don't trust you, and if I think at any time you are being less than truthful, I will dump you in the Seine. Understood? I don't like you, but unfortunately, we need each other. Don't get out of line because it won't take much for me to kill you; I am almost there already."

"Yes, Mr. Wright, I understand," Lane said with a slight smile. "Can I have some more water?" He raised his glass. Mason swung his hand across the table and knocked the glass out of Lane's hand and onto the floor where it broke into several pieces. He stood up and walked away as Lane smiled to himself and resumed eating.

Mason walked over to the corner where he leaned against the wall, seething. He hated Lane's smugness, but he knew there was nothing he could do about it now. He looked over at Jacques who raised both of his hands in a "calm down" motion. Mason nodded his understanding. The map was the most important piece to this venture, and they needed that more than anything. But he also had no intention of letting Lane get away with killing an innocent man. He had an idea that he would keep to himself until the right time arose. Mason returned to the table and sat back down. He turned back to Lane. "So where are we headed?"

Chapter 13

"I'VE GOT IT; 9:30. I'LL BE THERE," Lane spoke briefly into the telephone receiver and hung up. He turned to the three men who had watched him closely as he made his call. "We are meeting at Montmartre."

"The church you mentioned?" Ganoux asked.

"Yes. I'll exchange the map for my money there," Lane said, nodding shortly.

Ganoux and Mason decided they would be the only ones to accompany Lane. How they would retrieve the other half of the map was a plan Mason was still working on.

"I am to ring the bell on the side entrance three times, the door will be unlocked. I will go in and meet with the man in his office. I'll leave the door unlocked and you can follow me in and wait outside the office until I return with my payment; then you can do as you please."

Mason and Ganoux agreed; they had to assume the man in the church, whether a man of God or not, would be armed. A priest who dabbled in smuggling had probably committed a sin or two over his lifetime so one more did not really matter; his road to heaven had probably already been closed.

Mason tucked his Colt inside his waistband. Ganoux assured Mason that he had everything he needed. Mason wondered how this quiet, laid-back man could ever muster the energy to kill someone. It worried him a little. He had seen Ganoux operate and knew he was a professional, he just wished Ganoux showed a little emotion now and then. Jacques pulled them aside for a last-minute chat.

"Get back here as soon as you have both pieces of the map.

Then, we will find a way to get to the chamber and the paintings."

They nodded and pushed Lane out of the warehouse and into the car. Mason checked Lane once again to make sure he had no weapons concealed on him. Mason had found an old map in the warehouse. Rolled-up in a cardboard sleeve, Lane would present this instead of the real thing. Lane was not happy about this. "The priest will open the sleeve to look at the map. If he realizes it is not what he was promised, things could get ugly quickly," he told them.

Mason, however, was not inclined to worry about Lane's problems.

As the unlikely trio pulled out of the warehouse and headed toward Paris, a light rain was still falling, and the warehouse district was empty. Ganoux drove, with Lane in the passenger seat. Mason sat in the back, his Colt resting against Lane's neck. He jabbed him gently every time they hit a bump just to remind him to keep his cool.

"You know, Wright, you don't need to do that; I am not going to do anything stupid."

"Oh, I know, Lane," Mason replied. "It is just a bad habit of mine. See I don't trust people. Isn't that right Paul?"

"Yes," Ganoux replied as he turned his head toward Lane. "Mason has a hard time with trusting people."

"Do you always let him run the show?" Lane asked snidely.

"It is his show to run. I am just along for the ride."

They turned right onto Lafayette Avenue and headed downtown. Lane watched the scenery and people pass by, heading home to dinner with a family, a glass of wine. How incredibly boring, he thought. He was glad he would never have to do that. He was a man free from commitments, free to come and go, available to the highest bidder. He surrounded himself with people who always had things to hide. No one asked questions, because the answers were ugly. It was true, he thought, *there is no honor among thieves.* Honor got you killed.

It was intelligence and manipulation that kept you alive. He had not chosen this life; this life had chosen him. He was very good at it and had developed a solid reputation for getting the job done. One day it would end—probably with a thud, possibly tonight. He had no regrets. The only child of immigrant parents, he had never had any close relationships so it would be fitting if he died scrambling for air while slowly freezing in the Seine. It would mirror his life, all alone as he disappeared below the ripples of frigid water. Who would know that he was gone? No one would care. What would happen to his possessions? Where would he end up; rotting on the bottom of the river, or would he wash up on the shore somewhere? He had accepted long ago that his life would end in a sad and twisted way. His fate was sealed; nothing he could say would save his soul. He did not believe in God, so it did not concern him all that much. If there really was a hell, he figured they would welcome him with open arms, and he would recognize half the people there.

A passing truck snapped Lane from his daze. He could still feel the Colt on his neck. He turned and gave Mason a smile. Mason did not return the gesture, he just put his knee into the back of the seat, lunging Lane forward. "Oh…, I am sorry; it's a little tight back here."

Ganoux signaled to turn left onto Rue Cardinet. They were about five minutes from the Church of Saint-Pierre. Mason looked at his watch, it was 9:07 p.m. Ganoux made the final turn onto Avenue de Roule; the church of Sacré-Coeur was visible in the distance, its spire towering over the tree line. The Sacré-Coeur Basilica overshadowed the Saint-Pierre and was the more widely known. Ganoux planned to park down the street. They could walk through the south gate of the gardens and up the steps to the back of the church. They pulled over to the curb of a quiet side street and sat there for a minute. Mason and Ganoux surveyed the area from inside the car. It was quiet with nobody in sight. A few cars passed the intersection up ahead. They were parked on a street lined with trees and adjacent to a park. A few houses had lights on but overall, a good spot to go unnoticed.

They agreed that Mason would go up to the church and canvas the area. Ganoux and Lane would follow at exactly 9:30 p.m. They would meet at the side door.

Mason got out of the back seat, quietly closed the door, and did a quick survey. The three houses with lights on were now two; one had turned dark. A stray cat ran across the street and into the bushes; at the end of the street a car went through the intersection and continued on its way. The street was quiet, maybe too quiet, but that did provide a measure of cover. Mason walked back up the street toward the side gate. The cobblestone under his feet was shiny with rain. As he reached the side entrance, he could see through the trees, no one was there so he proceeded toward the main gate for a closer look at the area.

The gardens around the church were dotted with benches in a circular pattern; a large, stone statue of St. Pierre rising nearly ten feet on a pedestal was just visible through the trees. Between the benches were statues of past priests who had served there. A small cemetery was to the left of the walkway, with tilted gravestones and crosses. Mason entered the church property. At the main entrance two large wrought iron gates were permanently open and anchored to the stone wall. He quickly moved into the shadows of the trees and scanned the gardens. A gravel walkway hugged the perimeter giving people access to the benches and statues. Mason was alone, except for the statues. Everything looked calm and quiet. He retreated down the street to the side gate and slowly pushed the wrought iron lock back until it dislodged the gate. The sound of creaky metal followed as he slowly opened the gate. The sound would be inaudible during a busy day, but at night it was like a scream. He started up the stone steps, worn from many years of use, and now, after the rain, damp and slippery. Moss covered the left side wall as branches hung down over it. Mason arrived at the second set of stairs and paused for a moment. A train horn was barely audible in the distance. He climbed the final five steps up on to a red brick path; the path led through the trees toward the entrance to the garden. Once again Mason glanced around at the statues. Nothing had changed, still no sign of activity anywhere. A second-floor light in the adjacent house turned off and caught Mason's attention for a brief second. He stopped and focused on the house...nothing...so he continued. He was about to enter the garden area, where he would be fully exposed; he veered off the path into the wooded area to circumvent the garden. He stayed close to the tree line as he passed the headstones in the cemetery. He stopped for a moment at the wrought iron sculpture of Jesus which was inset into the stone wall; the eyes of the Lord followed his every move. As he approached the end of the cemetery the side of the church came into view. The side door was under the bell tower, which towered to the sky and up to a pointed spire. Cutouts in the façade at the top housed the bells. They were visible through the rain, illuminated by spotlights as they loomed over the churchyard. Mason stopped across from the side door. He would wait for Ganoux and Lane here; he had a clear view of the walkway and the path to the door. He looked at his watch; it showed 9:22 p.m. As he waited, he listened for any sound at all from inside the church. The church was dark except for the spotlights on the façade. It looked abandoned. He turned to his left and could see the much larger Sacré Coeur, with its multiple white domes bathed in light looking down on him like a parent watching a child.

At 9:27 p.m. Lane appeared at the top of the second flight of steps onto the path, followed closely by Ganoux. They silently and slowly walked to the side door. Mason appeared from the tree line and met them. He looked in all directions as he walked across the grass. There were no signs of life.

At 9:29 p.m. Ganoux and Mason split up and retreated to opposite sides of the door in case it was opened. Lane looked at Mason, who returned the glance holding his Colt in his hand. Mason nodded to Lane who turned his head and reached for the bell. He pressed the button and a faint bell could be heard through the stone walls. He waited, then pressed it again, and then a third time. After waiting a few more seconds he reached for the large metal handle on the exterior of the door. He pressed the handle with his thumb, and the sound of a metal lock detaching could be heard. Lane slowly pushed the door open and stepped inside to the back of the nave. To the left was a set of stairs leading up to the bell tower. Two brass stands with a red velvet rope blocked the entrance to the stairs; a small sign read "Ne Pas Entrer." Lane stood in the travertine-tiled hallway for a moment, and then started to his right into the main nave, Mason and Ganoux a few steps behind him. They entered a side room where candles flickered against the stone walls. A statue of St. Pierre holding a child rose several feet above them against the wall. Lane pointed into the main area and headed back that way. The church was quiet and dimly lit. The dancing flames of the candles reflected colors off the walls. The nave was lined with large mahogany pews. Four large chandeliers hung from the arched, stone ceiling, each had three brass arms extending from the middle, with five candles apiece.

Lane proceeded to the center aisle as Mason and Ganoux stayed to the side, hidden behind the columns. Lane ventured closer to the altar, his footsteps echoing throughout the church. There was still no sign of life, exactly as he had said it would be. Lane reached the front of the church, walked to the right of the stone altar, past the looming mahogany pulpit, toward a dark wooden door that led behind the sanctuary. The three large, stained-glass windows glared down from above the altar at the three men. Ganoux and Mason followed slowly as Lane approached the doorway. They paused in an opening where a stone baptismal font stood alone under another stained-glass window. The stone church had an eerie coldness to it, as if it knew the nature of their business.

A faint light came through the doorway as Lane opened it. He glanced over at them, gave the most subtle of nods, and disappeared through the opening. Mason quickly and silently tiptoed over to the door, he listened for any sound and heard nothing. Ganoux followed him and they stood with their backs against the wall. Mason motioned that he would take a look, and cautiously peered around the doorway. He glanced around the corner and saw a hallway that led to a door, which was open, about twenty feet away. Lane was nowhere to be found. Mason quietly walked into the hallway and approached the doorway. He could hear faint voices talking in the room. He inched closer to the opening and the voices became clearer. A man was thanking Lane for a job well done.

"My people will be very pleased. They shall look to do business again," the voice said.

"Thank you, Father," Lane responded. "I shall look forward to it. Good night."

At that instant Mason walked around the corner into the room with his Colt pointed straight ahead. Lane froze, staring at Mason.

"Who is this man?" said the voice from over Lane's shoulder.

"He is your next appointment," said Lane as he started to exit the room.

Mason stopped him. "Not so fast."

"We had a deal," Lane said coldly staring at Mason.

"Yes, I know, I agreed to let you get paid, I never agreed to let you leave. Get against the wall."

Ganoux entered, a weapon in his hand, and walked past Mason toward the priest.

"Show me your hands!"

The priest backed up, fear in his eyes, "What is going on here? I am a man of God."

"You are no more a man of God than I am so be quiet. I need the map. The one that you just paid him for," Ganoux replied.

"What map? What is going on here?"

Ganoux stopped and pointed the gun at the priest's head, "Where....is....it?"

The priest relented, "Okay, please do not shoot. I have it here in my drawer." The priest lowered his right hand.

"He's lying," Lane said from across the room. "He stored it in the cabinet behind him." Ganoux briefly looked over at Lane as a shot rang out across the room. The priest had pulled a gun from his robe and fired. Ganoux hit the floor. Mason crouched down and raised his gun. He fired one shot and the priest fell behind his desk.

Mason rushed over to Ganoux, he was lying dazed on the floor. "Are you all right?" he asked in a panicked tone.

"I think so. My ears are ringing; I can't really hear."

"You are not shot? Are you sure?" Mason said

"Yes," Ganoux said, nodding.

Mason stood up and turned toward Lane, who a minute before had been standing hands up, his back against the wall. He was no longer standing; he was in a heap on the floor, blood all over his shirt, and gasping for air. Mason grabbed a cloth from the top of a cabinet and applied pressure to the wound, but it was no use. A couple of gulps and blood flowed out of the sides of Lane's mouth, his head falling to the side and his eyes glazing over. Mason leaned back and dropped the cloth onto Lane's bloody chest.

He stood up and turned back toward Ganoux who was behind the desk tending to the priest, who lay on the ground holding his stomach. He reached for Ganoux and tried to speak. *"Credo in unum Deum, Patrem omnipotentem, factorem…"* His voice trailed off as he coughed.

"Where is the map?" Ganoux asked as he held the priest.

The priest managed a bloody smile and shook his head back and forth. His body went limp and his head hit the floor.

"Dammit," Mason yelled as he stood over them.

Ganoux stood up and wiped his hands on the priest's robe. He looked at Mason who was shaking his head. "Check the cabinet; see if it is in there."

Ganoux walked over to the wooden cabinet. It had three

drawers and was covered with a white cloth, a small statue of Mary on top. He tried the top drawer and it was locked. He tried the second and third: the same. He turned, opened the top drawer of the desk and rifled through it looking for a key: nothing. He did the same with the other drawers with the same result. Turning his attention to the priest, he knelt down and felt for pockets in the robe. Finding nothing he lifted the priest's head and noticed a chain hanging around his neck. He ripped it off, and to his surprise, dangling from the end of the chain was a set of keys. He found the smallest of the four and tried it in the cabinet. The lock popped out. Ganoux quickly opened the top drawer. He pushed some files to the side and noticed two cardboard rolls very similar to the one in which their map was stored. He grabbed one roll and popped the top off. Gently removing the scroll inside, he placed it on the desk. It partially unrolled by itself. Mason walked over and held one end as he rolled out the scroll. He looked down and recognized it right away: the missing half of the catacombs map.

Chapter 14

MASON LOOKED UP FROM THE DESK. He looked around the room and then turned to Ganoux. "Let's leave them, whoever finds them will think they shot each other for some reason." He leaned down and checked the priest for identification. He found a wallet in an inner pocket of the priest's robe, filled with cash—a large amount of cash—more cash than you would find on ten priests, Mason thought. Something told Mason that this priest was no man of the cloth, or if he was, he adhered to a different set of principles. What kind of a priest carries a gun and loads of cash? He stuck the wallet in his jacket and looked up, "What do you think we should do?"

"Give me your gun," Ganoux said, extending his hand. Mason removed the Luger which he had taken from Kolter in Central Park, flipped the pistol so the handle was facing away, and handed it over. Ganoux walked over and wiped down the Luger with a cloth, and then stuck the gun in Lane's hand. "We need to leave this here. Without it, they will know someone else was here; this way there are two bodies, two bullets, and two guns; they will wrap it up quick, probably chalk it up to a robbery gone bad. The church won't want the attention so it will go away fast."

They gathered the map and quietly exited back into the church. Walking down the aisle away from the altar, Mason felt a chill come over him, as if the church knew what had transpired and was letting him know it disapproved. He resisted the urge to scream at the top of his lungs. He had been in Paris for less than a day, and was a witness to three dead bodies, not exactly how he hoped the trip would start.

"Mason, we should be going," Ganoux said from the entrance to the candle room. Mason agreed and hurried toward the exit. They opened the door slowly and peered outside. Everything seemed as quiet as when they arrived. They walked outside, closed the door, and headed down the path. At the bottom of the steps they turned right and went directly to their car. As far as Mason could tell, it was just another weeknight in Paris, quiet and damp.

The ride back to the warehouse was quiet. Both Mason and Ganoux knew that their little errand had gone terribly wrong. Yes, they had the map, but they had left two dead bodies in a church, a church that was going to play heavily into their plan going forward.

Ganoux honked twice as they pulled in the driveway to the warehouse. The large door opened as Collette pushed it with all her might. Once inside the three of them made their way into the main area where Jacques was sitting sipping some tea and reading some papers on the table in front of him. Collette offered them tea and began to pour two cups, while sliding a plate of biscuits across the table.

"By the looks on your faces I can tell something has happened," Jacques said as he removed his glasses with a look of concern.

Mason put the cardboard sleeve on the table and looked over at Ganoux. "We were able to get the map, but we had things go a little sideways at the church."

Jacques interrupted, "Where is Lane? You did not let him go, did you?"

"He is lying on the floor of the church office with a bullet in his chest."

"You killed him?"

"No, I didn't, the priest did."

Jacques looked confused. "The priest from the church shot Lane? Where is the priest now?"

"He's dead, Mason replied in a somber voice.

"Lane killed him?" Jacques said trying to piece everything together.

"No, I did."

Jacques looked at him more than a little bit confused.

"The priest he was meeting with turned out to be armed. When we entered the room, Lane tried to tell us where the map was hidden, and the priest shot him out of nowhere. I returned fire before the priest had a chance to turn his gun on us. We wiped down the gun and left it with Lane. The police will think they shot each other in a robbery attempt."

"Well, let's hope so. Did anyone see either one of you? We don't need people poking around asking questions," Jacques said as he sipped some more tea.

"No, we made sure we went unseen. Also, I have my doubts about the man being a priest. I took his wallet and he had almost one thousand francs in it. Either he is helping himself to the collection plate, or he was merely playing the role of a priest. His name is Andrew Loch; does that ring a bell?"

"No, I don't think so. Perhaps, Paul can run it through the police records."

"I, for one, am happy that Lane is no longer living; he was a piece of filth," Collette chimed in. "You stole a wallet from a priest? Mason, how could you?"

"He tried to kill me, and no, he was definitely not a priest," Mason said, defending his actions sarcastically.

"Ok, let's just relax a bit. We will look at the maps together and figure out a passage to the chamber so we can retrieve the art works. Hopefully, that is the end of the body count, and we can proceed without incident. We still need to dispose of Mr. Dever and his car out front." Jacques stood up and grabbed a biscuit.

"I will get the other half of the map," Mason said as he walked over to his bag, which was sitting on the floor in the corner. He returned with a large envelope and removed its contents. He unfolded the piece of parchment and proceeded to flatten it out on the table with his hands; the sound of crumpling paper filled the air. Collette went to find some heavy books to put on the corners of the rolled-up half. Ganoux unrolled the scroll from the church, and he and Mason lined up the matching areas of the sides of both maps. Collette found some books and they held down the four corners of one side. Mason was still flattening out the other half.

Everyone sat down at the table except for Jacques, who hovered over the map like a professor getting ready to teach his pupils. He began by pointing out the entrance from the Saint-Pierre mausoleum, where they entered to hide the art. As far as he knew it was the only entrance in existence. They would need to gain access to the mausoleum and enter the catacombs through the bottom floor. Once inside, they would have to use flashlights to guide their way as the catacombs would be pitch black at night. There were two air ducts providing oxygen to the catacombs and during the day some light, but they were far apart and nowhere near where they were headed; besides, they were heavily protected with iron bars to deter anyone from going in. The French government had feared a buildup of toxic gas in a sealed grave, so they had constructed two towers to provide a release of gas, and allow some oxygen in.

Jacques put on his glasses and began to follow various paths from the entrance around the main hallway, which was now blocked by a pile of rock, bone and dirt. It was like walking through a maze; he would follow a path until he hit a dead end, then start over. Finally, he managed to reach the chamber. The route looked pretty easy. The hardest part would be getting in; once in, Mason and Ganoux would only have to make three turns to circumvent the blocked hallway and reach the chamber.

Mason, Collette, and Ganoux watched patiently as Jacques did some measurements on paper and mapped out the route. Mason snacked on a biscuit, dropping crumbs on the table. One large piece hit the table and rolled onto the catacomb map. Everyone looked up at him.

"Sorry," he said as he wiped it away. Collette just shook her head. Mason assumed she was over the fact that he had been less than forthcoming with all the information he had possessed back in New York. Ganoux sat staring at the map and sipping his tea. He looked as relaxed as ever, and Mason wondered if he was actually a machine devoid of emotion. Even after almost being shot point blank he remained calm, as Mason was running around in a panic. He knew that Paul Ganoux was going to be a valuable man to accompany him on this venture. Ganoux knew where they were going, and Mason felt comfortable following his lead. They made a good team. Mason chuckled to himself as he thought back to his threat to throw Ganoux out of the plane into the Atlantic Ocean if he did not trust him. Well, Mason had trusted him with his life in these last twenty-four hours, and Ganoux had proved more than a little trustworthy so Mason now considered Ganoux a friend.

Jacques broke the silence, "The path seems to be pretty clear, three turns and a straight walk to the entrance of the chamber. Two of the paintings have been removed from their frames and the canvas has been pried from the wooden supports. They are rolled up and have been sealed in two metal, airtight containers. They are not to be opened, understand? We can't risk them being ruined by light or flame or toxic air. The third is in its own container and should be removed first. I think you will need to make two trips. The metal containers have some weight to them, and I don't believe you can carry all of them plus flashlights in one trip. Are there any questions?"

Mason and Ganoux shook their heads.

"Good. I think you should try to make the trip tomorrow night. Collette, Anna, and I will return to the farm. The two of you should meet us there once you have everything. From there we can figure out how to best get the pieces out of France."

Jacques turned to Collette, "We will leave first thing in the morning."

Everyone stood up from the table and agreed that the plan

seemed pretty straightforward. They all needed their rest, and Mason was looking forward to some sleep; he was starting to feel his eyes getting heavy. Collette and Jacques took the bedroom, while Mason and Ganoux would sleep on the floor in the main area. Collette brought out some blankets and Mason grabbed a few cushions from the chairs to use as pillows. It had been quite the eventful first day in Paris, and Mason knew it would probably remain that way; nothing seemed to be going smoothly. He dozed off into a deep sleep and waited for Madame X to come calling; he needed her to tell him everything would be all right.

Chapter 15

MASON AWOKE TO THE SMELL of breakfast coming from the kitchen. He rolled over on the couch and saw Ganoux sitting at the table sipping a cup of coffee and browsing through the pages of the morning news. He looked as if he had been awake for hours, relaxed as ever. Mason once again wondered if he was indeed human. Last night had been a near disaster and had shaken Mason. He realized yesterday, as bullets rang out through the church, there was no guarantee he would make it out of France in one piece, but he was committed to the plan and needed to regain his focus. The two dead bodies in the church would surely raise some questions, and since they needed to return to the area tonight their task had just gotten a little more complicated.

Ganoux noticed Mason stirring and offered a "good morning." Mason returned the greeting as he sat down next to him. "Anything in the news about a small church in Montmartre?"

"Nothing," Ganoux replied. "I suspect that it happened too late for any newspaper and, as I said, it will be kept quiet, so I don't expect to read anything about it."

"Well, let's hope that is indeed the case," Mason replied as he slowly nodded his head.

"Good morning, gentleman," Jacques said as he entered the room with two bowls in his hands. He placed a bowl of bread and a bowl of eggs down on the table. Collette and Anna followed with more food. Everyone sat and ate and tried to discuss anything except the night before and the coming night.

After breakfast Jacques and Collette began packing the car

for the trip to the family farm. Once done, Jacques pulled Ganoux and Mason aside. "I want you two to promise me that if you run into anything suspicious tonight you abort the mission. If there are still police around the scene, you abort. I repeat, do not go into the catacombs if you have the slightest bad feeling. This is too important, and I will not risk the two of you getting caught, or worse. Understand?"

Both men nodded, and Jacques patted both of them on the shoulders. "Good luck," he said as he turned to walk away.

"Oh...one more thing," he said in a firm whisper as he turned and walked back toward them. "No more dead bodies."

With that Jacques called out to Collette, "Time to go my dear." Collette and Anna emerged with coats on and bags in hand. Jacques helped Anna with her bag as Collette came over to Mason.

"Please be careful tonight," she said as she kissed him on the cheek. Mason returned her glance silently and nodded. She looked at Ganoux. "You as well. I will see both of you tomorrow."

She turned and walked away. Mason followed and helped load the car and watched them drive out of the warehouse. He waved as they pulled away, eventually closing the large wooden doors.

Back inside, he and Ganoux sat down, positioned the map of the catacombs on the table and began to discuss their plan. They went over the map several times until they both could recite the directions from memory. Jacques had brought them everything they would need. They still needed to dispose of Dever's body and car. Ganoux knew of a lake in which they could conceal both. They agreed that Mason would drive Dever's car and follow Ganoux out of town.

"The stench in that car is awful, how am I supposed to drive with the smell of a rotting corpse?" he said.

"Breathe through your mouth," Ganoux replied, still staring at the map.

"Breathe through my mouth? That's your advice? And this

comes from your wealth of experience driving stolen cars containing rotting corpses?" Mason said sarcastically.

"Yes, that's my advice, breathe through your mouth, you'll be fine," Ganoux returned the sarcasm.

As the day progressed the two men relaxed and went over their plan several times. As dusk approached, they gathered their things and loaded the car. Mason would follow Ganoux to the lake, and they would dispose of Dever's car, then together drive to Montmartre. He felt a slight sense of remorse for just depositing this poor man's corpse into the bottom of a lake, unfortunately there was little they could do otherwise.

Mason pulled on gloves for the ride. He started the car and cranked down both front windows, betting on the cold air being a better option than a rotting corpse. Ganoux backed out of the garage and locked the warehouse doors. He pulled next to Mason and rolled down the window, "Are you ready?"

Mason nodded, and they pulled away. Mason tried to heed the advice of his partner and breathe through his mouth. He was having trouble concentrating as the stench engulfed the car. He shook his head and followed the car in front. They reached the outskirts of Paris and moved onto some winding country roads. Making a right, Ganoux led them up a small hill and pulled into a clearing at the top. Mason pulled in behind him and Ganoux motioned for him to drive toward the edge of the hill.

They exited their vehicles and Mason walked around taking some deep breaths as he cleared his lungs. Ganoux laughed as he watched Mason regain his normal breathing.

Mason looked over. "You enjoying this?"

"Yes, actually," Ganoux replied, still smiling.

Mason shook his head and walked back toward Dever's car. Ganoux got in and started it. He inched up and turned the car, so it was facing straight down the hill. The moonlight reflected off the lake below, the drop was about fifty feet; it started with a subtle decline and then dropped off significantly until reaching the lakeside. It would be a quick descent for

Dever. Ganoux put the car in neutral and both men went to the back bumper. Ganoux leaned over and placed his hands on the bumper. He backed up a step and bent down readying himself to push when Mason grabbed his arm. "Shouldn't we say something before just sending this guy into the lake?"

Ganoux stood up. "By all means," he said motioning to Mason. "You know more about the man than I do so I will leave it to you."

Mason looked at him for a second and then at the car, "Well, Mr. Dever, we are sorry you got involved in our mess. Sounds like you were a nice man and a successful radio salesman. We apologize that we couldn't give you a better burial. Rest in peace."

Mason looked over and shrugged his shoulders looking for approval.

"Very touching," Ganoux said with a drip of sarcasm.

Mason shot him a look and then bent down to put his hands on the bumper. Both men began to push the car forward until it started to roll on its own. They stood up and released their hands and the car rumbled down the hill, picking up speed until it splashed into the lake. The water swallowed the car quickly and soon there were only ripples in the lake as it sank beneath the water line. Both men stood and watched for a minute in silence, and then glanced around the area. Only silence surrounded them, so they headed back to the car, as the moonlight rippled across the water.

Back in the car, they rumbled back down the gravel road path to the main road, turned and headed back into Paris, toward Montmartre. Not much conversation was exchanged as they drove into the city.

They approached the hills of Montmartre about twenty minutes into the trip. They began the ascent up the cobblestone roads to the top. Montmartre is a maze of tiny roads, lined with shops and restaurants, snaking their way up to the top of the mountain. From the top you have spectacular views over Paris.

They turned on to the Rue du Cardinal Dubois and then on

to Rue du Mont Cenis. Ganoux pulled over at the end of a block within walking distance of the cemetery, the trees lining their side of the road provided some measure of cover for when they returned.

Mason exited the car first and went to the trunk, slowly scanning his surroundings. He waited a minute until Ganoux joined him at the rear of the car. Once satisfied they were alone, they opened the trunk and grabbed their gear.

The two men walked up Rue du St. Louis until they reached the steps to the cemetery. After one last look around, they started up the steps. The path to the cemetery was laid with old red brick, the moss between them thick from the recent rain. They walked softly as they reached the clearing of the cemetery. The tombstones sunk in the ground were tilted and old, some had the names weathered off while others were cracked and broken. Mason absorbed some of the names as they passed the gravestones…Dubois, Francois, and Kiely. He added Lane and Dever to that list as he recalled the events of the past twenty-four hours.

The mausoleum was located across the road from the Church of Saint-Pierre, on the other side of a small cemetery. The church had long stopped burials in the cemetery, and many of the headstones were faded and worn. The mausoleum was still operating, but at a much-diminished capacity. The main building was a reflecting area rather than an actual mausoleum. Services were held inside four times a year to remember loved ones and allow families to light candles for the dead. The last ceremony had occurred a few days ago, which meant the mausoleum should be peaceful and quiet, just waiting for the two art smugglers to show up to disturb it.

The two men walked through the main area of the cemetery and turned left toward the mausoleum. The gothic building rose out of the ground to a spire. Two wrought iron gates protected the entrance. They walked by the main entrance and along the side until arriving at a door toward the rear of the left side.

Jacques had assured them the door would be unlocked. Ganoux grabbed the handle as Mason kept a lookout. The lock clicked, and Mason breathed a small sigh of relief. Pushing the door open, Ganoux entered. They found themselves in a small stone-carved hallway. Both men walked down the hallway as quietly as they could. It led to a main area where some stone benches sat in the middle of the room. Next to the benches were large vases of flowers. Candles flickered against the stone and glass of the structure and the familiar smell of burning church candles filled the room.

They were to find a small staircase toward the back of the main room, so they slowly walked in that direction. The flames danced as Mason walked past, noticing the plaques on the walls. Names of the dead stared back at him. So far, his trip to Paris had become a visit with the dead or dying. Mason reached the stairs and went first, heading down to the burial chamber where they would find the entrance to the catacombs.

At the bottom of the spiral stairs, Mason pulled his rucksack off his shoulder and placed it on the ground. He opened it and grabbed his flashlight. They were underground so the beams from their flashlights would not be seen. Mason's military flashlight beamed across the room and illuminated the back door to the mausoleum office. The large above-ground stone tombs dominated both sides of the room.

He reached the door and tried the handle…nothing. He tried again…nothing. He started shaking the door handle when Ganoux reached over and provided a key. Mason shot him a disapproving glance.

"I thought you were going to rip the handle off for a moment," Ganoux said with a slight chuckle. Mason ignored his comment and unlocked the door. They entered the office where two large desks sat opposite one another against each wall. A stone altar sat in between against the back wall. What a dreary place to work, Mason thought as he looked around. After all, it was a mausoleum, so the motif mirrored the setting.

They began unpacking their things: rope, water containers,

weapons. Mason paused and looked around. He saw the desks, two bookshelves, the altar, and a large wooden cross hanging on the wall. What he didn't see was a way out of the room.

"I thought the entrance was off this room?" he said, turning to Ganoux.

"It is," Ganoux replied as he tucked his pant legs into his socks.

"Why are you doing that?" Mason said pointing at Ganoux's ankles, almost not wanting to know the answer.

"Rats...they bite if you step on them."

"You're serious, aren't you?"

"Yes, I am," he replied as he finished tucking in his pants.

Mason just stared at him. "Wonderful," he said sarcastically. "Which brings me back to my original question, where is the entrance?"

Ganoux led him over to the altar. They separated to each side. Ganoux motioned to him to grab a side.

"We need to push it out of the way."

Mason grabbed his side and Ganoux the other. They pushed and pulled until the altar moved slightly. They rested for a moment and then tried again. The altar slid across the stone floor slowly. The sound of stone dragging across the floor filled the room. Ganoux bent down and removed the rug which lay in front of the altar. He removed his knife and pried up a floorboard, exposing a metal handle. He grabbed the handle, asked Mason to move back, and lifted it. The floorboards opened as part of a door, and Ganoux propped it against the wall, exposing a black hole in the floor. The door lined up with the floorboards so when closed it was undetectable. They retrieved their things and stood over the hole.

"Ready?" Ganoux said.

Mason nodded as Ganoux turned around and pointed the beam of the flashlight down the hole. A wooden ladder was mounted to the floorboards from below and leaned against the opening in the floor. Cobwebs and dust were everywhere.

Ganoux bent down and cleared some away with his hands. After briefly looking up at Mason, he turned and crouched down. Ganoux grabbed the sides of the opening and slowly started down the oak ladder, the creaking sounds of old wood filled the room. Eight rungs later he yelled up to Mason, "Your turn."

Mason looked around one more time and then backed down the ladder. As he entered the catacombs, he remembered Ganoux's words of wisdom: "Breathe through your mouth."

Chapter 16

ONCE THEY WERE BOTH ON THE GROUND, they turned their flashlights toward the only way they could go. Both men knew from going over the plan so many times that the third opening on the right was the first turn. Mason looked around; he could see rats scurrying about and lots of cobwebs, some so big they almost covered the entire opening of the corridor. Ganoux had his knife out, which he used to break the webs apart. Mason took a deep breath through his nose and realized it was not nearly as bad as the stench emanating from the trunk of Johnathan Dever's car had been. He relaxed and focused on what they needed to do. Ganoux was leading as he had firsthand knowledge of the catacombs. He seemed very comfortable. He casually stepped over the rats and through the webs. Mason was transfixed by everything that moved. For a place of the dead everything seemed to be alive. He wasn't particularly squeamish, but the number of things crawling around made him a little uneasy. Water droplets from the ceiling above pooled on the ground at several areas as they walked. They had definitely found the right place to hide something; no one in their right mind would come down.

They reached the third turn and went to the right. Ganoux tied the end of the rope to a stone, which was protruding from the floor. He began to release some slack, then cut it with his knife. He was going to mark every turn they made with a piece of rope to make sure they did not lose their bearings. He wrapped the rope around the corner so they would remember which way to go. He then turned and continued.

It was here that the bones began to appear. The walls were

virtually covered with the remains of the dead, thousands of bones made up the walls, as if they were stone. They were all neatly tucked away as to hold the maximum capacity. Layers and layers of femur bones made up the base level, which extended about three feet up from the ground. Then several rows of skulls neatly tucked side by side, many of them with their teeth intact. Whoever had the job of organizing the bones was very good at one of the more morbid occupations you could imagine. Mason wondered how you became the bone storage guy. Did you volunteer or was it the shortest straw? Just as he was lost in this thought he walked right into a web, and it covered part of his face. He batted at his head as he tried to get it off. He was still picking it out of his hair when Ganoux glanced back and chuckled.

"Yeah, very funny," Mason said as he wiped his head one more time. They continued about twenty feet to the next turn. They went to the right, and then a quick left. They passed a cut out opening on the right. Mason flashed some light in, and there was a stone tablet in front of the wall of bones. It read:

OSSEMENTS DE LANCIEN CIMETIERE
ST. JACQUES DU HAUT PAS
DEPOSESEN1850 DANS L'OUSSUAIRE
DE L'OUEST ET TRANSFERES
EN 7 1859

Tablets throughout the catacombs had been erected by the French government to keep track of where each set of bones came from. When the bones were moved from cemeteries in the heart of the city to the underground, ossuary maintenance men oversaw organizing the bones, and the priest from a local church would bless the bones upon entrance. Local nuns from a convent would volunteer to assist in any capacity, often providing candlelight to the ossuary maintenance men. The catacombs had been open to the public only a few times and only to a small area of the tomb itself. The last visitation, according to Jacques, was in 1935. Ganoux managed to be one of the lucky few to get underground, Jacques had made sure of it. Once underground, he feigned interest in the bones while keeping a close eye on everyone. He made sure no one tried to access the forbidden part of the catacombs, so their secret chamber remained just that...a secret. Mason began walking forward again wondering how many bodies worth of bones were down here, easily thousands, he thought.

The only sound you could hear was their feet stepping in the various puddles of water that had filtered down through the earth. Water was either dripping down the walls of bones, or from the ceiling. Mason followed Ganoux as they continued through the tunnels. They had to be getting close, he thought as he ducked under another web. Ganoux calmly walked through the corridors as if he was strolling through a park on a sunny spring day.

They reached the end of the corridor and turned right. Ganoux stopped and shined his light to the left. You could see where the corridor had caved in. A large pile of rock, bone, and dirt blocked the way. Turning back, he said, "It's just ahead on the left." Mason could see the opening coming closer, about ten feet away.

They reached the opening to the antechamber, and stood next to each other shining their lights in. The room was the biggest they had come upon, and clearly set up differently than the others. The walls had wooden coffins placed in cutouts on the left, while bones were neatly stacked on the right. There was a large sarcophagus on the floor, with two smaller ones on either side. Ganoux walked over to the one on the left and put his things down. Mason followed, shining his light throughout the cave: at the ceiling, the walls, behind him. He was fascinated by the setup of the room. He wondered who got to be entombed here, definitely the high society. In his mind, a tomb was a tomb, but he had to admit this chamber had more dignity than having your bones piled up in the wall.

Ganoux broke the silence, "So everything is in this one. We'll take the top off carefully and move it over to the side. Be very careful, it is not that heavy, but it may be brittle, we don't want it to break in our hands. Let's try to be respectful, after all, this is a burial chamber."

Mason agreed, and they positioned themselves at either end. The top was surprisingly light, Mason thought. They removed it easily and placed it on the floor to the side. Ganoux shined his light inside the coffin, and it revealed two metal tubes about two feet long, and a wooden box approximately two feet by three feet. He reached down inside and retrieved one of the tubes. It was covered in dust. He handed it to Mason and reached down to grab the other. The metal tube had some weight to it, and Mason placed it on the dirt floor. He grabbed the second one from Ganoux and placed it next to the other one. Ganoux reached in a third time and removed the box. "This one goes first. I will take the box, and you take one of the tubes."

Mason reached down and paused before he picked one up. He never envisioned he would become an art thief. He knew this was for the greater good, but he was still stealing national treasures from France, and the feeling made him more than a little uneasy. He wondered if he would ever see the inside of the tubes and the box. He almost did not want to know which priceless paintings he was pilfering; it was better if he just pretended all the containers were empty. He wondered if his dad would approve. His father believed in the value of preserving the parts of history that are essential for civilizations to move forward. There are certain aspects of society that cannot ever be destroyed, the greatness of the artists and their creations must always be preserved, and to do that, every last resort must be undertaken. Well, Mason thought, this was about as last a resort as he could possibly imagine. He was in an underground tomb holding on to the thought that he was preserving history. He trusted everyone involved, but still needed some more answers. The questions had been piling up in his mind over the last few days, and the answers were few and far between, while the questions kept mounting.

Gathering their lights, Mason and Ganoux turned and left

the room. They followed the ropes back to the ladder while dodging the moving floor and the dripping ceiling. Once at the ladder, Ganoux reached in his pack and removed a cloth blanket. He laid it out on the ground and placed the box on it. Mason put the metal tube down as well. So far so good he thought as they headed back. He looked at his watch; they had been down in the catacombs for twenty-seven minutes. Figuring one hour to retrieve everything, they were right on schedule.

Walking back to the antechamber, Mason felt more confident. He walked briskly and avoided all the webs and the rats. He was starting to feel comfortable down here, but he also could not wait to be back above ground.

They reached the chamber and placed the top back on the sarcophagus, grabbed the other tube, and headed back to the ladder. Ganoux removed the ropes as they passed them. Even though no one was allowed down here, he was going to leave it as they found it. They reached the ladder and paused for a moment. Still the only sounds were things scurrying about; everything was going just as they planned.

Ganoux climbed up the ladder and slowly stuck his head back through the opening into the mausoleum office. He quietly looked around; they were alone. Mason picked up the wooden box. It was lighter than the metal tubes; he climbed on the first two rungs and held it up the ladder. Ganoux reached down from above and grabbed it with both hands. He disappeared for a few seconds and then reappeared. Mason grabbed a metal tube and they did the same exchange. The other tube was sent up the ladder, and Mason took one final look around to make sure they did not leave anything. He started back up the ladder, and Ganoux appeared above him. He reached down and grabbed Mason by the arm, helping to pull him back up into the room. Mason exhaled and dusted himself off. He was more than happy to be out of the catacombs.

Ganoux closed the trap door and replaced the piece of the wood floor. Mason helped him put the altar back in place. It sank back into the grooves it had created over many years. Mason grabbed the candlesticks and placed them on the altar. With everything back in place, they carried everything back to the door. They filled their bags with all their supplies and secured them on their backs. When they were ready, Ganoux slowly opened the door from the office into the hallway. The dimly lit hallway was silent and free of scurrying rodents. Mason grabbed one metal tube, and Mr. Ganoux grabbed the poplar box. They brought both up the stairs and down the hall to the door to the mausoleum. There were still no sounds, so they put them on the floor and Mason went back for the other tube.

It had been almost one hour since they came in, and they were both ready to get out of there. Once everything was back at the door, Ganoux removed the key and slowly unlocked the door. The sound of the lock opening echoed throughout the hallway. It was so quiet underground that the noise of the lock seemed incredibly loud. They waited a moment before opening the door. Ganoux peered out from behind the door and then opened it fully. They were back in the mausoleum. The flickering candles welcomed them back to civilization. Mason agreed to do the first run to the car. He looked out the side door and across the cemetery. His night among the dead was almost complete. A few trips to the car; and then back to the warehouse.

Mason started out carrying one metal tube. The airtight tube probably weighed twenty pounds and it was easy to carry but took both hands. His head pivoted like a top in every direction. He saw nothing strange, so he bent down and began to briskly move amongst the tombstones. He caught a glimpse of some of the names as he walked by Devoreaux, Lemoux, Bastille; he wondered what these families would think as he smuggled stolen art out of the mausoleum across their graves. He felt as if he could see them shaking their heads as he passed. He apologized under his breath and continued on. He reached the tree line and eventually the steps down to the street. He crouched in the trees as he peered down the steps. He could hear the distant sound of cars and a train horn. He saw no sign of life, so he headed down the steps. The car was still sitting in the same spot and nobody else was on the street.

At the car, he opened the trunk and placed the metal tube inside. Mason closed the trunk quietly and looked at the houses. They were all dark; no lights were on at all except two of the houses had a front light on. A cat ran across the street; it was not all black, so he felt good about that.

He met Ganoux back at the church and grabbed the other tube. Ganoux carried the wooden box as they walked briskly through the cemetery. They reached the car and placed the two items in the trunk. There were no signs of anything out of the ordinary so Ganoux started the car and they slowly pulled away from the curb. Neither man said a thing as they headed back to the warehouse.

Mason's thoughts plagued him during the whole ride back to the warehouse. He did not have regrets, he just wondered about going forward, and he could not wait to get out to the country and reunite with Jacques, Collette, and Anna. He had the vision of his head on the platter again, but this time he could not see who was holding it. He closed his eyes and beckoned for Madame X. She faintly appeared and then abruptly disappeared as they entered the driveway to the warehouse. They unloaded everything and had a drink before bed. Neither man said much, even though there was so much to talk about. Mason curled up on the couch and was fast asleep. Ganoux stayed up with his thoughts for a bit, and then went to the bedroom. He closed the door and picked up the receiver to the phone. He dialed a few numbers, waited a few moments, and then said quietly, "It's done." He hung up the receiver, lay down on the bed and closed his eyes.

Chapter 17

MASON AWOKE ON THE COUCH around 8:30 the next morning. He rolled over and saw that the metal tubes and the crate were exactly where they had left them last night. Ganoux was nowhere to be seen so Mason assumed he was still sleeping. He wandered into the kitchen to find some coffee and something to eat. There was little, and he went down the hallway and peeked in the bedroom; the bed was made, and there was no sign of Ganoux. Mason was slightly annoyed after everything they risked last night that Ganoux would leave without telling him where and why he was going.

Mason went back into the main area and sat at the table. He examined the metal tubes more closely, each one was airtight and had small etchings on the ends: a series of letters and numerals. There was no way of knowing how long they had been down underground, and no way of knowing their contents. Were they famous pieces of art with questionable backgrounds or something else? To be honest, he did not know much about the contents for which he had put his life and reputation on the line. He was out of his comfort zone, smuggling God knows what, with a man he met two days ago, who he had threatened to throw out of a plane into the Atlantic Ocean. Ganoux was still a mystery. A very competent partner he had proven to be, but there were still too many unanswered questions about him.

Mason had talked to his father when he had first received the letter from Jacques Moulié. Aldon Wright knew about the situation and was quite excited for Mason to be involved and seemed quite jealous that he could not be involved himself. It was because of his respect for his father and for Moulié that

Mason was here; seeing Collette was a bonus. His father told him to be careful and keep his cards close. "Don't give up more than you're willing to pay," were his exact words. Though only twenty-eight, Mason had traveled extensively and knew the ways of the world, especially the art world. He had been in the art and archaeology world for most of his life and had found himself in some interesting situations.

When Mason was eleven years old, he and Collette were on a dig outside of Turin, Italy, with their fathers. The excavation spanned two plateaus separated by a ridge. A path led around the ridge to the previously discovered ruins, but the ridge could be easily scaled, and the two young kids preferred to scale the ridge and slide down the other side, rather than take the path. Mason and Collette would help when needed but experienced a lot of downtime; archaeology was not a very fast-moving profession. As their fathers were surveying a new plot to dig, Mason and Collette were playing hide and seek on the other side of the ridge in the previously discovered ruins. It was Collette's turn to hide, and Mason was counting to fifty when he heard some commotion coming from the other side of the ridge. He climbed to the top of the ridge to have a look. When he reached the top and looked over the edge to the other side, he noticed his father and Jacques talking to some men in uniforms. One man was very animated as he spoke. Jacques stepped forward to talk to the man, three of the other men removed their rifles and pointed them at Jacques and Aldon. Both men retreated with their hands up, as the lead man barked some orders in Italian. Mason slid down his side of the ridge and began running through the ruins whispering Collette's name as quietly and loudly as he could. He ran around the corners and into small excavated rooms, his whispers echoing against the old stone walls. Finally, Collette emerged. "That's not fair, you can't call my name."

"There are men with guns on the other side," Mason said between breaths.

"What are you talking about?" she asked, moving closer.

"Come on," Mason said, and the two of them ran toward the ridge and began to climb up. They reached the top and crawled the last few feet. Collette inched up and looked over the ridge from behind a rock. She saw their fathers standing there with arms raised, a man in uniform pacing back and forth in front of them, questioning them in Italian. Collette spoke three languages, Italian being one of them. She translated as the conversation progressed, mainly between the soldier and Jacques. The soldier was questioning the validity of their paperwork for them to be excavating the site. Jacques insisted everything was in order and threatened to call the Italian Prime Minister. The soldier was particularly interested in a vase which had been stolen from the Italian museum in Turin. Jacques assured the man that no vase was in their possession, and any artifact found was quickly documented and sent to the museum for inspection. The man in uniform was undeterred and became increasingly agitated.

Mason grabbed Collette's arm. "The three vases in the tent? Do you think that is what they are talking about?"

"I don't know," Collette whispered back.

Collette looked back down at the men, the leader spoke up. "Search the area."

She turned back to Mason, "Come on." They both started their slide back down to the bottom and began running through the ruins toward the tents set up for sleeping. They reached the main tent where Mason immediately located the vases on a table in the corner. They grabbed them and ran outside, turning right and running in the direction of the mountain caves. Climbing and stumbling over the rocky terrain, they reached the first cave. Quickly stashing the vases behind the boulders marking the entrance. they re-emerged from the caves, just as the soldiers were entering the ruins. Hiding behind a wall for a moment, they waited until the soldiers turned the opposite direction and then ran back into main tent. Both kids jumped on their cots and pretended to be resting as a soldier entered. The soldier barked something in Italian and began searching the tent. He grabbed a blanket from Collette's cot as she huddled in the corner. He ripped it off the cot, almost taking her with it. The soldier walked over to the table and using his forearm, he wiped all the artifacts into the blanket, wrapped it up, and left. Collette was still shaking on her cot as Mason came over. He sat down next to her and put his hand on her shoulder "You okay?" he said with genuine concern. She nodded and they both stood up. There was some more commotion outside and men yelling. It eventually dissipated, and the two of them walked slowly to the entrance. Jacques came running in, almost knocking them over.

"Oh, thank the Lord, you are both okay. Aldon, they're in here," he yelled toward the opening in the tent. Mason's father ran in and exhaled once he realized they were all right.

"Daddy, who were those men?' Collette asked.

"They were most likely thieves posing as soldiers. They come to digs posing as official government personnel, confiscate artifacts and then sell them to the highest bidder."

"Oh no, they got the vases," Aldon said, exasperated.

Jacques turned and lowered his head in dismay.

Mason spoke up "Dad, we took the vases and hid them in the caves."

"You did what?" Aldon asked.

"We moved them before the men came in here."

Aldon chuckled and turned to Jacques, "My friend, we have some very smart and brave kids. Mason, that was very dangerous, but you both have done a great service to archaeology."

"We didn't want those men to have them," Mason said innocently.

Jacques smiled, "We wouldn't want those men to have them either." He walked over to both Mason and Collette.

"Thank you both."

Mason and Collette led their fathers to the vases in the

caves. The three were eventually donated to a smaller private museum for display. The Italian Museum of Turin had tried for many years unsuccessfully to have them returned. One of the vases was donated back to the Wright family for their role in preserving history, it currently rests in the front hall of Mason's apartment in New York.

Mason snapped back to reality and laughed to himself after reminiscing. He and Collette had preserved a small part of history, and he hoped his current situation would yield the same result. He was not entirely convinced and was still running on faith.

Mason moved over in front of the crate which presumably contained the third piece of art. It measured roughly two feet by three feet and was made of poplar, solid yet lightweight. He saw no markings on the crate and could tell it was made specifically for this purpose: airtight, a very professional job, clean lines and angles. There was no obvious way to open it, though he could tell the top from the bottom. The top had a two-inch raised edge all around the frame, while the bottom was smooth. Why was this piece crated when the others were rolled? Could it not be rolled up? Most paintings were on canvas, which could easily be removed from their frames and rolled. Not ideal for preservation purposes, but in this instance removing the art from their frames made everything easier and less conspicuous. This piece must have to lie flat, and therefore a crate made specifically for it was being used.

Just then Mason heard a car outside the large doors. He went to the window and saw Ganoux's car idling in the driveway. He heard the padlock on the doors being removed, and the doors open. Ganoux pulled in and shut the car off. Mason stood at the top of the steps waiting for the explanation, like a housewife waiting to hear why her husband was out so late. Ganoux got out of the car and wished Mason a good morning. He did indeed have some bread and other items for breakfast.

"You should have told me you were going somewhere. You

could have left a note."

"Sorry, dear," Ganoux replied with a touch of sarcasm as he walked by him. "I wanted to get the paper to see if there were any stories about the church last night, plus I went to check out the two names to see if we can figure out who they are."

"Any luck?"

"Not on Andrew Loch."

"The priest?"

"Nothing on him, but your friend from the park, Franz Kolter, his real name is Alex Beichler, and he is a known associate of a very famous man in this city. Franz Leiter. M. Leiter, who the police refer to by his nickname "Lucky," is the biggest black-market dealer in France, possibly Western Europe."

"Why do they call him Lucky?"

"He was a great admirer of the American gangster Lucky Luciano. After hearing all the stories about him from the prohibition era, he nicknamed himself Lucky."

"Wow, that's very clever," Mason said sarcastically. "The French Lucky Luciano."

"Lucky is quite a character. He owns a few nightclubs where he does business. The nightclubs are all legitimate, so he has the cover for his other interests. He also is a friend to many powerful people in this city. He has bought protection from virtually everyone. Many times, they have tried to bring him down, and he always finds a way out. Evidence disappears, witnesses disappear, or the charges get dropped randomly because no one will go up against him—another reason why they call him Lucky. He is not the kind of man you want mad at you, but he can be helpful if you need information—of course, it will cost you."

"What do you think he wants with me?"

"I suspect he knows you have a connection to Jacques, and he is interested in acquiring some art, specifically information on when and where the museums are taking their art for safekeeping. With war on the horizon, he probably sees this as a business opportunity. If the Führer is truly an art collector, Lucky may try to make friends with him in order to stay in business. My guess is he wants the master list so he can go shopping."

Mason shook his head. "The French Lucky Luciano, you have got to be kidding me. Well, I guess we should get going as soon as possible in case Lucky comes looking for us. The quicker we are out of the city, the safer I will feel. A quick bite and we'll go. How long will it take us?"

"About three hours," Ganoux replied, "without traffic. The hardest part is getting out of the city. Once we are clear of that, it should be an easy ride. I will make up some breakfast while you get ready."

Mason went in the back to shower and get ready while Ganoux made eggs and potatoes. They were to lock up everything and turn on the outside light. They did not anticipate coming back. Mason's hope was they would have a short stop in the country, then back to the city by train, on to the airport, and home to New York.

After breakfast they loaded up the car and did one final sweep of the place to make sure nothing was left behind. They turned off everything, locked the doors, and pulled away. It was about 10:00 a.m., and the warehouse district was bustling with activity. Ganoux had suggested this location because of the amount of activity; nothing ever looked suspicious. They could slip in and out with no one even noticing.

The ride through Paris was slow, but a welcome distraction from sitting around. Mason looked out the window at all the people coming and going. You would never know that war was knocking on their door. Paris was alive with activity. Traffic was everywhere; people were everywhere, it was vibrant. The Eiffel Tower was visible in the distance. After one hour the city started to disappear behind them. They had reached the outer boroughs. Everything was quieter here as they approached the main highway out of town. It was a nice day with plenty of sunshine. Mason hoped this was a sign of better days ahead. He wanted some time without bodies, catacombs, guns, or the thought of Lucky coming after him. He had not been to the Moulié farm in many years. The last time was in his teens when he and his father stopped there on their way back to the States. The farm was isolated and large, surrounded by rolling hills. He was looking forward to some much-needed rest.

They reached the exit for the farmhouse and turned left. They entered the small town of Leoville. It was a typical quaint French town with one main road, a few restaurants, and a town square. As they drove through, Mason could see the small café with people sitting outside enjoying the beautiful French day. One particular man was seated reading the newspaper. The man noticed the car going by, and the face he had been waiting for. Mason Wright had arrived in Leoville and would be on his way to the Moulié farm up in the hills. The man quietly stood up, paid for his coffee, and went over to the black sedan parked around the corner. He retrieved his bag from the car and would await word back at his hotel on what he was to do next. The information he was given was correct. Mason Wright was working with Jacques Moulié.

Chapter 18

THEY ARRIVED AT THE FARMHOUSE after three and a half hours and pulled into the driveway under the metal arch that read: *Maison des Collines,* The Home of the Hills. The driveway began in the woods and eventually opened to the picturesque scene of green grass, rolling hills, and a large chateau style home. The house was stone with four brick chimney stacks rising over the gray, slate roof. Ivy covered the left side of the house while black shutters adorned the windows. Colorful flower boxes hung under the upstairs windows, and two large stone planters graced either side of the front door. To the right of the house was the barn, stone with large wooden doors; it was as if they had just driven into a painting.

As they pulled down the driveway, Collette came out the front door followed closely by Anna, and they waited for the car to come to a stop. Mason got out and stretched, raising his arms to the sky. Collette walked over and gave him a hug.

"How are you?" she asked.

"A little tired but I feel pretty good. How are things here?"

"We are doing well," Collette said as she glanced over at Anna.

Ganoux grabbed his bag, said hello, and headed for the house. Mason gathered his things and locked the car. They would wait until dark to unload the cargo. Inside, they sat down to a large buffet lunch with plates of cheese, bread and fruit. Mason did like this aspect of the adventure; he was eating better than he had in months. Two bottles of wine were open on the table. Jacques poured the wine and raised his glass in a toast to Mason and Ganoux. He thanked them on behalf of the people of

France and claimed one day they would be hailed as heroes. Mason accepted the thanks, even though he had no idea what he actually had done. He did not want to be hailed as a hero to the people of France; he just wanted to get out of their country in one piece. Some people become heroes posthumously, he thought sourly. He did not plan on becoming one of them, or to have people lay flowers on his grave.

After the meal they relaxed in the living room and listened to Anna play the piano. She had been taught by her mother, and for an eleven-year-old was quite good. They drank wine and enjoyed each other's company. Mason had not seen Mme. Moulié since he was a teenager, so he enjoyed catching up with her. Angeline Moulié was a beautiful woman in her sixties with graying hair, a slim figure, and gorgeous skin. Collette was definitely her daughter: They were similar in looks, voice and mannerisms. Angeline sat down next to Anna and they improvised a duet, further lightening the mood. It was good to be with friends, Mason thought; this was the first time he had relaxed since he got to France. It would not last. When night fell, they would begin the next phase of the plan.

After some much-needed downtime, the girls retired upstairs. Jacques, Ganoux, and Mason prepared to bring their cargo into the barn to discuss. The sun had set, and the moon was just coming out. It was the beginning of a beautiful night in the countryside.

As the moon rose in the sky, the gentleman from the café positioned himself at the tree line with an unobstructed view of the house. His orders were to watch and report back any activity he witnessed. He had a pair of military grade binoculars, which would put him right in the middle of the three men. If he could only read lips. He would lie there all night if he had to, but, was happy to learn he wouldn't have to as he noticed the front door open and the three men emerge. He recognized Mason and Jacques Moulié, but not the third man, who had been driving the car earlier. He looked to be in his forties with a slender build. The café man took notes and jotted down key characteristics, along with the time.

8:53 p.m.: Mason Wright, Jacques Moulié, and unknown third male exit the house and go to the car. They talk for a minute. Moulié walks to the barn doors, unlocks the padlock, and opens them. Wright and the unknown male open the trunk to the car. The unknown subject carries a large crate to the barn. Wright carries what looks like a metal tube to the barn, returns, and retrieves a similar one. Unknown subject returns to the car, closes the trunk, and locks the doors.

9:01 p.m.: The three men enter the barn and close the large door.

Inside, Mason and Ganoux placed the poplar box on a bench in the back of the barn. Jacques entered the horse stall and pulled down on a large hook, which had horse reigns draped over it. He held it for a moment and then released it. The hook slid back up into place, and at the same time a large workbench against the wall began to slide sideways. Mason quickly turned and saw the bench sliding away to expose a set of stairs leading down.

"I had this built years ago before the Great War. Thankfully, I did not need it, but I always knew it would come into good use at some point," Jacques said.

The three men walked to the stairs and looked down. A stone cellar was visible about ten feet below. Jacques asked the men to bring the items down the stairs; they would open everything down below. Jacques grabbed one metal tube, Mason the other, and Ganoux the poplar box. Once in the cellar, they set the items on a table in the middle of the room.

The cellar beneath the barn was quite large and made of limestone. On one side there were shelves lined with supplies and glass jars. A small wood-burning stove was in the corner with the piping leading out through the wall. The piping led out back to a small creek, which ran behind the house. If they ever needed it, they would only use it at night, as the smoke would be visible during the day. At night, the smoke would be obscured by darkness. Two small beds were on the other wall, complete with blankets. A radio lay on one of them. Mason wondered if it was the Bedford 200. The cellar was cool and dry, and two lights hung overhead, one directly over the large wooden table.

Jacques flipped a switch at the top of the steps, and the workbench above slid back into place. It was time to get down to business.

Outside the man at the tree line kept taking his notes.

9:21p.m.: Still in the barn.

Jacques laid down a cloth over the table and brought over a small hammer and chisel. He moved the tubes to one side of the table and the poplar box to the other. He stared at the two men for a moment and took a deep breath before he spoke.

Jacques began by thanking Mason once again for being there and helping in this time of need. He began to explain why they were here.

"About one year ago, after Germany annexed the Sudetenland, I met with the Council for Preservation in Paris. The men at this meeting were all directors at various museums across France. We decided that a plan must be created for all the precious art in each museum to be moved to several secret locations in the advent of war. Several scenarios were discussed, and I formulated a plan with Jean Paul Laveaux, and Mark Lafite. Jean Paul is the director of the Museum de Antiques in Paris, Mark is the director of acquisitions for the Claude Renoir museum in Lyon. I have known Jean Paul for twenty years and we worked together extensively on many exhibits. In fact, Mason, your father knows him quite well, also. Mark has worked with us for seven years and has successfully updated many museums' information to bring the documentation of their collections into a much more efficient system. He is the "youngblood" of the group.

We decided to each formulate a plan and present our

findings to the council. After a few weeks we reconvened in Paris to talk about our progress. We decided on three main sites to start and began the exhausting chore of picking which pieces should go where. We created a master list for each plan. The two lists would only be known to us. Jean Paul and I had suspicions about the council, because we had been dealing with an ever-growing set of issues with some of the members. Certain men did not like the direction some museums had taken and wanted more input into the acquisition decisions. Being the two senior members, we felt the push from the younger ones, and quickly began to distrust most of them. Many had personal interests as well as outside influence pushing them in certain directions. We had to include one member in these decisions, and Mark was the most bearable man we could work with.

Due to the distrust within the council, Jean Paul and I created a false master list and locked it in the vault in the Louvre. Our suspicions were confirmed when a few weeks later the list disappeared. Someone has the master list and probably is offering it up to the highest bidder. We listed abandoned mines, warehouses, and factories in rural parts of the country, which would never be found because they don't exist. I was put in charge of safekeeping the two authentic lists, and therefore overseeing the safe return of any museum piece, which is removed."

Mason listened intently and nodded as the story was told. He was waiting for the part where they got to the three pieces sitting on the table in front of him.

Jacques continued. "So, with the help of Paul here, we decided to hide the lists down in the catacombs, the last place anyone would think of—at least that is what we thought. Recently, as I told you, our suspicions grew when someone started poking around asking about excavating the catacombs. We knew they had to be moved."

Jacques grabbed the first metal tube, and with the help of a pipe wrench, began to unscrew the top. Once open, he reached in and slowly removed a canvas roll. He discarded the tube and unrolled the canvas to reveal a painting. Mason looked curiously at it; he did not recognize the painting or the artist. He thought that he had risked everything for a famous painting or portrait, but what he was staring at was not very good at all. It looked as though it had been painted by a child, bad lines, and bad shading, not exactly a masterpiece. He hoped he had not risked his life for this—there had to be more to the story.

Jacques opened the second tube and unrolled a second terrible painting: a portrait of a woman looking out from her balcony over the landscape. Mason was less than impressed and was getting increasingly agitated that he had risked his life for this. Madame X, this was not. Mason was not an artist, but he knew art, and the value of good art, and the difference between amateur art and a real masterpiece. These two paintings fell somewhere in between a first-time painter and a person with no artistic talent whatsoever. Mason awaited the explanation on why he had been brought across the ocean to smuggle two terrible paintings out of France. If he were French, he would willingly part with these two from his collection; they were not exactly national treasures.

Jacques must have recognized the disgusted look on Mason's face. "Do you recognize either one of these, Mason?"

"No, sir, I can't even place a time period."

"I am not surprised, because I painted these myself a few months ago. We needed two paintings for our plan, so I whipped these up in about one month. Not bad, wouldn't you say?"

Mason thought to himself, "*No, not too bad...awful.*"

"Yes, they are quite good," Mason said trying to be convincing.

"Quite good?" Jacques asked. "They are not quite good, they are quite terrible. There is a reason I am in charge of protecting art and not responsible for producing any."

Mason exhaled and laughed, "Yes, they are not good, which leads me to the question, why are you storing worthless paintings in airtight metal tubes below Paris in a royal sarcophagus?"

"Ahhh…the big question. Why?" Jacques turned over one of the paintings and moved a small light over it. He slowly shined the light on the edge of the canvas, revealing a barely visible seam on its back. "Mason, you are looking at two worthless paintings that are priceless. Sewn inside of each of these is the master art list that Jean Paul, Mark, and I created."

Mason looked up, and Jacques returned his stare with a serious nod.

"Wow!"

"Yes, wow," Jacques replied. "You must take these lists back with you to New York and guard them with your life. The heart of France's humanity is sewn into these paintings. War will take many things from us, but I will not let it take this," Jacques said as he touched the table.

Mason silently acknowledged his plea as the full weight of this job now began to take its toll. Mason was now in charge of the largest art collection in Europe.

Jacques picked up the hammer and chisel and very carefully began to open the poplar box still sitting on the table. What was in it? Mason wondered. He was already slightly shaken by the contents of the first two packages.

Jacques removed the top with the utmost care. Something inside was wrapped in a canvas cloth. Jacques removed it carefully. Ganoux upended the box and Jacques carefully placed the wrapped item on it. He looked up at Mason.

"I know I am asking a tremendous amount from you, and I need to ask you for one more favor. I need you to take care of someone for me. A woman who is known the world over, I want you to take her back to New York with you. I have spoken to your father, and he has agreed to keep an eye on her for me. She will be safe with him. I trust and respect few people in this world, but your father is at the top of that list."

Mason slowly nodded as he looked at Jacques. Ganoux stared at Mason, and the looks on both their faces told Mason this was not just some ordinary woman.

With that, he began to remove the canvas wrapping. Mason's face went white as the blood drained from it when he saw what was under the wrapping. This was definitely not a Jacques Moulié original. This was one of the most famous women in the world, with her dark shoulder length hair, her crossed hands, and her wry smile. Mason was staring at a painting with an incredible history. This portrait had been stolen, owned by kings, once hung in Napoleon's bedroom, and was possibly the most famous painting in the world. It was known to many as La Gioconda but known to the rest of the world as Leonardo Da Vinci's Mona Lisa.

Chapter 19

MASON WAS SPEECHLESS. This could not possibly be the real thing. He had seen her once but from far away. Ever since her theft in 1911 and subsequent return in 1913, security had been very tight. He looked up at Jacques, "This isn't…"

Jacques cut him off, "Yes, Mason, it is."

"How did you…? Why do you…?" Mason stumbled over his words; he had a million questions but could not seem to get them out. He tried swallowing through the lump in his throat.

"I have had her for some time now. I made the decision, along with Jean Paul from the Museum de Antiques, that it was too valuable, and too risky, to go back on display. We hired a master forger, who we found through Ganoux; we paid him cash, and he created the Mona Lisa which now hangs in the Louvre. I could not bear the thought of her being stolen or destroyed by the ever-approaching war in Europe."

"Has anybody suspected the Louvre piece is a forgery?"

"No, not that I know of. The man who did this was quite good. He went to great lengths to duplicate it. Even I could not tell them apart. I told him he has a future in art if he wanted to legitimize his business. He told me the black market was more profitable. I hated to deal with someone like that, but I saw no other option. Jean Paul and I made the switch when it was due for a cleaning, then we simply brought the new one in and hung it back up and carried out the original in the bottom of a suitcase. I stored her down here until we could find a more suitable location."

"How am I supposed to get this out of the country?"

"The same way it was stolen in the first place. I have a

trunk with a false bottom, which fits the painting perfectly. I will explain everything when we get back inside. I wanted you to see her and realize how incredibly important this is. You will merely be escorting her home with you. Everything has been taken care of."

Mason leaned over and took a closer look at La Gioconda. He had never been that impressed by her, but he had to admit, seeing her up close, he was starting to change his mind. He understood now what all the fuss was about: the wry smile, the draped hands, the long hair. His mind drifted back to the Solario painting in the Metropolitan Museum. His head was still on the silver platter, but it was now being carried by a fifteenth century woman named Lisa, and she was smiling slightly at him. She was about to be stolen for the second time.

The Mona Lisa was stolen from the Louvre on August 21, 1911, by Vincenzo Peruggia, an employee of the museum, who walked out with it under his coat after regular working hours. He kept the painting in a trunk at his apartment for two years before attempting to sell it to the owners of the Uffizi Gallery in Florence. Peruggia served six months in prison and was hailed as a hero back home in Italy for trying to return her to her homeland. One of the suspects was an up-and-coming painter named Pablo Picasso, along with a poet named Guillaume Apollinaire. Both were questioned and later released.

Jacques wrapped the painting back up carefully in the canvas, put her back in the crate, and they retired inside so Jacques could explain the next move. Mason was even more shaken now that he knew why he was in France. Before Mona Lisa, Collette had been the only woman who had ever made him this nervous. He didn't like the way he was feeling. Jacques kept thanking him for doing this great service to France, but Mason felt a little bit like a common thief. He was now the keeper of one of the greatest secrets in French history: the prized Mona Lisa, in perhaps the most famous museum in the world, the Louvre, was not real.

They closed the door to the bunker and moved the work bench back into place. As they exited the barn into the French evening, the man lying in the tree line some hundred feet away, quietly jotted down some more notes:

10:47 p.m.: Leaving barn, heading to house. NO CRATE.

Once inside, Mason and Jacques, along with Ganoux, retired to the study, a wood-paneled room lined with bookcases and an inlaid wood-paneled ceiling. The bookcases were ten feet tall, reaching from floor to ceiling and filled with books covering all periods of history, particularly art history. Jacques was an expert in Etruscan art, and several excellent examples graced the shelves. One of the pieces Mason recognized from an excavation both he and his father had helped complete, the excavation, in fact, where he and Collette became quite close over the year and a half they spent in the Italian hills outside Rome. The vase in Mason's front hall back in New York was from the same dig. He told everyone that he had wanted it because it was his first real find on an actual archaeological excavation, but actually, it just reminded him of Collette.

Jacques opened a bottle of wine and began the conversation as if he was making a speech to first century Roman troops.

"We are about to undertake an extraordinary act of courage," Jacques began. "The enemies will be plentiful, the road will be difficult, but with men of virtue such as yourselves, the glory will be great."

I'm being primed for battle with Gaul by Julius Cesar, Mason thought hiding a grin.

"The entire country of France will be indebted to you, and history shall see that you are not lost. This is a task of utmost importance, but you must undertake it in secrecy. Your safety and success depend on it. The future of France's cultural life is in your hands. Though this is a great burden to bear, you share it with great men throughout history, and for that you have my highest gratitude."

Mason nodded as he envisioned himself putting on the armor for battle. Ganoux sat stoically as usual, the weight of

France not affecting him at all. He did not seem to be the least bit concerned that the Mona Lisa was sitting in the bunker under the barn wrapped in canvas, and about to be smuggled out of France to upstate New York. Mason tried to remain calm as he sipped his wine.

Jacques continued, "Mason, two days from now you two will go to the Loire Valley to visit Jean Paul at his country chateau. You will pick up a suitcase, which has been fitted with a false bottom. The Mona Lisa will fit securely in the suitcase bottom and be covered by the inside lining of the suitcase. You will be traveling as an aspiring artist aboard the train from Loire to Paris. In your suitcase will be some personal items and the two paintings I created. You can never leave the suitcase alone or let someone else handle it. It must be within sight at all times. Once you reach Paris, Ganoux will drop you at the airport for your return trip home. You should be back in New York in five days. I have instructed Paul to accompany you at all times until your plane is in the air. I am sure by now you know how valuable he can be if anything goes awry. I have trusted him with my life, and therefore I trust him with yours."

"I also have been scanning the newspaper for any story about the little incident at the church three days ago, and luckily, I have seen no mention of anything. The war in Europe has dominated the newspapers, therefore a story about a robbery in Montmartre is inconsequential. Do you have any questions?"

"You trust Jean Paul?"

"Mason, I have known him for thirty years. I would not have involved him if I had the slightest doubt. He is a man of superior character, and a great admirer of your father. He is very much looking forward to meeting you."

"I am okay with everything," Mason said as he sat back in his chair.

"Great. I am tired after this night and am going to retire to bed. Paul, you are okay on the couch downstairs?"

Ganoux nodded. "Yes, sir. Thank you."

"Mason, you are set up in the guest room at the end of the hall on the second floor by the bathroom. Good night; I look forward to a relaxing tomorrow."

Jacques left the room followed by Mason. At the top of the stairs Jacques wished him a good night and headed for the master suite. Mason followed the hallway to the end where he found his bag, his things all laid out. He cleared off the bed and changed. He was quickly asleep after a long day.

Once all the lights were out in the chateau, the man watching from the tree line jotted down one final note:

1:26 a.m.: Lights out.

He gathered his things and quietly made his way back to the road where he walked about a mile back to his car which was parked in the brush. He started the engine and made his way back to town. He would report immediately about what he had witnessed. He believed that Mason Wright had just delivered something of terrific value to Jacques Moulié, and it was currently in the barn at the Maison de Collines.

Chapter 20

THE MAN FROM THE TREE LINE returned to his inn. He had requested a room overlooking the road and the square. The shops would be bustling with people and activity, easier to blend in. The square was accessed by the road to the north; it was the only road leading to Moulié's farm. He would sit on the balcony and wait until daybreak, watching to see if anyone came driving by.

At dawn he picked up the receiver in his room and dialed the number he had been given. The voice on the other end picked up after two rings. The man relayed his notes from the night before and the voice at the other end thanked him and gave him his next task. He was to monitor the comings and goings of the farm, specifically Mason Wright's. If Mason did leave, he was to follow carefully, and if possible, retrieve the contents of the crate by any means necessary—but quietly.

As he hung up the receiver he smiled; he knew they should have hired him first instead of Lane. He would prove to them what a valuable asset he could be. He would stay on the balcony ready to go at a moment's notice. His car was downstairs, and his bag was packed. Yes, he had thought of everything. He was confident that Mason Wright was no match for him, and he was anxious to prove it.

Mason faintly heard the knock on the door. He looked at the clock, it was 9:17. He heard the knock again, and Collette's voice as she opened the door. He rolled over to see her standing in the doorway; she had a faint smile as she glanced in. She looked beautiful. *How does she do that*? he thought to himself. She always looked good.

"Anna and I are going into town for some shopping; do you want to join us?"

A day of shopping with the girls was not what Mason had envisioned for his day, but he agreed to go. He just needed a few minutes to get freshened up. Collette told him to meet her downstairs.

Mason went into the bathroom and looked in the mirror. He did not look nearly as good as Collette. He washed up and tried to scrub some of the guilt off. So far in France he had witnessed the deaths of two men, dumped a third body into a lake, and illegally entered the catacombs to steal a priceless piece of art. It had not been the ideal vacation. Maybe today would be uneventful.

After getting ready, Mason headed down the main staircase. The eighteenth century chateau could be a museum. Each wall was decorated with artifacts from around the world. The main staircase wall featured an enormous tapestry, a recreation of a piece from the famous Bayeux tapestry, hung majestically on a wrought iron rod.

The Bayeux tapestry, believed to be commissioned in the eleventh century, shows the events leading up to the Norman conquest of England. Some two hundred and thirty feet long, it has about fifty scenes depicted. He believed the section he was looking at was of scene twenty, which shows Conan II surrendering to William at Dinan. Jacques had excavated a box containing the original tapestry in an old abandoned churchyard in the South of England. It had been severely damaged but currently hung in the British Museum. He had hired a master weaver to recreate the image as a reminder of his historic find.

The smell of fresh coffee brought Mason back into reality, and he continued down the stairs toward the kitchen. He passed Sonja, the housekeeper, who pleasantly said good morning. He followed the smell down the hallway through the dining room and into the kitchen. Ganoux was sitting at the table sipping an espresso. Collette and Anna were at the counter preparing a plate of fresh croissants. Mason announced his entrance with a good morning and sat down across the table from Ganoux.

"Anything interesting going on in the world?" he asked, quietly raising an eyebrow.

Ganoux shook his head and Mason nodded in approval. Their little run-in at the church was surely being kept quiet. It had been three days and no mention of it.

Collette placed the plate of croissants on the table and Mason immediately grabbed one. He was hungry so he ate it in two bites. Collette just looked at him with a disapproving glance and shook her head. Anna had not left her side since they met at the airport. Mason was amazed at how well she was doing under the circumstances. Collette had a very nurturing way about her, which made her easy to gravitate toward. Anna had clearly trusted her from the beginning. Mason understood why Collette felt so strongly about helping Anna in the first place. Collette had lost her sister, Louise, at a very early age and Collette had never been the same. Mason believed she continued to carry the guilt for what happened to Louise.

They were traveling with their family in the south of France when the family stopped in a small town for some rest. Collette and her sister Louise were playing down near the river, outside the chateau where they were staying. Collette was twelve years old, and Louise was nine years old at the time. They were chasing each other around the large French manicured gardens, just two children enjoying their innocence. Louise complained of feeling sick, so Collette stopped chasing her and they sat down on a stone bench to rest. Louise began to cry as she complained of pain, so Collette ran to the house to get their parents. Jacques came out first, and they were running through the gardens toward Louise. She was no longer sitting on the bench, they ran around a row of bushes reaching the bench, and Louise was lying on the ground. They arrived at her side and she was not breathing. Jacques scooped her up and ran to the car to take her to the hospital. Mrs. Moulié grabbed Collette, and the four of them sped off to the closest hospital. Collette was crying hysterically as she lay next to her sister stroking her hair. They arrived at the hospital and Louise was rushed into surgery to take pressure off her brain from a lack of oxygen. She was diagnosed with an unknown heart condition that no one in the family knew about. The overexertion on that day from running around in the heat caused her heart to enlarge, essentially causing a stroke. Louise never regained consciousness and died on the operating table. Collette was devastated and took several years to come to grips with the guilt of that day. Mason's father told him what happened, and he decided to never talk about it with her, unless she brought it up, which she never did. He understood when Collette saw Anna alone on the bench crying, she thought of her sister, and he knew she would never leave Anna sitting there alone, crying.

Mason was staring off into space when Collette announced that they would leave in five minutes, and he quickly downed another croissant. Ganoux would stay behind to watch the house. Jacques and his wife had some errands to run in the next town over and would not be back until dinner time.

January in France felt like November in New York. It was not cold by Mason's standards, but it was by French standards. The sun was out; it was going to be a nice day.

Mason, Collette, and Anna piled into Jacques' car and headed down the gravel driveway to the main road and turned left toward town. Mason rolled down the window and Collette immediately told him no. "We'll all be sick," she said.

"Sickness comes from germs, not from cold air," Mason replied definitively.

"Mason," she said in a don't push me kind of tone.

"Okay." He rolled the window back up as Anna giggled in the back seat.

~~~

As a car approached the main square, the church bells announced 10 a.m. The man on the balcony of the local inn watched as the little Renault parked and Mason, Collette and a young girl emerged. The man did not know who she was. He had not been told of a child. He watched with confusion. Possibly this young girl was Collette's sister? He sat back in his chair, raised his newspaper, and continued to watch the scene unfold.

The trio approached the flower stand and exchanged pleasantries with the owner; Collette gave him a hug and introduced him to the others. The florist turned around and retrieved two flowers, which he gave to Collette. She broke off the stem and placed the flower in her hair, then did the same for Anna. He offered one to Mason, who raised his hands and shook his head with a smile. The owner laughed as he turned back to Collette. They spoke for a while as Anna and Mason perused the stand. She seemed to love all the colors of the flowers: calendula, tulips, and of course, lavender, leaning down to smell each flower. While she was enjoying the sights and smells of the flower stand, the man noticed Mason scanning the square for anything or anyone suspicious. The man looked around also, but his gaze always returned to Mason and Anna. The elders of the town gathered, talking, on the steps of the church. Some men played cards at a table off to the left, and children were kicking a soccer ball around at the far end of the square away from most of the people.

From behind his newspaper, the man watched from the balcony as Mason feigned interest in the flowers and continued to survey the square. Seemingly satisfied with what he saw, Mason turned his attention back to the young girl.

Collette finished talking with the florist and joined them at the other end of the stand. Anna raised the lavender for Collette to smell, and they agreed to purchase some. Mason waited as they paid the owner and had the lavender wrapped. With the lavender secure, it was on to a local clothier where Mason's input was not requested. He headed to the café on the square.

The man on the balcony grabbed his hat and headed down to the square where he sat on a bench to get a closer look at Mason, who was sitting at an outside table sipping coffee and eating a muffin. The man began reading his newspaper. He smiled slightly as he read the articles about the advancing German army.

~~~

Mason sat quietly sipping his coffee and scanning the square, where the people seemed oblivious to the fact that war was at their door. The French had been building a barrier between themselves and Germany, known as the Maginot Line. It was a series of barbed wire barriers and bunkers designed to be impenetrable. They were confident that in the event of war, they were safe. Mason did not share their optimism. He had read about the German Blitzkrieg war in Poland and felt Hitler would stop at nothing to take over Europe.

Anna and Collette appeared carrying several packages. Apparently, they had succeeded in finding Anna "a few" things. Collette mentioned that she needed to pick up some groceries for the house. Mason volunteered to bring the packages to the car and then meet them at the fruit and vegetable stand. He grabbed everything and headed to the car. Anna and Collette strolled over to a series of wooden farm carts filled with produce. The choices were limited in January, but there was still enough to choose from. Collette engaged the owner in brief conversation while Anna wandered around the stand. She walked around the end of the last cart to look at the large purple eggplant. Noticing she could no longer see Collette, she turned to go back and bumped into a man standing next to her with a newspaper under his arm.

"Bonjour," he said.

Anna did not return the pleasantry but managed a small smile. The man asked for her name as he leaned down, blocking her into the corner between the stand and the walls of the church. Nervously, Anna looked past him for Collette.

"You're not from around here, are you? Sprechen sie Deutsch?" the man asked as he peered at her through his sunglasses. Anna stared back, increasingly uncomfortable. She tried to go around him, but he again blocked her path. He looked down at her for a moment and then stood up straight.

"Nice to meet you. Perhaps we will meet again," he said in German as he turned and walked away. Anna ran back to Collette.

"Anna, what's the matter?"

"There was a man, and he was asking me questions. He said he knew I was not from around here. He spoke to me in German."

Collette walked down to the end of the cart and looked around the corner. There was no one there. Anna motioned that he had gone around the corner off the square. Collette briefly looked around the corner. An old man with a cane walked toward her as well as a young couple holding hands. She looked at Anna and pointed to the aged man. Anna shook her head.

Collette grabbed Anna's hand, and they walked back to the stand. She quickly picked out some things as Mason appeared. She told Mason what happened. Concerned, he walked down to the corner and had a look: nothing. He turned and gazed across the square.

"We better get going," he said as he returned to Collette.

They finished their shopping and returned to the car, loaded everything, and headed out of the square and back to the farm.

~~~

Now back on his balcony, the man watched the car leave. He'd had a closer look at the young girl and was convinced she was German, possibly a Jewish girl. The Mouliés had taken in a German refugee. How nice, he thought. If he could not easily get the crate from the barn, he would simply take the girl and trade her for it.

Chapter 21

MASON, COLLETTE, AND ANNA returned from shopping in the early afternoon. Collette and Anna were still a bit shaken from the meeting with the strange man at the market; they went upstairs so Anna could try on her new clothes, while Mason went to the kitchen for a snack. He was convinced it was not a chance meeting; they had attracted attention, and attention was something Mason was trying desperately to avoid. Attention brought people, questions, and problems. He would discuss this with Jacques and Ganoux tonight after dinner. In the meantime, he headed to the sitting room couch for a nap.

He was awakened around 6 p.m. by delicious aromas coming from the kitchen. The Mouliés had returned home and dinner was ready: lamb chops, Lyonnaise potatoes, haricot verts, and a Saint-Émilion Bordeaux as a perfect accompaniment.

As everyone ate, Mason could feel himself gaining weight. He had not eaten like this in a long time. Since he had started his Paris vacation, each meal was better than the last. He laughed at the thought of his small apartment refrigerator filled with leftovers and restaurant food containers. Once everyone was seated in the dining room underneath the crystal chandelier and the molded plaster ceiling, Jacques toasted to their continued good health and the hope the world would somehow avoid another great war. Mason enjoyed watching Collette interact with her parents. The love they shared for each other was evident even in the most benign conversation. Everyone complimented Collette and Anna on the superb dinner.

As usual, Mason was the first one done with his meal. No

matter how slow he tried to eat, he was always finished before everyone else. He looked around and all the plates were still half full. He wondered when it would be appropriate to begin a second serving.

To his right, Anna was pushing her green beans around the outside of her plate with her fork, clearly not her favorite. Half her chop was gone, and no potatoes remained. Ganoux had a perfectly portioned plate, carefully separating each type of food. He had barely made it through half of his meal. Jacques was so busy talking, his plate looked as if he had just been served. Mme. Moulié had a small portion to begin with and was slowly making her way through. Collette also had a small portion of food and interspersed bites of food with hand gestures as she talked. Her fork was constantly raised in the air as she described something. Mason pretended to join the conversation and hoped nobody would notice his empty plate. He poured himself another glass of wine and thought how much his father would enjoy the meal, the company, and especially the wine.

Collette reached over and handed him the tray of lamb chops without missing a beat of her conversation with her father. She did not even look at him. Mason gave her a barely audible thank-you and proceeded to serve himself. He placed the plate of chops back in the middle of the table and looked to his right where Anna had already pushed the potatoes over to him. He looked at her and smiled as he grabbed the bowl. He noticed she was still pushing her beans around with her fork, so he leaned over and speared one with his. He picked it up and ate it. She looked up at him and he laughed, then tilted her plate, and the remaining beans slid off hers and onto his. She laughed shyly as she put her plate down. Collette looked over and congratulated her on a clean plate. Anna smiled as Mason agreed with Collette. With his plate replenished he rejoined the conversation. He assumed nobody noticed all this happening, but, of course, they all had.

After dinner there were homemade pastries. Mason tried to

show restraint but was no match for the pastries. Collette and Anna knew by now that the young gentleman from New York required larger portions than the rest, so they doubled on Mason's serving. Mason was thankful, and finally he was full. After dessert, Collette put Anna to bed and Mme. Moulié turned in early as well. Mason, Collette, Jacques, and Ganoux gathered in the living room by the fireplace to recap the day. Mason and Collette rehashed their experience in the square, and both Jacques and Ganoux agreed that this was no random incident. Jacques seemed concerned. He began to speak as he leaned back in his chair.

"Today I met with some friends and was told very disturbing news. Through a contact in Germany, some news has been received, which could affect everything we are doing. There are rumors of a document outlining the plans for a super museum of sorts in Austria. Apparently, Hitler wants to build the largest museum in history; it would dwarf anything that exists today. He envisions one city as the cultural center of the Third Reich. He wants generations to talk about the architecture and the sheer size and importance of his museum. He has hired several prominent architects to redesign the city of Linz, Austria, which will serve as the home of the so-called Führer Museum. I guess he thinks of this as a modern-day Library of Alexandria, or his own Taj Mahal." Jacques' voice dripped with sarcasm and disapproval.

"French Intelligence has acquired some of the information contained in these documents, known as the Linz Initiative. These papers outline the plan for the museum, and even worse, the method by which the museum will be filled. Hitler wants to display the largest collection of art and sculpture ever assembled, and he plans to steal most of it from the rest of Europe. This plan has already been enacted in Germany where several large Jewish collections have been liquidated and signed over to the Nazis. These families were promised freedom in exchange for their belongings. Many of these families saw no other way out of Germany so they did as they were told. Once all the items were turned over to the Nazis, they were either killed or sent to work camps. Nazi Germany now holds the ownership papers for several masterpieces. I am sure the same is happening in Poland right now. Under the cover of war, Nazi Germany is conducting the largest art theft in human history.

"There is rumor of a master list—a wish list of specific items, which some of the German leaders want to present to their Führer on his birthday in April. A small group of art dealers, spies, and soldiers have been put together for the sole purpose of finding the art on this list. We can assume that at the top of this list are the greatest works of the world. We must also assume that there are men in our very midst who are already tracking these items. Money can buy much information from weak people."

Jacques paused for a sip of wine, then continued.

"We know that Hitler was an amateur artist and was once enrolled in an art school in Germany. He traveled to Vienna at seventeen and applied for entrance to the Vienna School of Fine Arts, a most prestigious school. He was deemed unsatisfactory for admittance and returned to Germany a bitter man. His mother passed away shortly thereafter, further fueling his bitterness. He is seeking revenge on the art world for his own deficiencies."

"I have been unable to get in touch with Jean Paul. This is unlike him, we speak every other day. I fear something has happened to him. Mason, I need the two of you to go to his chateau first thing in the morning and check on him. He has your travel case, custom-made to hold the Mona Lisa. He may also have a further update on things. He was in charge of moving some famous paintings. If found out, he is in terrible danger. The Linz papers have now put a target on all our backs. I am certain they will stop at nothing to fill the list.

"Collette, the rest of us will meet them in Paris. Once all together, we will travel to London where we can feel safer than here. Lord willing, everything will work out and we will be in

London in a few days."

Collette nodded, but the look of fear on her face was clearly visible.

"Do not talk to anyone or trust anyone. Jean Paul has specific instructions to only speak with the two of you," Jacques added as he turned back to Mason and Ganoux. "He lives alone; there should be no one else at his house. If anyone else is there, he will not tell you anything. If you see someone in the house, assume the worst. If you see anyone else on the property, maybe posing as a gardener, a chauffeur, or maid, they have gotten to him. He may be older, but he is as strong as they come. He will not give up his secrets. He will die with them if he has to; I only pray that this is not the case."

Mason agreed with the plan. He wasn't thrilled with the prospect of leaving Collette. He was worried about her and Anna. Something did not add up. Franz Kolter holds them up in Central Park with a Luger. Kolter couldn't be a German spy; he was an idiot at best. His ties were to Lucky Franz Leiter. The man who shot Lane was German—and clearly not a priest—his name had been Andrew Loch, No connection to Lucky. Now a strange man shows up in the square speaking German to Anna and then disappears. Mason was willing to bet that Lane and the man from the square were connected, both hired by Andrew Loch or someone above him.

Could the Germans somehow know he would be traveling with a lovely lady in a frame at the bottom of his suitcase? If the Germans knew about the list or the Mona Lisa, then someone in Jacques' tight-knit circle had talked. Either way, Mason was becoming a very popular man, and if people knew he would be traveling with both the list and the Mona Lisa, he was sure his popularity was only going to get larger.

Chapter 22

MASON AND GANOUX HEADED OUT of the driveway at first light. The sun was barely visible over the hills and throwing long shadows on the landscape. Mason could smell the morning dew as he rolled down the window. It was a chilly morning, but the fresh air helped him clear his mind. It had been hard to say goodbye to Collette and Anna, but if everything went well, they would all be in London by the end of the week. The sound of the gravel under the tires as they turned onto the road to the square brought him back to reality and he closed his window as they gained speed. Ganoux, as usual, was a man of few words. Over the course of the drive they would figure out a plan for when they arrived at Jean Paul's chateau.

They had gone to the barn overnight and retrieved the two paintings, which Jacques had prepared. Mason chuckled again at the sight of them in all their hideous glory. The lists were neatly sewn in the back of each. Each list consisted of valuable art works, which were currently being relocated to safer havens. Mason would be the only person in the world with both lists. The entirety of France's art collection would be packed in plain sight in Mason's suitcase. They would pick up the custom-made case at Jean Paul's. He would also be providing any updates on the situation in case anything had changed. Mason and Jean Paul had never met, but Jean Paul knew Mason's father, Aldon. It seemed everywhere Mason went in the world of museums and art, his father preceded him.

As for the Mona Lisa, it was securely resting in the car trunk in its crate, still wrapped in canvas. Mason had admired the painting overnight and was slowly gaining an attachment to her. Madame X would always be his first love, but La Gioconda was flirting with him every chance she could. Mason came back to reality as Ganoux slowly entered the square and quietly drove over the cobblestones. He slowed briefly around the corner of the south end, and Mason eased himself out of the passenger side door as the car was still moving. Ganoux then pulled away and continued down the street where he pulled over and parked down an alley.

With the ease of a gymnast, Mason climbed the outside stairs of the church to a balcony perch over the square, barely making a sound. At this time of the morning there was very little activity. He could see Mme. Patine brushing the ground in front of her café as the birds gathered around hoping for a piece of freshly baked bread. A woman rode her bike through the square and exchanged greetings with her. The sun was showing between the steeples of the church and the spires shadowed the square, looking like two long knives gradually making their way up the façade of the buildings as the sun rose in the sky.

Mason was startled by the ringing of the 6:30 a.m. chime from the bell tower. He wondered how anyone could live with that noise every half hour. Most residents would argue that the ringing of the bells was a sign of comfort from God that everything was well. Mason hoped they would ring for the townsfolk for many generations to come, but he was glad he did not have to hear them every morning.

Mason quietly and discreetly peered over the stone balcony looking for anything suspicious. If they were indeed being watched, someone would appear and follow them out of town. Sure enough, the sound of the large wooden inn door opening caught Mason's attention as across the square a man emerged. He wore sunglasses and a hat. He walked directly over to a car, hopped in, started it, and pulled out on to the square toward the south end. He turned off the square directly under where Mason was crouched down, and leisurely pulled out of town.

Ganoux, in the alley where he waited, noticed the car pass by. A few minutes later, Mason appeared at the top of the alley and jogged down to the car. He hopped in and told Ganoux what he had seen. A man pulling out, at this time of the morning so shortly after their car had passed by, could be a coincidence, but probably not.

They headed out of town to try to catch up to this man and see if he was really looking for them. They backed up the alley and started out of town. They were looking for a black Peugeot. Ganoux slowly drove out of town until they reached the road to Paris. They drove for about five minutes until they noticed a car parked on the side of the road ahead, the front hood in an upward position. A man crouched over the engine and seemed to be tinkering with it. It was the black Peugeot.

Ganoux looked at Mason. "Do we stop, or do we keep going?"

"Keep going," Mason replied. "If he is following us his car problems will be fixed shortly and he will show up behind us."

Ganoux agreed and sped up a bit to create some distance. They passed a woman on her bike heading toward town, but other than that there was no one on the road. They continued on another ten minutes when a small black car appeared on the horizon behind them. Ganoux slowed down to allow the car to come into better view.

Mason turned around to glance out the back window, "Looks like our friend fixed his car."

Ganoux looked at Mason, smiled, and pressed the gas. "Let's find out."

He accelerated, and the car jolted forward, speeding up to sixty kilometers per hour. Mason continued to watch the car behind them.

"He looks to be speeding up," Mason said as he turned back around. Ganoux eased off the gas. They were heading into winding, mountain roads. If the car was still behind them after the turns, he had a plan.

They headed up a small hill into the mountains. A sign on the side of the road showed a picture of twisting roads ahead.

The tires screeched as they hugged the turns, and Mason held the grab bar in front of him with both hands. The steep edge of the road had no barrier; if they lost control, they were going off the road and down the hill. They reached the next set of turns, and Mason glanced back; the car was visible for a second and then obscured by the mountains. They were convinced the man in the car was following them; no one would drive through these turns like this without a reason. Mason was thrown toward the door as they made their last turn. He was pinned against the door as Ganoux accelerated out of the turn, smoke and gravel shooting everywhere as they hit the straightaway. Mason turned to the back window; sure-enough the Peugeot was right there, exploding through the plume of smoke like a tank on a battlefield.

"He's gaining on us," Mason said warningly, looking over at Ganoux, who pushed the pedal to the floor, speeding up. The Peugeot sped up with them. Mason could make out the silhouette of the driver. He looked to be in his forties, he had removed the hat, but was still wearing sunglasses. He had both hands on the wheel and was gaining fast.

Ganoux looked down quickly at the speedometer; they were going ninety kilometers an hour and the needle was fluttering. They were pushing maximum speed.

"He is getting closer," Mason yelled again.

"Hold on," Ganoux said as the sound of metal on metal jerked them forward. The Peugeot was ramming their bumper. Ganoux struggled to control the car. The Peugeot bounced off and fell back a few feet. Mason looked at the driver: He appeared cool and calm.

"Here he comes again," he said just before the second hit. Both men lurched forward as they were hit from behind. Their tires slid on the gravel every time they were rammed. Ganoux, watching in his rearview mirror, knew they could not keep this up. At this speed, one more hit and they would go careening off the road. He had to use this to his advantage.

"Tell me when he is accelerating again," he yelled to

Mason.

"Here he comes," Mason yelled back.

"Hold on!" Ganoux slammed on the brakes. The car jolted backwards toward the Peugeot.

The man in the Peugeot was accelerating for another hit when suddenly dust and gravel kicked up from the vehicle in front him as it jolted and skid. The man in the Peugeot was startled; he instinctively turned the wheel as he smashed into the back of Mason's car. The impact sent Mason and Ganoux into a tailspin and sliding across the road onto the grassy edge before Ganoux regained control and brought them back onto the road, the rear of the car sliding back and forth.

The Peugeot was not as lucky. The driver did everything he could to regain control, but having turned his wheels, his car started to turn, rolled over three times, and ended up in a ditch on the side of the road upside down, wheels still spinning and the horn blaring.

Ganoux stopped and backed up until they were close enough to see the driver. He was motionless. Mason grabbed his gun and jumped out. He ran over to the car and knelt down near the passenger door—the driver was obviously dead. Mason walked around to the driver's door, opened it, and felt for a pulse: nothing. He looked inside for any possessions: nothing. He stood up, glanced around the crash area, and noticed a bag lying in the tall grass. It must have ejected when the car was rolling. He walked over and bent down. The bag was open; papers had fallen from it and were fluttering in the wind. Mason grabbed everything he saw, shoved it back in the bag, and ran back to the car. He threw it in the back seat, got in the front, and they drove away.

Once on their way, Mason fumbled through the man's bag. He glanced at the papers and dug further, coming up with a gun. He pulled it out by the handle: It was a German Luger. Under the gun was a map of the village with a red circle around Moulié's chateau. On a notepad he had made notations, coordinated with times, about all the events from the night that Mason and Ganoux had arrived. This man had been watching them and was most likely the man from the square who had confronted Anna. At the top of the pad was a phone number, no doubt a contact number; that might come in handy, Mason thought. He took a deep breath as they continued down the road. They approached a sign that read Paris-44Km with an arrow pointing to the left, and the Loire Valley-90 Km with an arrow pointing to the right. Ganoux slowed a bit and veered right toward Jean Paul's chateau and the Loire Valley.

Chapter 23

AS MASON AND GANOUX REACHED the Loire Valley it began to rain. They were approaching the outskirts of Orleans, a city on the edge of the valley; they would stop for fuel and a quick bite, then proceed on to Jean Paul's. Ganoux pulled over near a small café and into a gas station. A man appeared from the open bay door and approached the car. Ganoux spoke to him in French and the man started the gas pump. As it was filling, the attendant washed their front and back windows, finishing just as the pump stopped. Ganoux paid the man and pulled across the street to the café.

They sat at a small wooden table in the corner and ordered coffee and rolls. They briefly talked about what to do when they arrived at Jean Paul's. After a short rest they paid and left to continue their trip. Once back on the road they would follow the A10 south for about twenty kilometers; Jean Paul lived in a chateau nestled in the countryside outside of Touraine, along the Cher River.

Mason took over the driving after lunch. They checked on their cargo in the trunk; she was doing fine, although she had been banged around as they outran the Peugeot, she was well protected in her crate. Mason surveyed the damage to the rear of the car. The bumper was severely dented, but still in one piece. If not for Ganoux's quick thinking they might not even be standing here.

The two reached the edge of Touraine and crossed the Cher River. After a few turns, they pulled onto Jean Paul's street. Mason proceeded slowly as they looked for Jean Paul's address, 74 Rue de Alpine Glen. The sound of the gravel under the tires and the smoke generated made it hard to arrive discreetly. Ganoux spotted a 56 mounted on a large stone column as they drove by. The imposing wrought iron gates were closed, blocking the entrance of a long driveway which disappeared around a bend and into the trees. He motioned for Mason to continue. As they approached the upcoming bend, Ganoux noticed a 65 on the next set of stone columns.

"He must be the next driveway," he said to Mason.

They proceeded around the bend and noticed the next driveway on the right. Mason paused as they passed the opening to 74 Rue de Alpine Glen. The wrought iron gates were pulled all the way open; it was the only driveway they had passed whose gates were open. Mason continued slowly as Ganoux stared down the driveway, which disappeared over a hill. He saw nothing: no activity or visible tire tracks. Mason drove down the road until he found a cut-out on the side where he could pull over. He turned the car around and parked behind some bushes, partially obscuring the car. The rain had picked up and the temperature had dropped, making for a cold, damp afternoon.

Mason suggested they split up and approach the house from opposite ends to check for activity. Ganoux agreed and said he would go back up the road to the entrance while Mason cut through the tree line.

"Let us meet back at the car in fifteen minutes," Ganoux said as they stepped out into the rain.

Mason gave a slight nod as he jogged across the street and into the trees. Ganoux started back up the gravel road just behind the tree line. The cold rain was turning the wet grass into a slippery mess; Ganoux lost his footing and caught himself against a cherry tree. The jolt shook the branches, dumping more water on him. He shook his head, regained his balance, and continued.

Meanwhile, Mason was walking slowly, crouching as he went. He was looking for the house, but all he saw were bushes and trees. A cold raindrop caught him off guard, and he hunched his shoulders as it ran down his back. He wiped some water from his face and pulled his jacket hood onto his head. The branches cracked under his weight even though he tried to walk lightly. He stopped to listen for activity nearby, but only heard the slapping of rain against the leaves of the trees along with a few birds chirping in the distance. Satisfied he was alone, Mason continued walking toward where he hoped would be the house. Jacques had talked of the beauty of Jean Paul's chateau, the circular conservatory and large, stained-glass windows of the ivy-covered façade. It sounded impressive and judging by some of the chateaus they had passed on the way, he figured he could not miss it. Finally reaching the end of the trees, Mason crouched down to one knee, staring at a large grassy area which gradually headed downhill. In the distance he could see the tops of chimneys attached to a very impressive slate roof. He was close but would have to continue over wide open terrain. He noticed a small set of gravestones to his left.

Mason jogged slowly over to the headstones, looking in every direction for anything resembling human activity. He reached the first headstone and he knelt behind it. The stone tablet was almost four feet tall and leaning forward. The inscription read 1834-1891 with the name of Sophie Laveaux. Jean Paul's mother, Mason assumed; it must be a family cemetery. There was a total of five headstones grouped together under a large tree. The house was a little more visible at this point and he could see the upstairs windows, the drawn curtains prevented him from seeing in. There was a light on in one of the rooms. He planned his next move, to a large tree about halfway to the house. He bid Sophie adieu and jogged slowly toward the tree.

Ganoux reached the entrance to Jean Paul's driveway. He could still see the car parked up the road about fifty feet. He looked down the driveway and inched his way onto the property. He could see the house in the distance. The driveway turned downward, then to the right, and disappeared into some trees. He could not get a good look at the house unless he went all the way past the trees. There seemed to be no one around. The rain came down heavier in the open grass. He went back to the opening of the driveway and looked both ways. There was no one around so he started walking toward the area where the trees started.

He followed the trees around the bend until he had a clear view of the house. The chateau was built in the traditional French style of all stone. The front was adorned with black shutters, and a covered stone entrance to pull under right in front of the main entrance. On the right side was a glass turret, which housed the conservatory. Several stained-glass windows were visible in what looked like the main stairwell. A black Mercedes Benz was parked in the gravel driveway next to a large fountain, which served as the centerpiece of the parking area. He saw no signs of activity, so he headed back up the property to the road and back to the car.

Mason reached the next tree and had a clear view of the back of the property. The large stone patio was surrounded by neatly manicured gardens, meticulously maintained from the green grass to the topiary bushes lining the stone walkways. The ivy on the side of the house was trimmed to expose the windows. Mason also saw no activity; he took a quick glance at his watch and decided to return to the car.

Ganoux was waiting in the car when Mason returned. They sat for a moment to dry off and figure out their next move. Mason suggested Ganoux approach the home on foot from the back, while Mason went to the front door. If all was clear, and Jean Paul was inside, he would motion to Ganoux from the back window overlooking the patio.

Ganoux agreed; he exited the car and disappeared into the trees. Mason started the car, checked both ways, and reversed from the side of the road. He headed toward the mouth of the driveway. Once he reached the gates he turned into the driveway and slowly headed toward the house.

He emerged from the trees and finally saw the house ahead.

The two-story chateau had at least six stone chimneys towering over the steep, black slate roof. Large stone steps came down from the front door to a covered stone entrance. The front door consisted of two large oak doors with large black wrought iron door knockers on both. The doors arched at the top forming a churchlike entrance. As Mason pulled into the parking area, he drove around a stone pool with a fountain in the middle. The fountain showed a woman with three small children playing in the water as it blew out the top and rained down on them. To the right of the main house was a single level section with a tall glass conservatory in the shape of a turret with a glass peaked roof. Mason pulled under the stone entrance and shut the car off. He paused for a moment to see if anyone appeared. The only sound he heard was that of the fountain. He got out and went around to the back of the car. He opened the trunk to check on the precious cargo. Still in one piece and secure. He closed the trunk, adjusted the Colt in his waistband and started up the large stone steps.

He looked at the massive doors for a doorbell of some kind. Finding nothing he reached for the iron knocker. He knocked a few times with the sound echoing through the entryway. He turned around and scoured the landscape. All seemed calm as a few birds flew by heading for shelter in the trees. The rain continued to fall; it did not look as if it was stopping anytime soon.

The sound of a lock turning made Mason turn back around. The right door began to open, and an older gentleman stood in the doorway.

"Hello, Mason, come in—Jean Paul Laveaux, nice to meet you," the gentleman said as he stepped aside to let Mason in. Mason stepped into the large stone foyer. He admired the large stained-glass window overlooking the staircase for a moment, then turned around to greet Jean Paul and found himself staring at a man holding a gun pointed directly at him.

"I'm sorry, Mason," Jean Paul said as he was pushed aside

by the man with the gun.

"I have been waiting for this moment," the man said as he approached.

Mason recognized the face immediately. It was Franz Kolter, the man he had last seen in New York while walking through Central Park with Collette. The man had tried to assault them, but Mason had managed to get the upper hand and left him in the company of some park vagrants. He worked for "Lucky" Franz Leiter.

Mason slowly put his hands up as the man came closer, reached in Mason's waistband and removed his gun.

"My orders are to keep you alive, or I would shoot you dead right now," Kolter said as he took Mason's gun.

"Did you enjoy your night in the park?" Mason asked with a slight grin. Kolter smacked Mason in the head with the butt of his gun; he fell backward and grabbed his mouth, wiping blood off and regained his balance.

"Once we are done with you, I will take great pleasure in killing you slowly," Kolter said, motioning Mason to join Jean Paul against the wall.

"That's not going to happen," Mason told him as he walked toward Jean Paul, both men still with their hands up.

"Oh yeah, why's that?" Kolter said with a wide grin.

"Because it is only a matter of time before the tables turn and I have a gun to your head," Mason said, steely-eyed.

Kolter laughed as he approached Mason a second time. This time the blow to the side of the head sent Mason crumbling to the ground; he blacked out before he hit the stone floor.

Chapter 24

GANOUX CROUCHED BEHIND A TREE waiting for Mason to appear in the window at the rear of the house. Mason should have been inside already, he thought, and decided to give it another couple of minutes. The rain was still coming down and though he heard no activity in the house, he was beginning to get a bad feeling about this.

A few more minutes went by, and he decided to approach the back of the house. He slowly made his way through the manicured gardens past the evenly situated rows of topiary bushes. He had just ducked behind a bench when he noticed the curtain in the back room begin to move. He watched as the curtain was slowly pulled back and a man he did not recognize scanned the area. Through the large glass windows Ganoux could see a man who looked to be in his forties clearly scouting the area. The man's gaze was focused and stern; he had a hard look about him. Ganoux crouched down as low as he could to remain out of sight.

After a few moments the man disappeared, and the curtains fell back into line, swinging back and forth for a moment as they relaxed back into form. Something had gone wrong. Mason was inside for sure, but the man who looked out the window was definitely not Jean Paul.

He paused for a minute and decided to gain entrance through the back of the house. He made his way across the gardens, resting at every available cover until he was directly above the steps to the basement door; a large set of stone steps descended in a slight oval to a landing below the ground. The rain was gathered at the bottom where a drain was clogged with moss and leaves. Ganoux carefully negotiated the wet steps down to the landing and his foot hit with a splash. The back door was a smaller version of the front doors, but without the knockers. A small window in the top of the door offered a view inside behind thick glass, while the outside was protected by wrought iron rungs. The glass was so dirty he could not see inside, but he could tell it was dark. With a deep breath he tried the handle; as he pressed down with his thumb the latch clicked, but the door did not budge. He leaned into it with his shoulder; it moved a bit. Trying to be as quiet as possible, he repeated his attempt, and the door opened enough for him to slip inside.

~~~

Mason slowly opened his eyes and lifted his head. As his awareness returned, he realized he was seated in a large wooden chair with his hands bound to the armrests. He heard men's voices talking behind him, and as his eyes slowly adjusted to the light, he looked to his left and saw Jean Paul sitting next to him in a similar situation, hands bound.

"Are you all right?" Jean Paul asked in a whisper.

Mason nodded. "You?" he asked Jean Paul.

"I'm okay."

"You two—quiet," said the annoyingly familiar voice of Kolter. He stepped in front of Mason, "Don't make me give you another knock on the head," he added, pretending to hit him again.

Mason did not flinch, just stared back at him.

"Easy there, Franz," said a voice from across the room that Mason did not recognize, a voice that belonged to a portly gentleman dressed in an oversized black pinstripe suit. The man walked over in front of him and slowly moved Kolter out of the way. "He does not like you."

"The feeling is mutual," Mason said, soliciting a slight smile out of the portly man.

"After what you did to him in the park in New York, I wouldn't like you, either." The man pulled a chair over, sat down in front of Jean Paul, and gently brushed the front of his suit as if to remove any dirt.

As Mason stared at the man he began to wonder when Ganoux would be joining this little gathering, and why it was taking him so long.

"So, do you know who I am?" the man in the chair said to Mason.

"I would say you are a man who needs a new tailor. Your suit—it's a little big?" Mason said, smiling.

"Oh, you're a funny guy?" the man replied with a grin.

"Some people think so," Mason said with a shrug.

"I see." The man stared at Mason, nodding. He pursed his lips and spoke. "Mason, my name is Franz Leiter. Most people call me 'Lucky.' I am a French businessman, and I believe you are in possession of something that I would like very much to acquire. I was a little skeptical that someone as adolescent as yourself would be trusted with such valuable information, but by showing up here I have to believe that you do indeed have the information I speak of."

"You have saved me the trouble of tracking down the Mona Lisa, and for that I am grateful. I came here to get the list from you, and I was astonished to find the Mona Lisa sitting in a suitcase on the dining room table. I can't believe you would leave something so valuable out in the open…that is bad for you, but quite good for me, one less beautiful painting I need to track down.

"Now as far as the main reason I came here, Mason, I am only going to ask you once for it. I very much suggest you cooperate, and we can all walk out of here in one piece. If you don't, unfortunately, you will be carried out of here in pieces, or possibly not at all. Do you understand, Mason?"

"I do, and I would very much like to cooperate, but I don't have the slightest idea what you're talking about. I am here visiting a friend of my father to talk about his experience during the Great War. I am afraid you'll just have to untie us and be on your way. Sorry, and as far as the Mona Lisa over there, take it. It's not real, anyway."

"Is that so? Mason, I may not look like a dangerous man to you, with my expensive suit and my calm demeanor. I have men here who will do whatever I say so don't make me do something we both don't want."

He took a breath and paused before speaking again. "Let us try this another way; I will explain it to you in the simplest of terms. You have a list that contains much of the art in France's museums and where it is going to be moved. I would like that list. If you don't tell me where it is right now, I will cut off a finger. Do you really want that to happen?"

"No, of course not; why would I want you to cut off your finger?" Mason said sarcastically.

"Oh, that's right, you're the funny guy. Mason, I will not be cutting off my finger, and I will not be cutting off your finger, I will be cutting off his finger," Lucky said motioning toward Jean Paul.

Lucky waved his hand and Kolter and another man in the room promptly walked over to Jean Paul. He removed a long knife from his waistband while the other man grabbed Jean Paul's hand. He grabbed four fingers, exposing the pinkie finger as Kolter gently rested the knife on it right above the knuckle.

Jean Paul pushed back in the chair. "No, please don't do this."

"Shut up," Lucky said as he turned back to Mason.

"Ok, funny guy, your call."

"Look, I told you, I don't know what you're talking about. I know you don't believe me, but I am telling you the truth; I swear I don't have any list. Whoever told you I did gave you bad information."

Lucky nodded, and Kolter began to press the knife against Jean Paul's pinkie finger. The skin separated, and blood pooled around the knuckle.

"Okay, okay, stop," Mason yelled.

Lucky turned toward Mason and raised his right hand.

Kolter pulled the knife away as blood dripped from Jean Paul's finger on to the eighteenth century Oriental rug.

"Either you tell me right now where this list is, or your family friend here will no longer be able to count to ten with his hands."

Suddenly Jean Paul spoke up, "He doesn't have the list. I do."

Mason quickly looked over at Jean Paul, "What are you doing?"

"It's all right, Mason. There is no need for anyone to get hurt here. We can work this out." He turned back to Lucky. "M. Leiter, I have the list you speak of. I was meeting Mason today to transfer it to him, but I plead with you not to take it from us. We put together this list so that we could preserve the artistic culture of France and keep it out of the hands of the German army. I never thought we would be in danger of losing it to a fellow Frenchman. I beg you not to do this."

Lucky stood up and removed a handkerchief from his pocket. He gave it to Kolter and nodded toward Jean Paul. Kolter cut the rope around Jean Paul's left wrist and wrapped the handkerchief around his hand; it quickly turned red.

"You should apply pressure to your finger, so it stops bleeding." Lucky motioned to the other hand, and with that Kolter cut the rope on the other wrist and Jean Paul grabbed his left hand with his right.

"At least we have one reasonable man here," Lucky said as he looked at Mason.

"Jean Paul, you ask why I want this list? I am a businessman, and when the German army comes knocking, I need some things to negotiate with. I care about one thing: money. I don't care who gives it to me, or who I do business with. The French government has failed our country; I am simply setting myself up for the next regime. I plan on staying in business for a long time, and this list will help me do that. Now, go get me the list."

Jean Paul shook his head with dismay as he stood up. Kolter put away his knife and grabbed his pistol. He motioned to Jean Paul to move.

"The list is in my office safe. It is just down the hall."

Lucky said to Kolter, "Go with him, and make it quick."

The other man stayed in the room, standing behind Mason with a gun in his hand. Another man was on the other side of the room near the opening to the study, gun in hand.

Lucky turned back to Mason. "Once I have the list, what am I going to do with you? You know I can't leave you alive. I don't worry about Jean Paul. The old man can barely walk, but you; I would worry you would come after me late one night, and I don't like that thought."

Mason just stared back at Lucky in silence.

"Not so funny anymore, are you?" Lucky said as he patted Mason on the knee. Lucky stood up and walked to the front window. He looked out, "I wish this rain would stop, it's quite depressing."

Chapter 25

GANOUX MADE HIS WAY UP the basement steps and stood at the top, the basement door slightly open. He could hear voices down the hall in the lighted living room. He could not make out what was being said, but he distinguished at least three people talking. Suddenly the floorboards creaked; someone was coming out of the living room. Jean Paul walked toward him, his hand wrapped in a bloody cloth. Quickly but quietly Ganoux closed the door as he noticed another man behind Jean Paul. The two men walked by the basement door and continued down the hallway in silence.

Once they were well past the door, he opened it again to have a look. He only heard one voice coming from the living room; it was not Mason's.

Ganoux decided to follow Jean Paul. He knew only one man had been with Jean Paul, and he liked those odds better. He still did not know how many men were in the living room.

Slowly and quietly Ganoux made his way down the hallway until he noticed a room on the right with the light on. He paused outside it.

"Hurry up," he heard a man say from inside the room.

"I'm going as fast as I can. You nearly cut my finger off, remember?" Jean Paul replied.

Ganoux inched closer. With his back tight against the wall and his gun in his right hand, he glanced across the hallway and noticed a wooden portrait of the Madonna and Child staring at him. He took that as a blessing as he turned and appeared in the doorway.

Jean Paul was at the far end of the room beside an open

wall safe, rummaging through some papers on one of the shelves. A man stood about ten feet in front of Ganoux with his back facing him; he held a gun in his right hand, pointed at Jean Paul.

Jean Paul turned and saw Ganoux in the doorway. He immediately began to cough and said, "I'm terribly sorry, I should not have smoked all those years."

"Hurry up," Kolter said impatiently.

As Jean Paul created his distraction, Ganoux approached the man from behind, smashing the butt of his pistol down on the back of the neck. Franz Kolter had no chance; his world went black and he crumpled to the floor as his gun silently fell to the carpet next to his motionless body.

Jean Paul smiled and silently said, "Thank you. Excellent timing. I was wondering where you were."

"What happened to your hand? Are you all right?" Ganoux asked anxiously, walking toward his friend.

"Fine, it is just a small nick. Good to see you, my friend," Jean Paul said as he reached out his hand. He quickly filled Ganoux in on what was happening. They grabbed Kolter's lifeless body and dragged it into the safe. They closed the door and quickly turned the dial, locking him inside. Jean Paul then closed the door, hiding the safe behind the oak panels.

Chapter 26

MASON LOOKED UP AS JEAN PAUL reappeared in the living room with a large envelope in his right hand. His left hand was still wrapped in Lucky's bloody handkerchief.

"That took you long enough," Lucky said, turning and approaching Jean Paul. "Where is Kolter?"

"Oh, don't worry about him, he is safe." Jean Paul chuckled as Ganoux entered behind him.

Lucky was startled by a new person entering the room, gun drawn. "Paul Ganoux, well, this is a surprise, I have not seen you in many years," Lucky said. Mason noticed the clear acknowledgment of some kind of history between the two. Lucky slowly raised his hands and retreated across the room.

"It's about time you showed up, where have you been?" Mason demanded.

Ganoux pointed to the man standing behind Mason and instructed him to throw his gun into the corner. The man obliged and raised his hands; he and Lucky moved to the front of the room and stood with their backs to the wall.

As Ganoux approached Mason a shot rang out from the other corner of the room as the third man entered from behind the curtained opening between the living room and study. The bullet flew by Ganoux's head, and the plaster wall broke apart as the bullet hit, a plume of smoke rising in the air. Ganoux dove behind a couch as the man fired again. Jean Paul fell to the ground as the second bullet struck him. He crawled behind a chair for cover as he grabbed his side. The man in the corner continued to shoot as the sound of gunfire filled the air.

Mason tipped over his chair and fell to the ground to avoid

the crossfire. From behind the couch, Ganoux fired in the direction of the gunman. The bullet missed, and a glass sconce exploded against the wall. Mason was caught in the middle of the hail of bullets as he lay on the floor, still strapped to the chair. He tried to make himself as small as possible. Bullets continued to fly as the man ran across the room, still shooting. Another lamp exploded, and the pieces rained down on Mason. He could feel the shards cutting his face as they fell.

Ganoux returned fire without looking, his right hand lifted over the couch. Lucky hit the floor and, on all fours, crawled over to Jean Paul. He grabbed the envelope from Jean Paul's hands, as his man continued to fire at Ganoux. The other man retrieved his gun from the corner and they both fired several rounds toward the couch. One bullet struck the wooden frame and splintered the side armrest.

Still firing, Lucky and his men ran out of the room, carrying the envelope and the painting, which Lucky grabbed off the dining room table near the door. The three men exited the front door and headed toward the garage area, the two men leading the way, Lucky, crouching, swerved back and forth as he ran.

At the garage they scrambled into a black sedan, and with a cloud of smoke, spun their wheels and sped down the driveway and out of sight.

Inside, Ganoux crossed to Jean Paul, where he lay moaning on the floor. His hand was still wrapped, and his shirt was soaked with blood on his side by his hip.

"How bad is it, are you okay?" Ganoux asked as he helped him up on to his knees.

"Never better," Jean Paul replied. "This is all so exciting for an old man like me." He lifted his shirt, exposing a wound on his side. "I think it just grazed me." He used the handkerchief to wipe away the blood.

Ganoux looked closely. It was not too serious. He grabbed a tablecloth which had lain under one of the shattered lamps, shook it out, and gave it to Jean Paul. "Apply pressure to it."

Jean Paul nodded and did as suggested.

"That was close," Ganoux said.

"Thank you again, my old friend. If you had not shown up, I am afraid this could have ended much worse," Jean Paul said as he rested his right hand on Ganoux's shoulder.

"Are you two done over there? I could use a hand," Mason said sarcastically from his chair on the floor. He was lying on his left side, still strapped to the chair trying to get loose. Blood dripped down his face from a cut under his eye.

Ganoux righted Mason's chair and cut the straps around his wrists with his knife. Mason stood up as he rubbed his left wrist with his right hand. "Thanks."

Ganoux nodded. "You okay?"

"Yeah, I'm fine," Mason said as he wiped the blood from his face

"Everyone is all right?" Jean Paul said as he joined them. "I don't know about you two, but I could use a drink."

Jean Paul poured three glasses of Scotch and brought them across the room, as glass cracked under his feet.

"I am sorry about the lamps," Ganoux said as he grabbed a glass.

"Oh, those lamps? Forget it. I am just happy no one hit the Scotch, it is much more valuable."

"So, what was in the envelope that Lucky ran out of here with?" Mason asked as he took a sip.

"My friends, Mr. Lucky is now in possession of a detailed list of all the art in France, which is being secretly moved in anticipation of war; very professional looking. Unfortunately for him, this list is a complete fabrication. He should realize this when he arrives at an abandoned chateau in the south of France. There, he will find nothing but cobwebs and rats as no one has lived there in years. I do wish I could see his face when he gets there.

"He also has the copy of the Mona Lisa, which has been hanging in the Louvre for years. It is a forgery, but I imagine

Lucky will never find that out and will sell it to the highest bidder. If the buyer does their homework, they will discover the painting is a fake. That may put Lucky out of the art business permanently."

The three men chuckled and toasted, clinking glasses.

"Hopefully, that takes care of him for a while. If I know Lucky, he will go there immediately, blinded by the thoughts of a fortune in stolen art. The forged painting was a nice touch, Jean Paul, good thinking on your part," Ganoux said, taking a sip of scotch.

"I left it on the dining room table for that specific reason. If I had any unwanted visitors, I would gladly give up the forgery to protect the original."

"What happened to my friend Franz Kolter?" Mason said.

"We knocked him out and locked him in the safe in my office. He should be coming to about now."

"He will be so happy to see me," Mason said as he took another sip of Scotch.

"We'd better figure out what to do with him and get out of here as soon as we can." Ganoux finished his glass. "We need to move quickly."

Jean Paul agreed. "I will get the suitcase; you two get the paintings from the car."

The three of them put down their glasses and dispersed. Jean Paul looked like the walking wounded as he hobbled out of the room. Ganoux looked at Mason, and the two of them shook their heads with a chuckle and headed for the front door. Jean Paul was quite a character.

They retrieved the art from the car and brought it into the dining room. They placed the three paintings side by side across the large maple dining room table. After unwrapping the two amateur Jacques Moulié originals, they uncrated the Mona Lisa.

Jean Paul returned with a slightly worn, heavy, leather case. He had cleaned up his wounds and was walking much better. He placed the case on the table and opened it. After picking at the bottom for a minute and unsnapping some straps, he removed the false bottom and exposed a two-inch deep area reinforced on each side with oak panels. It was the exact dimensions of the Mona Lisa.

Jean Paul silently gazed at the Mona Lisa as she stared back at him. "Magnificent, isn't she?" he said without breaking her gaze. "I have had the pleasure of sharing her company on many occasions. I never thought I would be hiding her away or saying goodbye. I know it is the only way to save her from a terrible fate."

He gently removed the painting from its crate and placed her in the opening at the bottom of the suitcase; she fit perfectly. Mason and Ganoux could feel the emotion in the air as they noticed Jean Paul's eyes well up. It was as if they were witnessing a final goodbye between two lovers who did not know if they would ever see each other again.

As Jean Paul took a deep breath, he grabbed the false bottom and returned it. After reattaching the straps, he closed the suitcase. He looked up at Mason and Ganoux. "Please take care of her."

They both nodded as Jean Paul wiped his eyes with a handkerchief. "Mason, you will pack the suitcase as if you are on holiday. You are an amateur painter and struggling artist. These two atrocious paintings should sit on top as they will dilute interest in your belongings. Anyone searching your case will take pity on your severe lack of talent as an artist and hopefully, send you on your way."

Mason nodded as Jean Paul continued, "You and Ganoux will follow me to Orleans where you will board the train to Paris. Once in Paris you will meet up with Jacques and his family. He will have your papers for your flight back to the America. Any questions?"

Both men shook their heads.

"Good. Let us get ready to leave. "

"We still have to deal with the man locked up in your safe," Ganoux mentioned as the three of them left the room.

"Let me talk to him, he is my problem. I'll deal with him," Mason said as he headed down the hallway. Both men followed him, and they entered the office. A faint voice could be heard behind the door to the walk-in safe.

Jean Paul turned the dial on the door to the left, back to the right, and slowly once again to the left. The clicking of the gears could be heard as Jean Paul backed off. "He is all yours," he said as Mason approached.

Ganoux handed Mason his gun and both he and Jean Paul backed away. Mason approached the safe and grabbed the handle with his left hand, turning until the lock disengaged. He pulled on the heavy metal door and it easily opened. Mason raised his gun and pointed it at Franz Kolter's head. Kolter stuttered at Mason in broken English.

"Shut up" was all Mason said as he got closer.

Kolter continued to stutter.

Mason entered the safe, cocking his weapon. "Shut... your...mouth," he said slowly and calmly.

Kolter shut it.

"You are a lucky man, Mr. Kolter. Do you know why?"

The man on the floor of the safe shook his head with a somewhat skeptical look.

"I am going to let you live in exchange for some information. If I find out that you lied to me, I will make it my personal mission to let your boss know that you gave up all his secrets. Then not only will you have to outrun me and the war, you will have to worry about Lucky coming after you. How long do you think you would last? Not long, I suspect. Understand?"

Kolter slowly nodded his head.

"Good," Mason said as he smiled.

Jean Paul and Ganoux left the room as Mason continued to question Kolter. They ventured back into the dining room and packed the suitcase with Mason's things and the two paintings. They closed the case. Ganoux picked it up, shook it a bit and was satisfied with the size and the weight.

Mason returned with Franz Kolter by his side, hands bound, and a cloth tied around his mouth. He did not make any sound as they walked in. Mason pushed him down into one of the chairs.

Ganoux handed Mason the suitcase. He grabbed it and held the case in his left hand as he switched the gun to his right. The case felt good. It was a little big, but not big enough to draw attention. He would blend in with the other travelers.

They gathered outside, and Jean Paul appeared with his car, ready to go. Mason and Ganoux loaded the case in the back seat of their car, and Kolter began to get in. Mason pulled him back. "Oh, no you don't. There is not enough room for you in there." He walked him to the back of the car and opened the trunk. He motioned with his gun as Kolter looked at him.

"Get in," he said, and he pushed him toward the trunk.

Kolter lay down in the trunk, and Mason smiled as he closed it.

Everyone was satisfied with the plan and ready to go. Jean Paul took a moment to say goodbye to his home, not knowing when he would return, or if he would have anything to return to. He locked the front door and settled into the front seat of his car. With that, Mason and Ganoux followed him out of the driveway, with the Mona Lisa in the back seat and Franz Kolter in the trunk.

Chapter 27

AS THE TWO MEN IN THE CAR and the one in the trunk drove down the main road toward Orleans there was not much conversation. Mason was wiped out from the day's events. They followed Jean Paul to a secluded area where they could dump Franz Kolter off. About thirty minutes into the trip they stopped on the outskirts of a small town called Cheverny. Mason got out and opened the trunk, dragged Kolter out, and threw him on the ground. After cutting his bonds, Mason put the knife back in his waistband, Kolter removed the cloth around his mouth, coughing and spitting.

"You almost choked me to death in that trunk," he said in between coughs.

"Almost—that is too bad," Mason said with very little emotion. "Do you remember what we talked about? Remember what I told you?"

"Yes," Kolter replied. "I understand, and I told you the truth."

"There is a train station in town. You can disappear from there. This better be the last time I see you, or next time I guarantee will be the last time you see anything."

Kolter nodded. "Thank you," he mumbled as he began to walk away.

Mason got back in the passenger seat and they drove away leaving Kolter limping down the road. Ganoux glanced over at Mason, "You are learning that there is always more than one solution to a problem. I know you wanted to put a bullet in his head, but then we would have another body to dispose of. He almost died in that safe, and he was so terrified of you we got some valuable information on Lucky. I know Lucky is a low-life, but he has connections everywhere, and if we run into more trouble, he may not be the worst person to reach out to. Of course, that is assuming he forgives us for sending him all over France looking for things that aren't there."

"I just want to get out of this country in one piece with everything and everybody. I hope we never see Lucky again. And you're right, I did want to put a bullet in Kolter's head, but I heard you on my shoulder telling me it was not worth it. I have enough going on in my head without the vision of Kolter being executed."

Ganoux agreed, and both men settled in for the hour ride to Orleans. Mason closed his eyes and called out to Madame X. She appeared quickly, and Mason dozed off.

He woke up as they hit a bump on the outskirts of Orleans.

"Sorry," Ganoux said as he slowed down.

Orleans, France, located on the Loire River, has long been a strategic city, which has seen its share of battles and conquests over the years. Julius Caesar took the city in 52 B.C. and destroyed it during the siege; he rebuilt it under the Roman Empire. Attila the Hun attacked it in 451, and Joan of Arc helped defend the city in 1429, during the Hundred Years War with England. War was once again coming to Orleans, Mason thought as he scanned the landscape.

The city was half empty as they drove over the Pont Rene Thinat. The Cathedral of St. Croix, built in 1529, towered over the city to the left as they crossed the bridge.

Jean Paul pulled over, parked, and limped to their driver's side window. Ganoux rolled down the glass.

"I will circle the station when we arrive to look for anyone suspicious. If I think it is safe, we will stop in front and drop you off. Is everyone good with that plan?" Jean Paul said as they turned onto the Avenue Jean Zay.

Mason and Mr. Ganoux agreed with the plan. Ganoux climbed into the back seat and Jean Paul assumed the driving duties.

He turned left onto the Boulevard Lamartine and drove by the Grand Cemetiere D'Orleans. Mason eyed the tombs and hoped he would not be occupying one anytime soon. As the Gare de Aubrais Station appeared just up ahead, the three men could now see where most of the people were: at the train station in the heart of the city.

Jean Paul drove by the station and turned around. He circled the front a few times and the three men seemed satisfied that it was okay to stop. Jean Paul pulled over at the side of the road.

"Well, I guess this is farewell," he said as he reached out his hand.

Mason shook it and nodded. Ganoux was already out of the car with the suitcase.

As Mason emerged from the front seat, Jean Paul called, "I almost forgot; you won't get far without these." He removed their tickets from his coat pocket and handed them to Mason. "Should be a private car for two."

Mason leaned in and said, "Thank you."

"Don't thank me, son," Jean Paul said as he smiled. "France thanks you."

Jean Paul pulled away as Mason and Ganoux turned and faced the crowded entrance to the station. Ganoux glanced at his watch and then at the ticket. They had thirty-six minutes until the train departed. Both he and Mason scanned the crowd in front of them for anyone who did not look as if they were traveling. They spotted a young man with a newspaper under his arm waiting off to the left. As they eyed him, a woman came up to him and they shared a warm embrace. The young couple turned and walked away from the station toward a waiting car. Mason and Ganoux looked at each other and nodded as they headed for the main entrance.

As they entered Gare de Aubrais station, they walked into a mass of people heading in all directions, pushing carts, dragging luggage and pulling children. Announcements could be heard in the distance as well as the sound of train horns. Mason and Ganoux stopped just inside the entrance and scanned the hordes of travelers in front of them. Nobody seemed to be paying any attention to the two men who had just entered the station. Men and women were coming and going through the main entrance, some with bags, some not, but all trying to get out of town. Mason felt comfortable he would blend right in as another passenger heading to Paris.

Ganoux broke the silence between them. "I will meet you on the train." Mason nodded, and Ganoux walked toward the ticketed passengers' entrance and quickly was swallowed up by the sea of humanity. Mason took one more look around and headed into the station. It would be impossible for him to tell if someone was watching. With his slightly oversized suitcase, Mason blended in as another traveler heading to Paris, although his suitcase was worth considerably more than the average person's.

A woman, who was yelling at her child to keep up, bumped into Mason as he stopped in front of the departure board. She said nothing as she dragged her child past. Mason gave her a sneer and looked up at the board. His train was right on schedule for departure on track two. He checked his watch and had twenty-four minutes until departure. He turned and walked away toward track two. The chaotic scene in the train station made it difficult to maneuver. Mason tried to wait until people dispersed, but it seemed the more people who left, the more entered the station. Mason had his one suitcase and he pushed his way through the crowds and down the stairs.

As he reached the busy track two, he put down his suitcase and looked back up the stairs for any familiar faces that might be following him. He recognized one, the woman still dragging her child, and hoped they were nowhere near him on the train.

Convinced he was not being watched, he removed his ticket, grabbed his suitcase, and approached train car #3. His ticket was for a private first-class cabin, he handed it to the conductor; he acknowledged the ticket and welcomed Mason aboard.

Once on the train, Mason walked to the right, down the corridor through the dining car and into first class. He found cabin six and grabbed the brass handle. Pulling it to the left he slid open the door to find an empty, clean cabin. He closed the door behind him, unsnapped the curtains and pulled them closed across the glass windows for some much-needed privacy.

Another check of his watch: sixteen minutes to departure and one step closer to home. Mason placed the suitcase on the bench seat and took a deep breath. He glanced out the large window; across the tracks was another train waiting for departure.

Mason sat down and wondered where Franz Kolter was at this moment, probably on a train heading somewhere. He detested the man and secretly hoped someone would throw him from his train. He thought of Jean Paul, a patriot of France that no one would ever know. He promised himself that if he made it through this, he would make sure France knew the incredible courage shown by this man. He thought of Collette and Anna, and hoped they were safe and not worrying about him. He smiled at the thought of seeing them again.

A subtle knock on the glass of the compartment door startled Mason. He checked his gun and slowly walked to the door. He pulled the curtains back and saw Ganoux outside. He unlocked the door and let him in.

"Everything okay?" Mason asked.

"Yes," Ganoux replied as he walked into the cabin. "I did not see anyone suspicious. So far, so good. Nice cabin." He sat down, looked as his watch: four minutes.

Mason nodded. "Really can't wait until we are moving."

"How is she?" Mr. Ganoux asked with a nod to the suitcase.

"I haven't checked."

With that Mason stood up and opened the case. He moved some clothes and removed the two canvas Moulié paintings, still marveling at how bad they were; it gave him a chuckle every time he saw them. Mason removed the rest of the clothes and started to unsnap the false bottom. He removed it and the lovely woman from Italy stared back at him with her wry smile.

A knock on the glass of the cabin door caused both men to look at the door. Ganoux walked over and pulled the curtain back. A conductor stared at him through the glass. Ganoux unlocked the door and stepped back. The door to their cabin slid open and a conductor walked in yelling, "Tickets." Mason tried closing the suitcase but the top was caught on the window sill, so it did not fully close.

The conductor walked in. "Welcome aboard, Monsieurs. Can I see your tickets?"

The man walked over to Mason and caught a glimpse of the Mona Lisa as he tried to shut the case. He looked from the case to Mason, perplexed.

"La Gioconda?" he asked.

Mason, through the lump in his throat, nodded yes, and tried to sound convincing, said, "Oh, this? Yes, I am an aspiring painter and have always been taken by her, so I decided to try to paint her."

"Well, let me have a look. I have seen her on many occasions; she is one of my favorite works. I have been several times to the Louvre to visit her. She is mesmerizing, isn't she?"

The conductor walked over for a closer look. Mason caught a glimpse of Ganoux who looked as if he would break the conductor's neck at any moment.

"Not bad," the conductor said as he looked in the suitcase.

"You need some more definition in the face, and your color is a bit off, but not bad at all. I like what you did with the wood, aging it, very convincing. Ahhh...and that smile, needs a little work but it is not bad at all. Are you enrolled in a school in America?"

"No, it's just a hobby," Mason said, trying to avoid any further conversation.

He smiled at Mason. "You have talent. Keep working at it."

Mason, while trying to decide whether to laugh or vomit, thanked the conductor.

"Are these your works also?" the man asked as he looked at the two canvases on the seats.

"Yes, some of my earlier works," Mason said, looking at Ganoux, who mouthed to Mason to get the man out. Mason shrugged his shoulders as if to say, "I am trying."

"Now these are impressive. Believe me, I know. I was not such a bad painter myself many years ago, and I know what separates an amateur from a professional. These are very nice. Oh yes. Very nice form and lines. You could benefit from some teaching, but you are on your way to a career."

Mason almost smacked the man on the side of the head for being such a moron but relented and played along. He thanked the man for his generous words.

"Well, gentleman, it was nice to meet you, and you, son, keep up the good work, maybe my children will be visiting the Louvre one day to see your works."

"Thank you, very generous," Mason said as he ushered the conductor out of the cabin.

He locked the door and turned around as Ganoux quickly put the case back together, loading all of Mason's things back in.

"I guess it is good that he knew absolutely nothing about art, or we could have been in serious trouble," Mason said as he sat down.

"We have to tell Jacques that he has an avid fan of his work collecting tickets on the Orleans to Paris rail line."

Mason laughed. "Yeah, he will get a kick out of that."

Both men settled down and tried to get some rest as the train moved closer to Paris.

Chapter 28

A HARD KNOCK ON THE CABIN DOOR startled Mason from a dream dinner with Madame X. He shook his head as he woke up and looked around but Ganoux was nowhere to be found. The knock came again, louder this time; Mason stood up and walked over to the sliding cabin door and pulled the curtains aside. He saw the conductor with zero art education, standing there.

The conductor smiled briefly, "I need to recheck your ticket, sir."

"Why?" Mason said annoyingly through the glass.

"I need to make sure the cabin number and the ticket match. There is a woman complaining that she has the wrong cabin and is insisting she be moved into your cabin; she claims it is hers. I am very sorry for the inconvenience."

Mason took a deep breath and shook his head in disgust as he let the curtains fall back into place. He secured his pistol in the small of his back as he unlatched the door and began sliding it open.

The door was pushed open and the conductor was thrown into the cabin, nearly knocking Mason over. The conductor fell to the ground and was quickly followed by two men in black suits, both holding Lugers.

"I am sorry," the conductor said. He was shaking and obviously terrified as he lay on his back on the floor.

Mason backed up a few steps and raised his hands.

The second man closed the cabin door and locked it, briefly looking through the curtain for anyone coming. Convinced they had raised no suspicions, he let the curtains flow back into place and gave his partner a nod of approval.

Mason looked at both men, noticing the similar features, square jaw, blond hair, soulless eyes. Neither of the men said a word as they turned their eyes to him. The conductor started to weep as one of the men told him to sit down and be quiet. The man had a heavy German accent. He motioned to the bench seat with the barrel of his Luger. The conductor was shaking so much he could barely move.

"Do it now," the man said firmly. The conductor managed to climb to his feet and sat down on the cabin's red leather bench seat. He was sniffling, trying to remain calm as tears streamed down his cheeks. Mason looked over as the poor man tried to compose himself with little success.

With his hands raised chest high, Mason turned back to the first man standing in front of him. He was over six feet with a strong physique; the second man, still standing in front of the cabin door, was easily six feet, five inches, and was built like a machine. He said nothing, only glaring with an ice-cold stare at Mason.

The first man gave an invisible sign and the man behind him walked over to Mason and removed the gun from his back; Mason's head was only chest high to the behemoth. Mason stared up at the man as he returned to his cabin door guard position.

"So, you are Mason Wright?" the first man said almost admiringly. "I must say you are much shorter than I thought." The man approached and walked behind him. Mason turned his body to follow the man's gaze.

"I have been told a great deal about you, your job at the museum, your unceremonious departure, and your little vacation here in France visiting friends. Interesting time to come on vacation as war approaches; most people are leaving Europe but not you, no, you have chosen to visit. How nice." The man proceeded full circle and stood back in front of Mason. "I do admire your loyalty to Jacques Moulié, and of course, Collette, she is quite beautiful," The man smiled slightly;

Mason envisioned snapping the man's neck as he took a step forward.

"Eh, Eh, Eh," the man said warningly as he raised his gun.

"What do you want?" Mason asked, his gaze never leaving the man's eyes. "Have you come to write my biography? You seem to know an awful lot about me."

"Actually Mason, if it were up to me, I would simply kill you. That will come soon enough once you give me what I have come for. I know you have the painting, where is it?"

"Painting? I have no idea what you're talking about." Mason slowly shook his head.

He wondered where Ganoux had disappeared to and hoped he would return soon; if not, Mason was in serious trouble.

The man looked over his shoulder. "Search the cabin." The larger man began rummaging through the overhead compartment, pulling things out and throwing them on the floor: magazines, an emergency kit, some blankets. He was not gentle in his search. Mason wondered why they felt the need to carry guns; whoever they were, all they needed was this guy. His physique was bursting through his suit as he stretched his arms and threw things around the cabin. The conductor, still sitting on the bench, moved out of the way as the man continued his search. After the overhead compartment was empty, the man pushed Mason aside as he moved across the cabin to the tall thin closet; Mason felt as if he had been hit with a cinder block, but it was only the man's forearm. Opening the closet, the man ripped out a blue suitcase and threw it on the bed. Mason stared at it, he had never seen it before, he wondered what happened to his suitcase; he suspected Ganoux had something to do with this.

As the man rifled through the suitcase, undershirts and socks flew through the air. Once empty, he turned it upside down and shook it. Satisfied there was nothing left he threw it on the ground at Mason's feet. Mason stepped back trying to avoid losing a foot.

Next, the man started pulling all the cushions off the bench; it was evident both men were getting increasingly agitated. He continued searching and found nothing, the conductor was dodging various items being thrown his way, more terrified every second.

After finding nothing the first man approached Mason; he pushed the barrel of his Luger into Mason's neck. They stared at each other for a moment; Mason saw the coldness of the man's soul as they moved within a few inches of each other. Mason was uneasy; this man was obviously capable of anything.

"Where is the Mona Lisa?" the man said, his voice indicating this was Mason's last chance.

Mason swallowed and leaned forward a bit, "I believe it is in the Louvre." He smiled slightly; the man was not amused. He cocked his pistol and offered one last statement. "Goodbye, Mr. Wright."

The words had barely left his lips when there was a screech of metal on metal as the train suddenly braked hard, slowing at an incredible pace. All four men were thrown against the walls as the train screeched to a stop. As the man with the Luger hit the wall, his gun went flying. He crumbled to the ground, unconscious and bleeding. Mason hit the wall with his shoulder; pain shot through his upper body. He was dazed as he hit the floor. The large man was thrown against the conductor as both men hit the open closet. The conductor fell to the ground halfway into the closet.

The large man hit the closet face first; shattering the door into pieces. The train came to a stop and the burning smell of the brakes filled the cabin. Mason regained his composure and jumped on the large man who was stunned by the door in the face. He tried to react, but Mason was on him quick and he repeatedly smashed the side of the man's head into the wall. The man used his forearm to throw Mason across the cabin and onto the bench. Mason looked around for a gun but, seeing nothing, he grabbed the empty suitcase and threw it at the large man stumbling toward him. He knocked it away with his arms and grabbed Mason by the neck; his hands were like a vice. Mason threw his elbow into the man's chest; it felt like elbowing a brick wall. The man barely moved and continued to squeeze Mason's neck. Grabbing the man's hands, Mason tried to pry them off, but he was beginning to lose consciousness.

Suddenly the window on the door to the cabin smashed open and a hand reached in and unlocked it. The door slid open and Ganoux appeared, gun in hand. He fired one shot and struck the man in the shoulder. The grip around Mason's neck instantly loosened. Mason quickly fell to the ground, coughing and gasping. A second shot rang out and the large man fell back onto the floor with blood dripping from his shoulder and his side. He lay there for a moment, trying unsuccessfully to get up.

The terrified conductor covered his ears and closed his eyes. Ganoux grabbed Mason's arm. "Come on, we have to go." Mason was still catching his breath as he got up from the floor. He coughed several times as he stood. He grabbed Ganoux's arm and in a hoarse whisper asked, "Where's the case?"

"I've got it, let's go," he yelled as the two men emerged from the cabin into the hallway. Several people were gathering there, having been awakened by all the commotion. Most of them were in sleeping clothes and dazed.

Ganoux led them through the wooden hallway, passing cabin after cabin. Mason bumped into a few people as he ran by; he glanced behind them but there was no sign of the men who confronted him. They reached the dining car and stopped. Mason was still coughing; his neck burned from almost being choked to death. They reached a table where a busboy was standing holding onto the brass rail above the seats. Ganoux reached under the table and pulled out the suitcase; he handed the busboy some cash, and he and Mason turned and ran.

They ran through the dining car, through the vestibule, and arrived at the reserved seating car which was filled with people and chaos; people's suitcases were strewn throughout the aisle.

Ganoux yelled out in French, "Please move, this is an emergency." He forced his way down the aisle with Mason on his heels. They stepped on and over people and luggage, apologizing every few feet. Mason was the target of some French insults as he pushed his way through. Ganoux stopped suddenly and Mason caught a glimpse of a man coming through the next cabin; the man was dressed the same as the other two men who had barged into his cabin. The man held a gun in the air and fired two shots straight up, causing screams as people ducked back into their seats, exposing the two of them. Mason ducked as Ganoux fired a shot toward the man, who jumped to the right as the bullet exploded into a seat cushion, sending seat stuffing into the air.

Mason and Ganoux turned and ran back in the direction of the dining car as a bullet flew past their heads and into the cabin wall. People were screaming, and Mason could feel Ganoux's hand in his back pushing him along. Once back in the dining car, Ganoux closed the door and locked it; this would not stop the man, but it might buy them a moment to think. Mason could see the men from his cabin barreling toward them from the other direction. They were trapped.

Looking around for something strong, Ganoux finally kicked a barstool several times, ripping it from its supports. He turned toward the window and swinging with all his might, threw the barstool into the window, cracking the glass. He pulled it back and smashed the window again, sending glass flying out into the night. Mason fired off round after round in the direction of the approaching men, who had ducked behind some seats and were returning fire.

Glass exploded behind them as the other man reached the locked door. He had shot out the window and reached in to unlock the door. Mason fired and struck the man in the shoulder. He fired another round and hit the man in the chest; the man fell to the ground and disappeared behind the partition. Ganoux grabbed a tablecloth and threw it over the broken glass in the opening of the window.

"Come on," he yelled at Mason as he climbed through the window and jumped down onto the loose stones next to the tracks. Mason handed him the suitcase and then fired a few more shots before he jumped out. He fell to the ground and rolled over a few times. The jolt sent a sharp pain through his neck, leaving him momentarily stunned and short of breath. He got to his knees and began to spit up some blood. Ganoux grabbed his arm and dragged him down the hill into the trees. Engineers from the train were running toward them yelling and waving their arms. Mason and Ganoux disappeared into the trees as shots rang out over their heads; leaves fell on top of them as the bullets hit the trees. Mason was feeling faint as he stumbled into the woods. Ganoux led him as they disappeared into the cover of the trees, Mason in one arm and the suitcase in the other.

Chapter 29

MASON AND GANOUX STUMBLED their way through the woods, Mason struggling to keep his balance. They could still hear the commotion at the train and had no idea how far behind the men with the guns were. Mason, coughing and wheezing, was forced to stop in a clearing and rest for a moment. Ganoux watched their back as Mason caught his breath.

"We really need to move, Mason!"

He nodded and stood up straight, grabbed the suitcase, and they continued through the woods, dodging branches and roots. The moon was full in the sky, providing the only light as they darted through the brush. Mason's chest burned with every breath, but he kept up with Ganoux. They had no idea where they were going, but they both knew they could not go back. Wherever these woods ended was where they were headed, and Mason hoped they got there soon.

Ganoux stopped in another clearing and Mason put the case down. He leaned over and put his hands on his knees. Having been almost choked to death ten minutes ago, he had trouble regaining his breath, he coughed and spit up saliva and blood.

"Where do we go from here?" he asked in between coughs and spits.

"There's a road up ahead. We can try to flag someone down."

"What if no one comes?"

"Can we have a little optimism, please? It is a busy road for trucks, someone will come by." The sound of rustling branches could be heard behind them in the distance. They looked at each other and continued toward the road.

Mason's legs and lungs were burning as they moved through the weeds, bushes, and trees. A root tripped him as he ran by; he went down along with the suitcase. Ganoux stopped and helped him up. Mason wiped some blood from his hands and nodded his thanks. Ganoux picked up the case and pushed Mason forward. He stumbled on like a drunk in an alley after a long night; the sounds of the men chasing came ever closer. Ganoux alternated keeping an eye on Mason with quick glances behind them.

Finally, they reached the end of the tree line and arrived in a grassy area next to a road. Mason collapsed in the clearing, vomiting in the grass. Ganoux put the case down and checked the rounds left in his gun. He turned and focused his aim on the tree line, where the sounds of the men coming were even louder. They were obviously closing in.

Mason shook his head, trying to regain his composure as he rolled onto his back. He opened his eyes wide as he heard an engine approach. He mustered all his strength, jumped up quickly, and saw headlights approaching from his left. He ran into the road waving his hands wildly back and forth. The headlights, approaching quickly, were joined by the sound of a horn. Mason stood his ground and a small delivery truck came to a stop in front of him. Mason ran to the driver's side as the man rolled down his window screaming in French. Ganoux ran over to calm him down, and finally he motioned for the two of them to climb in.

Mason ran to the passenger door and jumped in as a bullet raced by his head. The two men from the train had reached the clearing and were firing wildly at the truck. Ganoux pushed the driver to the middle and slid in his seat. The driver covered his head, clearly frightened as Ganoux fired two shots out the passenger window, while stepping on the gas pedal. The truck lurched forward, and with tires spinning, sped away. More shots rang out as the truck rumbled down the road, the side mirror blew out and the driver screamed as he cowered between them. The two men ran into the road and fired on the truck speeding away. Mason and Ganoux both sank in their seats as bullets flew by. As they gained speed the sound of bullets was replaced by the sound of the old man rambling on in French.

Mason looked across the cab at Ganoux. "Who were those guys, and how is that big guy still standing?"

"I don't know; German spies would be my guess."

Mason looked at the driver with annoyance. "Can you get this guy to shut up?"

"Soyez silencieux," Ganoux said a few times before the man finally stopped talking. He held a brief conversation with him before looking across at Mason, who was still coughing a bit. "You okay?"

Mason nodded. "The big guy nearly choked me to death. Where did you go, and how did you know to take the case?"

"When I went to the dining car to get some food for the cabin, I passed through the passenger car and noticed the small guy sitting quietly. He looked up at me as I went by; his eyes were not the eyes of a Frenchman, and definitely not the eyes of a family man. He had a cold stare. I watched him for a bit from afar and eventually the big guy joined him. They talked briefly, and the big guy got up and headed my way. I ducked into the kitchen as he passed and made my way back to our cabin. I knew those guys were looking for us. I grabbed a suitcase from the luggage rack and returned to the cabin. You were sound asleep, so I switched it out for ours and went back to the dining car. I told the bartender I would make it worth his while to watch the case and he put it behind the bar. When I went back to the passenger car both guys were gone. I looked for a bit and then went to the cabin where you were entertaining them. I pulled the emergency stop and well, you know the rest."

Mason stared over at Ganoux and he could not hide his annoyance. "I could have died in there; the big guy was going to snap my neck."

"I know that was very dangerous, and thankfully that did not happen," Ganoux replied with his eyes on the road.

Mason shook his head and stared out the window. Something wasn't right. His covert mission to France was anything but. People had confronted them at every turn, they seemed to be on everyone's radar. After being used as bait, he was beginning to wonder if his friend Ganoux was not as trustworthy as he had been led to believe.

Mason closed his eyes. His throat was sore, his whole body hurt, his lungs seemed five sizes too small, and he wondered if his biggest threat to this whole mission was currently driving them to Paris in a stolen delivery truck.

Chapter 30

MASON WOKE UP as they approached the outskirts of Paris. Their plan was to rendezvous at the warehouse where this all started. They would meet Jacques and Collette and figure out how to get Mason and the Mona Lisa out of the country.

"How are you feeling?" Ganoux said as he noticed Mason shuffling in his seat.

"Not great, but better." As Mason moved the owner of the truck also woke up, startled.

"We should be in Paris in twenty minutes or so. We'll go right to the warehouse and meet up with Jacques and Collette. The train we were on is scheduled to arrive within the hour. If someone is waiting for us at the station, they will know something went wrong when it does not show up. Pulling the brakes as I did surely threw them off schedule at the very least."

"We won't have much time before everyone comes looking for us."

Ganoux slowed down and pulled over to the side of the road, Mason listened with little comprehension as Ganoux spoke quickly in French to the truck's owner. The man said nothing but nodded his head in agreement. Ganoux got out of the driver side, and the truck's owner slid across the seat and exited the truck. Ganoux handed the man something and patted him on the shoulder, then climbed back in the driver's seat. The two men sped away in their stolen truck leaving the Frenchman on the corner.

"What did you say to him?" Mason asked as they drove away.

"I told him you wanted to put a bullet in his head, and I convinced you not to. He was terrified of you," his partner replied with a slight smirk.

"Very funny," Mason replied sarcastically.

"I told him we needed his truck for the night, and it was a matter of the highest priority in the defense of France. He was so scared he just nodded silently. I gave him some money for his troubles and reassured him of his patriotic duty. He was just happy to be alive, so I am not sure he understood a word I said."

The truck approached the road to the warehouse, it was early morning now, the district had not yet come to life. They pulled in front of the large wooden doors in the driveway of the warehouse.

Ganoux looked at his watch. "Our train is not due for twenty minutes, but they should be here already. They won't be expecting us, so be careful. We don't want Collette shooting you accidentally."

"I'll be fine, thanks."

Both men exited the truck and approached the doors; Mason carried the case as Ganoux pulled out his pistol. Standing in front of the large warehouse doors he fumbled for the keys to the padlock as Mason glanced around.

A truck rumbled down the road, causing both men to pause and look behind them. It passed and eventually drove out of sight. The chain rattled through the clasp as Ganoux pulled it out, grabbed the large steel handle, and slowly pulled the large, heavy door open. The door creaked, and Mason peered inside. He spotted Jacques' car parked in the bay. Ganoux started in and passed the parked car on the left, peering into the windows as he passed. Mason pulled the doors closed and locked them; he followed Ganoux past the car and up the stairs.

No sound came from the warehouse as both men climbed the stairs into the main room. Ganoux stopped suddenly and put out his right hand to stop Mason, who pushed through to see what had startled Ganoux. Lying on the floor, bloodied and bruised, was Jacques Moulié. He was tied to a chair, which had fallen on its side, he had a cloth in his mouth and his left eye was swollen shut. He was alive, but barely. Mason could see tears running down Jacques' face mixing with the blood. Ganoux removed the cloth from Jacques' mouth, causing him to cough up blood.

"They have her," Jacques said hoarsely and coughed again. "They took her." Ganoux untied his wrists, and Jacques grabbed onto him. "They took my girl," he said again as he started to cry.

Mason's face drained of color. Collette was gone, and he was to blame. His feelings for her were a big reason why he was in Paris in the first place. He had done this for her and now he might never see her again. His heart ached as he turned back to Jacques.

"Who took her, what did they say?" he asked urgently. His sense of heartache was being slowly replaced by rage and a desire for revenge. Suddenly his neck felt fine and the only thing that mattered was making these people pay. If they even so much as laid a hand on her, he would kill them all. Someone was going to pay dearly for doing this. He looked at Jacques again and calmly sat him down at the table. Ganoux returned from the kitchen with a wet towel and some water. Jacques wiped away the blood and tears and drank some water. He regained his breath and started to recount what had happened. His voice crackled as he spoke, still choking back tears.

"Collette and I arrived as planned. We pulled the car in and parked. Collette pulled the doors closed and I brought some things into the main room, I reached for the light switch and I was hit by something or someone. Next thing I knew I was tied to a chair and two men were standing over me. My face was bloody. One man stepped forward and in a heavy German accent told me they were taking my daughter. If I want to see her alive again, they will trade her for the Mona Lisa. I screamed at him and the other man started to beat me. I was yelling Collette's name as the man kept hitting me. His last punch knocked me over and he leaned down and said there was a phone number on the table. Have Mason Wright call when he arrives, we know he has the painting, only then will we give you instructions for a switch. The last thing he told me was, 'No tricks or we will kill your daughter, understand?' He patted my cheek and then stuffed a cloth in my mouth."

Mason found the paper with the phone number. He showed it to Ganoux. The rage on his face was visible to everyone in the room. Trying to remain calm, Mason asked, "What did these men look like?"

"Both men wore long black leather coats; they had German accents. They were armed, and they were emotionless. Mason, you have to get her back."

"We will get her back," Mason said as he turned to Ganoux. "Any ideas?"

"We have to think about this. They want the painting so they will not do anything to her. We can assure them we have the painting, and we will make the switch, but we are going to need help. These people have been on us since the beginning. I have no idea how that is possible."

"I don't know, but the man who attacked Collette here, the man in the square who chased us in his car, the men on the train, they have all been after us and the painting. I'm tired of it, and this time we are going after them with everything we have. They have messed with me for the last time." Mason's face told Ganoux that he meant business. He envisioned the Solario painting again; this time he was holding it, and there were several heads on the platter.

Ganoux quietly nodded in agreement as they began to plan. After a few moments of talk, Mason grabbed the piece of paper and dialed the number. The rotary phone seemed to take forever to connect, and Mason grew more enraged with every second. He tapped his fingers on the wall as he stood by the phone. It began to ring on the other end. Ganoux, on the receiver in the kitchen, also listened intently.

After the third ring a voice picked up on the other end. "I am glad you decided to call, Mason, I was beginning to think you were finding the painting more important than your girlfriend."

If he could have, Mason would have reached through the phone and strangled the man right there. "Let me talk to her," he said calmly.

"No, I don't think so," the voice said with a slight chuckle. "I assure you she is fine. She is quite lovely you know, and very pretty. It would be a shame to take some of that beauty away. Mason, listen to me carefully, what I am proposing is a simple trade. We both possess beautiful women. You deliver me the one that I want, and I will give you back yours." The man continued with the specifics, time, location, and who should come. Mason agreed and gave the man one last piece of advice.

"If you hurt her in any way, I will hunt you down and you will feel more pain than you can possibly imagine."

The man chuckled. "Mason you are letting your emotions get in the way. The only reason I took Collette is because I knew it would be you who would come for her. I am very much looking forward to meeting you. Just bring the painting and I won't have to hurt your girlfriend."

The phone went silent. Mason hung up and punched the wall.

He turned around, "Once we have Collette back, I am going to kill all of them."

Ganoux returned from the kitchen; he and Jacques nodded at Mason. This had become personal for all of them, and they shared Mason's sentiments. Blood was about to be shed, and people were going to die.

They were to deliver the painting to an address outside Paris, where Collette would also be released. They had about four hours before the 5 a.m. meeting. They needed some things, and with very little choice, they decided it was time to go see someone for help.

They bid farewell to Jacques and the warehouse, locked the large wooden doors, and drove away, Mason in the stolen truck and Ganoux following in Jacques' car. They needed guns and men, and they knew where to find both. They dumped the truck on a corner as promised to the old man; they hoped he would find it in one piece. It was a small measure of thanks to the old man who stopped and helped them back to Paris. Then both men proceeded in Jacques' car on their way to see a man whose help they would need, knowing full well it was the last thing this man would want to do. Mason had a plan, he just hoped it would work. His thoughts bounced back and forth between getting Collette back and vengeance. He was confident he would attain both.

Chapter 31

MASON AND GANOUX DROVE across town to the entertainment district and parked in front of the American Club D'Paris. The night club was closed for the evening to patrons, but a club as unique as this one never truly closed; it was open for business twenty-four hours a day.

The after-hours club was much different than the regular everyday business. During the evening hours the club specialized in drinks, dancing, and cabaret. The club catered to the Paris elite, the politicians, the police, and the gangsters, all rubbing shoulders together trading stories, favors, and cash. The club's owner loved the attention that came with his clientele; he moved from table to table delivering bottles of French champagne and greasing the palms of the men who allowed him to operate slightly above the law. Once the operating hours ended the business of the club turned from music and drinking to illegal items, stolen goods, drugs, and prostitution.

The club's owner was not going to be happy to see Mason walk through his door; in fact, it was extremely dangerous for him to be there at all. Mason had little choice, he needed a favor and only one man in Paris was capable of providing him with information, men, and weapons. That man was Franz "Lucky" Leiter.

Mason exited the vehicle and slowly approached the front entrance, the lights on the marquee were flashing with the names of the show and band performing each night. The colors of the French flag and the American flag flashed across the background. Mason shook his head as he looked at it. Lucky loved American gangsters and had copied a theater marquee from Chicago and dropped it right in the heart of Paris.

As he approached the front glass doors, Mason secured his pistol in his waistband. The left of the three front doors began to open as he approached, and a man Mason recognized from Jean Paul's living room approached. He was pretty sure it was the man who had taken a shot at him while he was tied to the chair. Mason did not forget the faces of people who tried to kill him; fortunately, they were few and far between.

The man extended his arm and pressed his hand against Mason's chest. Mason stopped, glanced down at the man's arm, and slowly looked up.

"We are closed," the man said in a heavy accent.

"No, you're not." Mason replied, and in a split second grabbed the man's arm by the wrist, and with a quick twist and a punch, dislocated the man's elbow and slowly dropped him to the ground. The man lay there moaning as Mason stepped over him into the club. As the door closed behind him another man approached saying something in French. Mason pulled out his pistol and pointed it at the man's face. "Take me to Lucky."

"Lucky is not here," the man said in severely broken English.

Mason turned the man around and disarmed him. He put his gun into the man's back and with his right arm pushed him forward into the club. They reached a curtain which separated the atrium from the main club. Mason pushed the man through the curtain and followed close behind. Two men were seated at a table eating as Mason entered with the stumbling man in front of him. They jumped up with their guns drawn. Mason pointed his pistol in their direction and fired one silenced shot which ricocheted off the wall behind them. Both men raised their hands.

"Put them down on the floor," Mason said as he pushed his man over toward the other two. The man on the right nodded to the others as they put their guns on the floor. Mason walked over and picked up the guns, unloaded the clips from both, and threw them aside. The man on the right appeared to be in charge so Mason walked up to him and pointed his gun into the man's face, "Take me to Lucky."

"He is not here," the man replied as he leaned back away from the barrel of Mason's gun. Mason smirked and fired one shot just past the man's ear. The man stumbled and fell backward, "OK, OK. He is in the back, I will take you."

Mason followed the man down a few steps, across the dance floor and down a hallway to the left of the stage. Music could be heard coming from a room at the end of the hall. It grew louder as they got closer. The man stopped and motioned in the direction of the closed door.

Mason looked at the door and with a quick motion knocked the man out with the butt of his gun. The man clumped to the ground with a thud.

Mason grabbed the handle to the office and raised his pistol. He opened the door slowly and the sound of American music filled the air. The lights were dimmed, and the smell of a stale cigar filled the air. As Mason stepped into the office and across the room, he could see Lucky seated behind his desk with cigar in hand and eyes closed, he was moaning, and his head was slowly moving. Mason quietly approached the desk and could see the reason why Lucky was completely unaware of his presence: a woman was on her knees with her head in his lap. Mason smiled at the absurdity of this situation. Lucky was an older overweight pig of a man. *This poor woman,* thought Mason as he tried to decide the best way to announce his arrival. He decided to have some fun. He raised his pistol and fired one shot directly over Lucky's head and into the wall.

Lucky's eyes opened, and he screamed as he fell backwards off his chair. The woman fell to the ground and grabbed the sides of her head. Mason looked at her. "Get out of here."

She grabbed her clothes from the ground and ran out of the room in her lingerie.

Lucky was still rolling around on the ground trying to get

his bearings. He stood up with fear in his eyes as his pants fell to the ground. What was left of his hair was standing up on his head; he looked like a man who was just awakened from a deep sleep.

Mason smiled as Lucky reached down for his pants.

"Hello, Lucky, is this a bad time?"

Lucky stared at Mason with disbelief. "If I made a list of all the people in the world who might walk into my office tonight, you, Mason Wright, would not be on it."

"Surprise, surprise," Mason said as he smiled. "Sorry to interrupt your little liaison."

"Yes, your timing was not great, and what was with the gunshot? You almost gave me a heart attack." Lucky dusted himself off, without looking at Mason, and added, "So, I have to ask, what brings you to my office at four in the morning?"

"I need a favor," Mason replied, knowing full well the absurdity of that statement.

Lucky turned and picked up his desk chair. He sat down and reclined as he looked up at Mason.

"You need a favor? Are you kidding me? You do realize a couple days ago I had you tied to a chair and almost killed you, right? A request for a favor I was not expecting. A bullet to the head perhaps, but not a favor."

"No, I'm not kidding. Revenge is reserved for those who have no other options, I still have a choice, and I do need your help. I have an urgent matter and could use some weapons and a few men, but most of all I need something which you took from me a couple days ago when we were down in the Loire."

Lucky stared straight at Mason with a quizzical look. "OK, go on."

Mason placed his gun on the desk and pulled up a chair. "I don't have much time, the Mona Lisa painting you took from me in the Loire? I need it back. I have a situation where I need to use it in a switch for someone. You can take it back once the switch has been made."

Lucky managed a slight grin. "Is it really considered stealing if the person you took it from has stolen it himself? Mason, I would love to help you, but I already have a buyer and unless you can up the price, I don't believe I can help you."

"It's not worth the wood it is painted on. It is a fake—a very good fake—but it is no less a fake."

"Do you think I am a fool? The painting is very real and is going to fetch me quite a nice price. I never understood the draw of it, she's not very beautiful, but my buyer disagrees and has the offer to prove it," Lucky said as he stood up and walked over to his liquor cabinet. He poured himself some bourbon and motioned to Mason with a glass, "Bourbon?"

"No," he replied as Lucky sat back down at his desk. He leaned into a few inches from Lucky. "The painting is not real because I have the real one, and no, I don't think you're a fool. In fact, I don't think you care if it is real or not as long as it sells."

Mason paused and looked at all the pictures on the wall around the office, American actresses and gangsters dominated the landscape. His gaze eventually returned to Lucky. He placed his hand on his gun and stared straight into Lucky's bloodshot eyes. "Lucky where is the painting? I need it and I am leaving here with it." He picked up his gun and put a bullet through the Bourbon bottle on the cabinet. It exploded as bourbon and glass sprayed everywhere.

"OK," Lucky said as he backed away from the desk. "I have it, but you've got to promise me I can get it back."

"That depends on you," Mason said as leaned back in his chair and explained the situation and their plan. It took some convincing but eventually Lucky nodded as if they were suddenly committed partners. After the brief conversation both men felt confident that their unlikely partnership might work out. Mason would get Collette back, Lucky would get his fake Mona Lisa back, and then they would part ways and hope the upcoming war did not kill them both.

Mason left Lucky's office with a forged Mona Lisa, a deal

with the devil, and a vision of all their heads on one large platter being delivered by a hand belonging to the unknown someone who was behind this whole situation—someone Mason would meet soon enough. Getting Collette back was first and foremost in his mind, if that happened, he would deal with whatever came next. Several days ago, she had stood in his apartment and actually intimated that this would be fun. A few dead bodies later, several close calls, too many bullets fired, and now an abduction, it was not fun anymore. It was serious and possibly deadly for all those involved.

He walked out of the club with an exact replica of the suitcase he had been lugging around France for the last few days, Ganoux was waiting and beginning to be concerned over the time that had passed.

Mason placed the suitcase in the back seat and sat in the front. Ganoux looked at him. "Everything OK?"

"Yes, we are all set. If somehow Lucky holds up his end of the bargain, we at least will have a chance."

Ganoux stared at him silently for a moment, "Do you think that is going to happen?"

Mason looked at Ganoux. "You know what? Strangely, I do. Lucky wants his money so if there is one thing for sure, he will do what he needs to make sure his fake painting comes back to him."

They drove away as Mason filled him in on his meeting with Lucky, the plan, and the timing. Ganoux nodded slowly, his distrust in the plan, and Lucky, evident. A Parisian gangster was the glue that would keep this plan together. If Lucky did not come through, they were dead already.

Chapter 32

THEY DROVE OUT OF TOWN and arrived at the address they had been given ten minutes earlier. Ganoux parked down the road from the front entrance. Mason remained stoic in the passenger seat, his thoughts on Collette, as Ganoux rehearsed their plan over and over.

"I got it," Mason finally said, cutting him off before he began the third go-around.

Five minutes later, Mason got out of the car with the suitcase. He knew the forgery was good but was not sure what kind of scrutiny it would be given or if it would pass inspection. If it did not pass the test, he and Collette would die together without her truly knowing how he felt about her.

He approached the entrance to the home and checked the address: 293 Rue Floret. The stone column rose about ten feet in the air and towered over Mason as he stared at it. The long gravel driveway curved about fifty feet down the hill and disappeared toward the house, which was barely visible through the trees. *Does every house outside of Paris have large stone columns and driveways that disappear?* Mason wondered. He felt as though he was back at Jean Paul's.

Mason slowly started up the driveway, the gravel crunching under his feet. He reached the turn in the driveway and the house appeared in the distance, drenched in the moonlight. The meeting was scheduled for 5 a.m. He checked his watch: 4:56 a.m. As Mason approached the house the three gables at the front rose above the stone roof. Three double stone chimneys could be seen at the top of the roof line. The house was painted a light cream color with maroon wooden shutters around every window.

Mason stopped in front of the large granite steps and took a deep breath. He had no intention of dying here, but he would need help from several people to avoid that happening.

He climbed the steps to the front door, which creaked and began to open. A man motioned for him to enter the foyer. Mason entered. Once inside, the door closed, and Mason stood in a large foyer two stories high with a grand wooden staircase spiraling its way up to the second floor. He noticed a large oil painting on the wall above him of a mother and child in the garden with their dog asleep at their feet. He thought of the irony of such innocence in a situation derived from hatred and greed.

Another man appeared from the corner to the left and approached Mason.

"Put the case down and raise your hands over your head," he said with a heavy German accent. Mason obeyed and placed the suitcase on the carpet next to his right leg. He raised his arms as the man checked him for weapons, Mason was unarmed for the first time on this trip. He did not like the feeling of being so vulnerable, but that was the plan, and he did not want to jeopardize Collette in any way.

Satisfied, the man motioned for him to move. He picked up the case and proceeded down the wood-paneled hallway. With a slight nudge from the man he was pushed through an opening into a large room dotted with bookcases on each wall. Two other men stood at the entrance as Mason walked through. His heart was beating as if a marching band was charging through his chest.

As he entered the middle of the room, a gentleman rose from a leather chair; Mason did not recognize him. He was over six feet tall, short cropped hair, dark eyes, and an arrogance to his smirk. The man reached out his hand to introduce himself as Mason stared at him.

"Mason, it is so nice to finally meet you. My name is

Johan Kliest. I have been following your every move since you arrived in Paris. It is nice to finally talk to you face to face," the man said with a smile.

"Where is Collette?" Mason said with the warmness of a block of ice, leaving Kliest's hand in midair.

"Can I offer you a drink?" Kliest lowered his arm and walked over to a large silver cart with some brandy and crystal glasses.

"I want to see Collette," Mason repeated.

"My dear boy, this will go much more smoothly if you relax a bit; Collette is fine. She is beautifully unharmed. We are merely conducting business, none of this is personal. I admire you going through all this dirty work for a woman." Kliest stood in front of Mason with a crystal carafe containing a tawny-colored brandy. The condescending tone further enraged Mason. He wanted to break the carafe over the man's skull.

After a few moments Kliest relented. "Fine, fine, we shall proceed to the reason for which we have all come." He motioned to a man in the corner who disappeared through a door.

Mason's gaze did not leave Kliest.

"Mason, I want to ask you something," Kliest said. "Why would an American come all the way to France and get involved in this when you could be home in New York working in your museum and enjoying a peaceful life? This is not your fight."

"Believe me, I don't want to be here," Mason said softly, "but because of people like you, I need to be here. The only thing needed for evil to succeed is for good men to do nothing. I am one of the good men, you are not so I have come here to do something and make sure you and your people pay for what you are doing."

"There is so much you do not know, Mason. In time you will understand that all we have in this world is not given to us; it must be taken. We are merely taking what we believe to be entitled to."

Mason's blood had begun to boil when Kliest's man returned with Collette. She was bound at her hands and had a cloth tied around her mouth. Her eyes were red, and Mason could tell she was crying.

Mason gave her a reassuring glance and asked her if she was ok. She nodded as tears rolled down her face. Now that Collette was here, Mason began to calm down; the drums in his chest slowly marched away.

"Where is the painting?" Kliest asked, turning back to Mason.

Mason walked over to the table and placed the case down, then turned and walked back.

"Open it," Kliest said, losing patience.

Mason turned back and stopped at the table. He opened the case and removed the false bottom, he folded back the cloth, exposing the forged version of Da Vinci's masterpiece and removed it from the case. He placed the case back on the floor a few feet from the table and backed away.

Kliest looked closely at the painting and his eyes grew wide. "Tell her it is here," he said.

Mason kept his eyes on Collette as Kliest inspected the Mona Lisa. He was growing impatient and tried to move things along.

"Can we get going with this. Do your inspection and let..." He was interrupted by a voice who entered the room.

"Hello, Mason," said the familiar female voice. Mason's face went white with shock.

He turned his head and watched his old boss enter the room: Dr. Margaret Heckler.

Mason's eyes followed her as she walked across the room. She was dressed in a black jacket with a white blouse as if she had come from work at the museum. She walked confidently across the room with the sound of her heels tapping the wood floor.

She stopped in front of Mason. "I've seen you look better,

a trying few days?"

"What are you doing here?" Mason stuttered as she smiled at him.

"I have come to collect the masterpiece you have been so generous to bring us. I will be accompanying her on a journey back to Berlin. My Führer is anxious to meet her."

"You have spent your entire career fighting for the preservation of countless national treasures, how could you be behind this?" Mason's disdain was easy to see.

"Mason, please don't lecture me. You don't know anything about me. I have spent twenty years caring for my mother who suffered a total emotional breakdown after witnessing the torture and killing of her husband, my father, in cold blood by allied troops in World War I. My father was executed for no reason. So, when the Führer asked that all Germans return to the Fatherland, I answered the call. He is going to build the single most important museum in the history of mankind. The Führer Museum will house the greatest art collection the world has ever seen, and this lovely lady here on the table will be one of its most famous pieces."

"You disgust me," Mason said as he shook his head slowly.

"I liked you, Mason, I did, but you kept getting in the way. When I found you in the records room that night, I knew that was it, I had to get you out of the museum. You had the instinct to piece together the mystery of where the Mona Lisa really was. I knew the one in the Louvre was fake; I had the opportunity to study it. I have been searching for the real one for years. When I realized you took the catacombs map, I simply put my people on you from the moment you left. You have proven to be a tough adversary, but in the end, you led me right to it."

"She has nothing to do with your father's death," Mason said motioning to Collette. "You have your prize, let her go. I will stay until you are finished with me."

Dr. Heckler turned and looked at Collette. "No, I don't think so. I think we shall all wait a few minutes more until I have a look at the painting."

Mason needed to have the last word. "You have just discredited your entire career on a fruitless act of revenge. History will soon forget your achievements and only know your failures, all you are now is a common thief."

"How I choose to exact revenge is up to me. My place in history is only just beginning. I will be credited with running the greatest museum in the history of the world so spare me your career retrospectives."

She turned to Kliest. "Watch him while I inspect the painting."

Kliest stepped forward with his weapon pulled. Mason backed away from the painting, making sure his steps took him closer to the door. Kliest followed and stood next to him, the empty suitcase sat on the floor between them and the table.

Dr. Heckler opened her bag and removed a large magnifying glass as she slipped her glasses on and leaned over the painting.

Mason glanced at Collette and kept her attention while Dr. Heckler inspected the painting. After a few minutes Dr. Heckler stood up and removed her glasses. She turned to Kliest and was about to say something when Mason yelled, "Get down."

Collette dropped to the floor as Mason removed a small device from his sleeve. He pressed the button and the empty suitcase exploded. Kliest stumbled backward as the explosion sent pieces of the suitcase in every direction. Mason stepped forward and grabbed Kliest's gun with his left hand and with his right he punched him in the jaw, sending him toppling over a chair. Mason dropped to the ground, slid on his back, and fired two shots at the man behind him. Kliest crawled across the floor and dove behind a couch on the right side of the room. Mason fired in Kliest's direction. One of Kliest's men crouched down; he had a clear shot at Mason. He tried to pull the trigger when his shoulder exploded as a bullet struck him and knocked him off his feet. Two men rushed into the room followed by

Ganoux. They fired in every direction as men dropped everywhere.

Dr. Heckler lay crumpled on the floor near the table, having taken the worst of the blast. Her clothes were ripped and covered in blood. Kliest continued firing toward Mason as his other men kept Ganoux and Lucky's men bogged down in the corner. Shards of wood and glass were everywhere as lamps exploded and furniture was torn apart by bullets. Mason continued firing as he tried to make his way in the direction of Collette. He stood and unloaded his gun at the men on the other side of the room and ran across and dove on the floor by Collette, grabbed her, and dragged her behind the large sofa on her side of the room. He tore off the cloth and made sure she was okay. She huddled behind the couch as Mason fired blindly over the couch. The familiar sound of an empty gun followed: click, click, click. He was out of ammunition.

Ganoux and Lucky's two men were in trouble in the corner. They were crouched behind a dresser, which they had thrown to the ground and were taking heavy fire from two of Kliest's heavily armed men.

Kliest, meanwhile, saw his opportunity and ran to the basement door, opened it, and jumped down the steps. His men continued firing until Mason found a loaded pistol nearby. He crawled over and picked it up. He leaned around the sofa and unloaded two rounds into the face of the unsuspecting man, who fell dead. The other man was startled by the shots from Mason's direction; that gave the time for Ganoux to put a bullet into his chest from across the room. The man staggered backwards as a lone bullet to the head finished him. He fell against the wall, leaving blood on the wall as he slid down to the floor.

With the shooting finished, Mason went back to Collette and propped her up. He untied her hands and she wrapped them around him. She sobbed uncontrollably and managed a "thank you" in between sobs. He held her tight and vowed to never let her go again. He kissed her as she cried, and she wiped some blood from his face. As they were mid-embrace, Ganoux walked over to them. "Are you two okay?"

They both nodded and slowly got back up to their feet. Lucky's men came over and Mason thanked them for helping. He walked over to the body of Margaret Heckler, her legs were torn apart by the blast. He crouched down and searched for a pulse, there was none. He shook his head at the thought of her running the Führer Museum. He stared at her lifeless body for a moment. *Such a brilliant antiquities expert*, he thought, *corrupted by greed like so many others in history.*

He stood up and looked at the table, the Mona Lisa lying there still in one piece, completely oblivious to the chaos surrounding her. Mason walked over and inspected the painting, she stared back at him with that wry smile. He wiped away some dust and shards from the chaos; she was still in one piece. Lucky would get his painting back after all.

Chapter 33

"I HAVE TO GO AFTER HIM," Mason said as everyone gathered around the Mona Lisa.

"No, Mason, please. It's over; let's just get out of here," Collette begged.

"No, it's not over. That man is going to pay for what he did to you."

Mason asked Ganoux to stay with Collette and motioned to Lucky's men to follow him toward the basement door. The three men listened for a moment before Mason started down the stairs, each stair creaking as he walked. He stopped on the fifth stair down and listened again: only silence. He continued and reached the bottom of the stairs, and noticed the temperature was ten degrees cooler. Mason was standing in a cold, stone basement with a dirt floor. Furniture covered in thick dust was to the right, while old rusted gardening tools hung from nails on the left. The basement extended the length of the house and two dangling bulbs provided the only source of light. The coolness and the musty smell reminded Mason of the catacombs, minus the bones.

Mason motioned to Lucky's men to come down once he was sure the basement was clear. The three men spread out and started to make their way across the basement. There was no sign of Kliest anywhere, it was as if he had vanished into thin air. They reached the other end of the basement and found some old boxes and a wooden trunk. Mason raised his hand to stop the other men and pointed toward the trunk. He slowly approached it and cocked his weapon. In one quick motion he raised the top of the trunk and pointed his gun inside. There was no one, just a clump of old clothes and the smell of the years of decay. He turned back to Lucky's men, who both stared back with confused looks. An old stone fireplace was mounted against the wall and Mason approached it for a closer look. He ran his hand over the top and down the sides. He stopped about midway down the left side. Standing up, he grabbed the edge of the mantle and pulled it toward him, surprising Lucky's men and himself as the fireplace moved a few inches. All three stepped back and raised their weapons.

Mason slowly walked back to the fireplace and again pulled it from the wall, exposing a large opening behind it. He leaned in and saw a tunnel leading away from the house, veering to the left and out of sight. Once again, there was no sign of Kliest. For a minute, Mason contemplated pursuing him into the tunnel, but realized it was too dangerous. He had no idea where it led, or who was waiting at the other end, so he pushed the fireplace back into place. It closed and clicked like a large door.

The three men started back across the basement and up the stairs. They rejoined Ganoux and Collette in the main room. Bodies, bullets, and blood were everywhere.

"Did you find him?" Ganoux said as they entered the room.

"No, there is a secret passageway leading out from the house, he's gone, and who knows where. Something tells me he will be back so we should get out of here."

Ganoux agreed. Lucky's men left first with their forgery. Mason watched as they drove out of the driveway. Convinced they were alone, he called for Collette and Ganoux. The three of them exited the house through the front door and on to the gravel driveway. The morning sun was barely visible on the horizon.

Collette was remarkably composed as they stood on the driveway. She stopped Mason and looked him in the eyes. "I

Love you," she said quietly as she kissed him. They embraced for what seemed like a lifetime until Ganoux cleared his throat, essentially saying "let's go"

The three started down the driveway with guns drawn, each person focused on a different direction. The quiet calm of dawn was littered with the sounds of birds, but no humans. They reached the car and Mason walked around the back to the trunk, he opened it and saw his suitcase sitting there, untouched.

Could it really be over, he wondered? Had he really survived this ordeal? Could he now leave France in peace with the painting, and safely get it back to New York?

Kliest would continue his purge of Europe's greatest treasures, and Mason would do everything in his power to stop him. Mason had looked Kliest in the eye and seen the evil in his soul. This was a terrible man, capable of anything, and Mason knew they would meet again someday. He envisioned the Solario painting once more, the silver platter held Kliest's head on it as Mason held the tray. He would get his revenge somehow, but first, he needed to travel with a lovely lady back to America. He smiled and slammed the trunk closed.

Chapter 34

One Week Later
Geneva, NY

MASON STEPPED BACK TO LOOK at the painting. He had picked the perfect spot, directly above the dresser, across from his father's bed in the master bedroom of their home in Geneva, New York.

He, Collette, and Anna had made the drive from New York City and arrived this morning. The surprise had been reserved for Mason's father, Aldon Wright. The Mona Lisa was now hanging in his bedroom where it would remain safe from the outside world.

Collette wrapped her arms around Mason's left arm and leaned on him as they stared at the painting. Anna looked back and forth between the painting and Collette; she smiled when Collette caught her eye. Collette motioned her over and embraced her with her right arm, pulling her in close. Mason's father had a tear in his eye as they stood silently admiring the slight wry smile of the lady staring back at them.

"This was your mother's favorite painting. She would never believe that it is hanging in our bedroom."

Betty, the longtime Wright family housekeeper, leaned her head in the door to see if anyone needed anything. She noticed the four of them staring at the wall.

"Betty, come in, please," Aldon Wright said as he motioned for her to enter.

She entered the room and noticed the painting on the wall. She put her hand over her mouth, and her eyes opened wide, "Oh...the Mona Lisa. I have always loved this painting, she is beautiful. Unfortunately, I will never get to France to see her, especially now."

She leaned in and admired the painting. "Mrs. Wright would have loved to see this," she said, getting emotional.

"Did you have it made?" she asked turning to Aldon.

"A gift from an old friend," Aldon said. "Betty, take a good look at it, it is remarkably realistic, reminds me of the real thing."

Betty wiped a tear away as she admired La Gioconda. The five stood in silence for a few minutes as Mason gathered his thoughts.

He kissed Collette on her head and turned back to the Mona Lisa hanging on the wall. Such a simple portrait of an unremarkable lady, she had no idea the adventure she put him through to keep her safe. Mason, Collette, Anna, Betty, and Aldon stood there for a few more moments in silence as La Gioconda smiled back at them with gratitude, she was home, safe and sound.

They packed the car and headed back to the city. Mason had one more stop to make, a promise to an old friend.

A short time later he sat in Director Montgomery's office recounting the adventure he had just returned from. The director sat there hanging on every word.

"Mason, I must say that is quite a story, and I am a bit jealous. Those sorts of adventures are behind me, I'm afraid."

Mason laughed, "Don't be too jealous, I did almost die several times."

He stood up and walked over to the tube he had brought with him, uncorked the top, and pulled out two old pieces of parchment.

"I did promise to return what I borrowed so here they are in one piece—well, two pieces." He handed both scrolls to the director who carefully placed them on his desk.

"So, Mason, what is next for you?"

"I will accompany Collette and Anna back to England where we will join her parents. I have volunteered to help the war effort however I can. We also have promised Anna we will look for her family, which will not be easy. I will also be looking into Kliest. I won't sleep soundly again until I deal with him."

"Well, we sure got Dr. Heckler wrong, she seemed like such a quiet scholar dedicated to her work. Who knew she would be wrapped up in this?" Montgomery shook his head.

"I always wondered about her, but yes, I would have never guessed," Mason said as he stood up.

He extended his hand, and the director nearly broke it with his handshake.

"Be careful, son, last time you left my office, I told you that you were entering a world filled with shady characters. I was right, and now you are part of that world so watch your back. There will be many people looking for you; don't let them find you."

Mason left the office, and Anna and Collette were waiting outside. He walked down the steps of the museum just as he had a couple of weeks ago. This time, however, he was not worried about what was going on in his life, he was exactly where he wanted to be, walking with Collette and Anna up Fifth Avenue in the greatest city in the world.

About the Author

Steven Knapp was born in New Jersey. After living overseas for the better part of the first decade of his life in Belgium, Germany and Brazil, he returned to New Jersey. The experience of living overseas stayed with Steven, as he as always loved to travel.

A graduate of Seton Hall University with a B.A. in Psychology, he has been the owner of Steven Knapp Home Improvements LLC, for over 22 years. He started writing six years ago with no experience and just a story to tell. Steven is an avid reader with a special interest in the lesser known stories of World War II era history. *The Bones of Saint Pierre* is his debut novel, part of The Mason Wright Series. He is currently working on the second book in the series while continuing to run his home improvement business, where he puts his creativity to work to help his clients bring their ideas to life.

Steven resides in New Jersey with his wife of 17 years, Lori, and their two cats, Sylvester and Bam. Spending time with family and friends, visiting New York City and listening to live music are some of the places you will find them when not at home.